Bloodstains *with* Brontë

Also by Katherine Bolger Hyde

Arsenic with Austen

Bloodstains *with* Brontë

A Crime with the Classics Mystery

KATHERINE BOLGER HYDE

Minotaur Books

New York

BLOODSTAINS WITH BRONTË. Copyright © 2017 by Katherine Bolger Hyde. All rights reserved. Printed in the United States of America. For information, address St. Martin's Press, 175 Fifth Avenue, New York, N.Y. 10010.

www.minotaurbooks.com

Library of Congress Cataloging-in-Publication Data

Names: Hyde, Katherine Bolger, author.
Title: Bloodstains with Bronte : a crime with the classics mystery / Katherine Bolger Hyde.
Description: First edition. | New York : Minotaur Books, 2017.
Identifiers: LCCN 2017024857 | ISBN 978-1-250-06548-3 (hardcover) | ISBN 978-1-4668-7243-1 (ebook)
Subjects: LCSH: Murder—Investigation—Fiction. | GSAFD: Mystery fiction.
Classification: LCC PS3608.Y367 B58 2017 | DDC 813/.6—dc23
LC record available at https://lccn.loc.gov/2017024857

Our books may be purchased in bulk for promotional, educational, or business use. Please contact your local bookseller or the Macmillan Corporate and Premium Sales Department at 1-800-221-7945, extension 5442, or by email at MacmillanSpecialMarkets@macmillan.com.

First Edition: December 2017

10 9 8 7 6 5 4 3 2 1

To John,
who makes everything possible.

• Acknowledgments •

It takes a village to make a book. In this case, my village was populated by my family, the Rockaway gang (you know who you are), Molly King, Charise Olson and the members of the Santa Cruz Writers Who Lunch, and my beta readers, Susan Shisler, Bev. Cooke, Carrie Padgett, and Carol Loewen. What little I know about construction and remodeling is thanks to Mark Roberts; any errors are, of course, my own. The idea of a fundraising murder mystery play was first floated in real life by Charise Olson.

Also in the village are my wonderful agent, Kimberley Cameron, my gracious editor, Marcia Markham, her untiring assistants, Quressa Robinson and Nettie Finn, my publicist, Sarah Schoof, and the rest of the folks at Minotaur, many of whose names I do not know but whose efforts on behalf of the book I am grateful for nevertheless.

Lastly, the village includes you, the reader. Welcome to Stony Beach. I hope you enjoy your stay.

Bloodstains *with* Brontë

I heard, also, the fir bough repeat its teasing sound . . . "I
must stop it, nevertheless!" I muttered, knocking my knuckles through the glass, and stretching an arm out to seize
the importunate branch; instead of which, my fingers closed
on the fingers of a little, ice-cold hand! The intense horror
of nightmare came over me . . . a most melancholy voice
sobbed, "Let me in—let me in!"

—*Wuthering Heights*

Emily awoke disoriented in the moonlit room. The shadows,
all in the wrong places, seemed plucked from her unquiet
dream. And that sound—that high, keening, human wail rising
above the shriek of the storm—did it come from the dream
world or the waking one?

She reached to her right to turn on the lamp, but her hand
met empty space. Groping to the left she found a switch, and
the room came into focus along with her mind. Aunt Beatrice's
room. Of course. She had moved down here yesterday in prep-
aration for the remodeling on the third floor.

But the wail that had awakened her still sounded in her ears.
Lizzie? Her infant lungs were powerful, but Emily had never
heard her make a sound like that. Her young life could not have
seen the depth of anguish contained in that wail.

Emily slid her feet into her slippers, wincing at the chill, and wrapped her ancient fraying bathrobe around her. Following the sound, she groped her way down the back stairs and into the kitchen. The wail did seem to be issuing from Katie and Lizzie's room next door.

Emily tiptoed to the bedroom door and eased it open a crack. She could see Lizzie in the cradle, sprawled on her back with all her limbs flung out, her breath soughing softly through her open mouth. Emily inched the door farther till she could see the bed. Katie lay tangled in a shroud of sheets, eyes closed but head tossing on the pillow. And that heartrending keening was issuing from her throat.

Oh, Katie. Emily had guessed there must have been difficult times in Katie's past—it wasn't likely her parents would have been perfectly loving and supportive for nineteen years before suddenly throwing her out with her newborn child—but this sound spoke of an even deeper pain, one mixed with terror and hopelessness. Emily tiptoed up to the bed, touched Katie's hand, and softly called her name.

The tossing stopped, and the wail subsided to a whimper. Emily smoothed the sweat-soaked bangs from Katie's forehead and kissed it. "Katie. Wake up. It's only a dream."

This time Katie's eyelids fluttered, then opened. She blinked several times before focusing on Emily's face. Then she sat bolt upright. "Mrs. C! What's wrong? Is it Lizzie? Is the house on fire?"

"No, no, nothing like that. I heard you—I think you were having a nightmare."

Katie passed a hand across her face and shivered. Emily grabbed Katie's robe from the bedside chair and wrapped it around her shoulders. "Yes . . . a nightmare . . ." Katie pulled the robe around herself and shrank into it.

"You need some cocoa. I'll be right back."

Emily ducked into the kitchen and put the kettle on. Had Katie had such nightmares before? Emily doubted she would have heard her from her third-floor tower bedroom. The girl seemed content and carefree during the day, often singing as she went about her household chores—which made this descent into terror even more troubling. Emily had never yet had cause to regret her impulsive decision to hire Katie as housekeeper when she'd turned up, friendless and homeless with a seven-week-old baby, on the doorstep of Windy Corner last summer. Since then she'd come to see Katie almost as a daughter and Lizzie as a beloved grandchild. But was it possible Katie had buried issues that Emily, for all her love for both mother and baby, would not be able to help her with?

The kettle's whistle made Emily jump as it echoed Katie's nightmare wail. She mixed up two mugs of cocoa, took them both back to the bedroom, and handed one to Katie, who still sat upright, clutching her robe about her and shivering. She wrapped her hands around the mug and sipped gratefully.

"That nightmare must have been a doozy," Emily said. "You seemed really upset."

"Yeah. A doozy."

"Want to tell me about it?"

Katie looked up at her, her eyes full of the same keening her waking had silenced. Her lips parted, as if the words were hovering there, waiting for a chance to escape. But the lip-gates shut firmly down, and she shook her head. "Thanks, but it's already fading. I don't want to call it back."

Emily swallowed her own hurt, wishing she were Katie's real mother rather than her pretend-adoptive one so she would have the right to coax her into confidence. She would have to give the girl time and hope eventually she would trust Emily enough to share whatever was eating her up from the inside.

two

There was no possibility of taking a walk that day . . . the
cold winter wind had brought with it clouds so sombre,
and a rain so penetrating, that further outdoor exercise was
now out of the question.

—*Jane Eyre*

Emily had to rise early next morning despite her broken
night's sleep. Today was Monday, the day the remodeling of
her inherited Victorian mansion into a writers' retreat was set
to begin. They'd had workers on the property for weeks already,
refurbishing the old chauffeur's apartment over the carriage
house into a snug little nest for Katie and Lizzie, so they could
have some privacy and their current bedroom could be used for
retreat guests. But today would be the first time Emily's own
personal space would be invaded. The next phase of the plan
was to turn the third floor into a private retreat for Emily, add-
ing a sitting room and full bath to the dear little tower bedroom
she was already using.

For the first time a flash of doubt assailed her: Why had
she decided to turn her home into a semipublic space? Oh, yes,
the guilt. The unreasoning guilt of someone who had always

merely subsisted over becoming suddenly wealthy, with a gorgeous home much too large for her, but which she loved far too much to give up. The guilt was only compounded by the fact that Emily had inherited Windy Corner (along with a large chunk of the nearby village of Stony Beach) as a result of her dear aunt Beatrice being murdered. The only way she could live there in good conscience was to share it. She would just have to buck up and endure the remodeling as best she could; but her old, quiet, safely boring life in the literature department at Reed College in Portland looked strangely attractive by contrast.

Emily was finishing her breakfast in the dining room when she heard the sounds of truck engines, doors slamming, and booted feet clomping up the porch steps. She sighed as she addressed Bustopher Jones, the aging, portly tuxedo cat she'd inherited with the house, who sat by her chair doing a poor imitation of a cat with no interest in table scraps. "No rest for the wicked, Bustopher. Here come the troops."

She pushed to her feet and entered the hall just as Katie came out of the kitchen. Emily opened the door while Katie hung back by the stairs. Jeremiah Edwards, the contractor who was handling her remodeling project, ducked his towering head beneath the lintel and pulled off his cap as he stomped the water off his boots on the mat. Two young men Emily didn't recognize hovered behind him.

"All done with the garage apartment, ma'am. Except the painting, as per your instructions." Edwards nodded toward Katie. She had insisted on doing her own painting in her new home, and in fact had finished the first coat in the living room over the weekend. "Brought in some new fellas for the work upstairs. This here's Roman Martinez—" He pulled forward a swarthy young man not much taller than Emily herself, who also doffed his cap. He nodded briefly at Emily, then his black eyes fastened on Katie's face and stayed there.

"And this is Jake Newhouse." The other young man, who'd been hidden behind Edwards, stepped forward. Emily heard Katie's sharp intake of breath and shot a glance at her. The girl had gone whiter than Beatrice's bone china. She put out a hand and gripped the newel of the banister next to her.

Emily turned frowning eyes on Jake Newhouse. Six feet tall at a guess, well built, blond and tanned, and much too handsome for his own good. The smile with which he ogled Katie made Emily want to punch him. She'd have to keep an eye on this one.

Edwards, seeing Katie's face, frowned down at Jake from his height of six foot five. Emily was comforted to think he would be keeping an eye on this one, too. Edwards hitched his jeans up on his skinny hips and said, "Best get to work. Idle hands are the devil's workshop." With a nod to Emily, he started up the stairs, treading carefully on the plastic sheeting he'd laid down the week before to protect the treads from all the tromping boots.

As Jake approached, Katie turned and fled to the kitchen. Jake followed her with his eyes, smirking and whistling some unknown tune. Emily deliberately placed herself in his line of sight and summoned her best imitation of Aunt Beatrice's signature glare. He dropped his eyes and his whistle and followed his boss on up.

Roman trailed after them, also watching Katie but with a strikingly different expression—like a starving man who sees food just out of reach. Goodness, what was it about that girl? She was lovely, certainly, but hardly a femme fatale—more like the girl next door.

When all the men had disappeared upstairs, Emily headed toward the kitchen to find Katie leaning over the sink. Hurriedly Katie turned the faucet on full blast with her left hand while she wiped her mouth with her right. The unmistakable stench of vomit rose from the drain.

"Katie, what's wrong?"

She kept her back turned to Emily. "Just a tricky tummy. Maybe I picked up a flu bug somewhere. Better stay back; I don't want you to catch it."

"Picked up where? You never leave the house. It's that Jake, isn't it? You know him?"

Lizzie whimpered from her play space on a blanket under the table. Katie turned, avoiding Emily's gaze, and knelt to pick her up. She clutched her daughter to her chest, burying her face in Lizzie's fuzz of red-gold hair. "It's nothing. I'm fine. I've seen J—" She made a choking sound. "I've seen him around, that's all. From high school."

Emily was baffled, and a little hurt. More proof she hadn't yet won Katie's full confidence in the four months they'd shared this house. Katie was more like a daughter to her than an employee; but apparently the feeling wasn't fully reciprocated.

On the other hand, daughters didn't always tell their mothers everything. Especially where young men were concerned.

She put her arm around the girl's shoulders. "Katie, you know you can trust me, don't you? I only want to help."

"I know. And thank you. But there's really nothing to tell." Katie kissed Lizzie and put her back on the floor. "I'd better get busy. Lots to do. Have to finish up here so I can go paint when Lizzie goes down for her nap." She turned to the sink and began to pile dirty dishes into it haphazardly. She turned the faucet on again, full hot, and plunged her ungloved hands into the steaming water.

Emily knew when she was beaten. She blew Lizzie a kiss and left the room.

~

PROPERTY OF KATIE PARKER—PRIVATE! KEEP OUT!

I never thought I'd write in this journal again. Never thought I'd have time, after Lizzie was born. Certainly never thought I'd have the need.

But now I have the need.

He's here.

Mr. Edwards brought in more guys to work on Mrs. C's new apartment upstairs, and he was one of them. Last night's nightmare come to life.

When I first saw him, I thought I was back in that nightmare. Then I thought I was going to faint. Then I thought I was going to puke. Which I did.

I wish I could have kept my cool, not let him know it bothered me to see him again. Then maybe he would have had the grace to be embarrassed. But no. I was trembling and I'm sure as white as new paint, and he—he smiled at me. That horrid, greasy, knowing smile. That was what turned my stomach.

If I asked Mrs. C, I'm sure she'd give Mr. Edwards a hint to get him off the job. But then I'd have to tell her why. And I don't think I can do that. I can't even write the words in this journal. I'll just have to try to avoid him, I guess. It's a big house, and the work is all upstairs. I should be able to stay out of his way.

But if he so much as looks at Lizzie—I won't answer for my actions.

Emily's own part of the overall project of turning Windy Corner into a writers' retreat was to plan the redecoration of the bedrooms. She and Katie had decided to theme each of the six guest rooms around a different classic author. Some of them were already furnished appropriately and would only need a few extra touches—Aunt Beatrice's room could become the Forster room with ease, and the front bedroom with the balcony evoked the red-room from *Jane Eyre* so strongly Emily shivered whenever she went in there. It was a natural for the Brontë room.

But the other rooms—Austen, Montgomery, and Dostoevsky upstairs, and Dickens on the main floor—would need more work, and Emily was clueless as to how to begin. She'd always had a passive interest in decorating but had never had the time or money to indulge it. Her first step in any new endeavor was always to read about it, so now she turned her attention to the ranks of books in Beatrice's library.

Her search was fruitless, however. Only serious literature was allowed to grace these venerable shelves. She would have to pay a visit to Ben Johnson, Stony Beach's bookseller. He might not have what she needed, either, but he would know how to get it. And by this time she was feeling desperate to get out of the house. The sounds of demolition from the third floor were filtering down more insistently than she had hoped.

She moved to the library windows, a broad semicircle that looked out over the ocean. The bangs and crashes from upstairs had diverted her attention from the steadier drumming of the rain slanting in sheets against the glass, driven by what looked to her landlubber's eyes like a gale-force wind. She could barely see the ocean, though it crashed to shore only a few hundred yards away, but what she could see of it was a froth of white-caps. If the Brontës had lived on the Oregon coast, this would have been the weather they gloried in. Too stormy to make that trip to Ben's bookstore now.

Emily sighed and returned to her chair in front of the fire, wincing at a particularly reverberating crash from upstairs. If only she'd had the foresight to lay in a stock of earplugs. Another errand to do when the weather cleared.

Before she could pick up her knitting, Levin leapt onto her lap, rubbing his sleek gray cheek against hers before circling and settling down for a nap. Kitty, his nearly identical sister, already dozed on the opposite chair, snuggled up to Bustopher Jones. The harmony between the two cats she'd brought with her from Portland and Bustopher, the original king of the house, was a small miracle among the many that had brought Emily to this place. She should be grateful. But at the moment she was merely annoyed.

She reached for the nearest book and read the same page three times without absorbing a word. Finally another sound shrilled over the hammers and the rain: the telephone. She leapt to answer it, dislodging an indignant Levin. Even talking to a telemarketer could provide a welcome distraction from all this noise.

"Hey, beautiful."

Luke's favorite endearment for her, left over from their halcyon days as teenage lovers but still uttered with complete sincerity, always sent a thrill through Emily. "Luke! You're a sound for sore ears. I swear, this remodeling is going to put me in my grave right next to Aunt Beatrice. And this is only the first day."

"I thought they were still working on the carriage house. They're in the main house now?"

"Yeah, they finished up Katie's apartment Friday. Except for the painting—she's doing that herself."

"So where are they starting with your place?"

"Third floor. They're tearing down walls today, then they'll start framing in the bathroom and sitting room. I've moved into Beatrice's bedroom for the duration." Even now, more than four months after her death, the room was still full of the old woman's presence. And her belongings, which Emily would have to start clearing out soon.

"How about I come take you away from it all? We can go to the Crab Pot for lunch."

"In this weather? Aren't you afraid your car will be blown off the road?"

"Heck, this is just a little breeze. It's only October. You should see the kind of weather we get after Christmas."

"Well, if you say so. Would you mind if we stopped by the bookstore and the drugstore on the way?"

"How about on the way back? I'm not sure my stomach can stand to wait for you to get through in that bookstore."

Emily laughed. She wasn't an avid clothes shopper like so many women, but let her loose in a bookstore or a yarn shop and hours could pass before she knew it. "Fine. Let me make sure Katie doesn't already have something going for lunch."

She laid down the phone and stepped through the hall into the kitchen. "Katie? Would it mess up your plans if I went out to lunch?"

Katie's brunette ponytail swung as she turned from the stove to face Emily. Her cheeks had not regained their usual rosy color after this morning's baffling episode, but she spoke cheerfully enough. "Not a bit. I was just going to do soup and sandwiches. The soup'll keep."

Lizzie gurgled a greeting from her blanket under the table. Emily bent down and waggled her fingers at her, then returned to the phone. "Katie says I'm free to go."

"Be there in five minutes."

Emily hurried up the stairs and into Beatrice's room to change. The Crab Pot was hardly formal dining, but she always wanted to look her best for Luke. She exchanged her chinos for a calf-length, flared brown tweed skirt and her old ratty sweater for a lovely pumpkin-colored mohair one she'd finished knitting the week before. She just had time to tuck a few stray copper curls back into her loose, high bun before she heard the doorbell.

By the time she reached the landing, Katie, holding Lizzie on her hip, had already opened the door to Luke. Emily couldn't see Luke, but she heard his playful tone. "Hey there, little lady. I see you've got everything at Windy Corner under control, as usual." *Little lady?* It wasn't like Luke to address Katie that way. Then he added, "With a little help from your mom."

Katie laughed. "Yeah, we have a great system—she makes the messes, I clean them up. And the rest of the house in the process."

"I hear you're doing your own painting, too. I bet Lizzie'll be a big help there. She'll test all the colors for you, won't you, peanut?"

"Yeah, on her clothes, on her hair . . . As far as painting goes, she's helping me by napping through the whole thing."

Emily descended the last leg of the stairs as Katie stood back to let Luke in. After thirty-five years—most of which, granted, they'd spent apart—the sight of Luke's tall form still quickened Emily's blood. His youthful good looks had coarsened with the years, and his once-abundant brown hair was now sparse and graying, clipped close to his head and topped by a khaki sheriff's cap; but the teasing light in his gray eyes when he gazed at her was just as bright and compelling as it had been when they were teens. Looking at him, Emily could not bring herself to regret the chain of events that had brought her back to Stony Beach—it had brought her back to Luke as well.

Katie evaporated toward the kitchen as Emily went to meet Luke. He took her in his arms. "Mmm, I like this sweater. Real soft." He kissed her. "Almost as soft as you."

She returned the kiss, then pulled back. "You, on the other hand, are soaking wet."

"Sorry 'bout that. House like this in this climate, I'm surprised you don't have one of those whatchamacallits where you can get from the car to the house under cover."

"A *porte cochère*? That's not a bad idea. Though I'm not sure it would harmonize with the style of the house. You see those more with neoclassical than Queen Anne."

"Whatever." He pulled her raincoat off the coatrack. "Your mackintosh, my lady." He held the coat while she slipped her arms into the sleeves.

"Thank you, my lord." Emily's taste for British television was beginning to rub off on Luke. So far she'd introduced him to *Jeeves and Wooster, Downton Abbey,* and *Inspector Lewis.* His tolerance for mystery shows was limited, as they inevitably fudged on the details of true police work; but he'd watch almost anything for the sake of getting her to cuddle up with him on his plushy sofa in front of his big-screen high-definition TV.

The Crab Pot was on the south end of downtown Stony Beach, a couple of miles from Windy Corner, which stood alone at the end of a stretch of undeveloped land to the north of town. Emily gripped the grab bar of the sheriff's department SUV throughout the ride as if by doing so she could keep the car's wheels anchored to the road. She was sure if the wind didn't blow them away, they'd hydroplane on one of the sheets of water flowing across the pavement and end up in the lake, which ran along the inland side of the highway most of the way into town. But Luke's driving proved equal to the situation, and when they pulled into the parking lot of the Crab Pot, only one space was open. Apparently the locals agreed with Luke that this was "just a little breeze." And besides, at this time of year, the Crab Pot was the only open restaurant in town.

They made a mad dash for the door and shook themselves like dogs in the entry before hanging up their raincoats and hats and heading to Luke's usual table at the back. Emily had the menu pretty well memorized by now, but she pulled a laminated card from the stand on the vinyl-topped table anyway and ran her eyes down the list of a dozen lunch options. She settled on clam chowder in a sourdough bowl. That ought to warm her up.

Sunny, the diner's sole waiter, shuffled up to their table holding two plastic glasses of water in his one good hand. He plunked the glasses down, then stood silent, hitching up the shoulder of his ratty, ill-fitting overalls as he waited for their order. "Clam chowder and coffee, please," Emily said.

"The same. And don't forget the oyster crackers." Luke winked at Emily. One always had to ask for the extras with

Sunny, even though they were supposed to be included with the meal. Sunny grunted and shuffled off.

Luke sat back in his chair, hands in pockets, tilting the chair onto its back legs. He whistled softly under his breath as his eyes sparkled at her.

Emily raised an eyebrow at him. Luke was normally cheerful, but this was a bit much even for him. "What has you looking like the cat that got the cream?"

"Oh, nothing much." He let his chair down with a thud and leaned toward her. "I'm just stoked that you're going ahead with your third-floor apartment. Means you're planning to stick around."

Emily started. It certainly did appear to mean that, but she wasn't conscious of having made such a decision. She'd applied for a sabbatical back in June, when it became clear that the seismic shift her life had undergone made an immediate return to Reed unthinkable. But even as she went ahead with the transformation of Windy Corner into a retreat center, she'd never actually decided to extend her sabbatical into full retirement.

Not that she had any compelling reason not to do so—Philip, her husband of three contented decades, had died two years before, and her one close friend at Reed, Marguerite Grenier of the French department, was perfectly happy to visit Emily at Windy Corner as often as required. And the work of teaching literature had lost most of its savor at some indefinite time in the past. Retirement looked attractive on most fronts; but the idea of permanently abandoning Portland with its vibrant cultural life was one she wasn't quite ready to entertain.

She gave Luke an ambiguous smile. The arrival of their food saved her from having to give a definitive reply. Once Sunny had slammed down their plates and shuffled off, Emily cast about for a way to change the subject. The new young workers she'd been introduced to that morning popped into her mind. "Do you know anything about Jake Newhouse?"

Luke snorted. "I know he's trouble. Why?"

"What kind of trouble? He's working on my house."

"Girl trouble, mostly. I don't think you need to worry about him stealing or anything. But you might want to keep Katie out of his way."

"That's just it—the way they both reacted when they saw each other this morning, I'd swear there's some history between them." She described the scene. "But Katie wouldn't tell me anything except that she knew him slightly from high school."

"There's not a pretty girl in this county Jake hasn't at least tried to get to know more than slightly. I've heard some nasty stories—there'd be more than one case against him for date rape if the girls dared to come forward. But in a little place like this, where everybody knows everybody's business, testifying in a rape trial'd be almost worse for the girl than the rape itself. Fries my bacon the way rape victims get treated in the courts, but doesn't seem to be anything I can do about it."

Emily stopped with a spoonful of chowder halfway to her mouth. "I hate to think Katie could have been one of his victims. But she's never told me anything about Lizzie's father. Do you think—?"

"It's possible. Though I don't know of any redheaded New-houses."

She put down her spoon. Her appetite had followed her imagination into the no-man's-land of what might have befallen her beloved Katie in the past. "I'd better ask Jeremiah Edwards to get rid of him."

"Well, now, there you could be unleashing some pretty

vicious attack dogs. Jake's daddy's a lawyer. Family's big stuff around here. Unless you could show some kind of misconduct on the job itself, he'd likely sue you and Edwards from here to Christmas for wrongful dismissal."

Emily stared at Luke. "So I have to wait until Jake actually attacks Katie to get rid of him?"

Luke winced. "Let's hope it doesn't come to that. My bet is he's a lazy bugger. Maybe Edwards'll be able to sack him for loafing on the job."

"I'll have a word with Jeremiah. I just wish Jake had never set foot in the place." Attack dogs or no attack dogs, she would have to find some way to get rid of that boy.

three

A half-civilized ferocity lurked yet in the depressed brows
and eyes full of black fire.

—*Wuthering Heights*

After lunch, Luke dropped her off in front of Stony Beach
Books, saying he'd do an errand of his own and come back
for her. The storefronts to the left and right of the bookstore
turned dark window faces to the gloomy street. Ben Johnson was
one of the few shopkeepers in this seasonal tourist town who
kept his store open year-round. Winter or summer made little
difference to him, since his bookshop was as much a warehouse
for the used books he sold online as a true retail outlet. When the
bell over the door tinkled, he emerged from the back room to
greet Emily, a wide smile illumining his ascetically handsome
mocha brown face. He stopped a few feet away from her so she
could look him in the eye without craning her neck too badly.

"Emily! What can I do for you?"

"I'm looking for anything on period decor. Mostly nineteenth
century, with a little late-eighteenth and early-twentieth thrown

in. Not modern interpretations of those periods, but the real thing."

Ben ran a hand over his two-inch-long dreads. He'd started growing them since the summer. Emily suspected she knew why. "Wow, I don't know if I have anything like that. But I'm sure I could find it for you if you can give me some time."

"How much time?"

"I don't know, a week or two maybe? Of course, if you're in a hurry, you could always look for yourself online."

Emily grimaced. *Online* was a four-letter word to her. "Could you look for me? I'm clueless when it comes to online shopping. I would just run into Portland to Powell's, but I hate to leave town while they're working on the house."

"No problem. Come on back." Ben led the way into his office, where a tiny computer desk was wedged between a packing table and stacks of boxes. "Do you have anything specific in mind, or shall we just browse?"

"If there are books about where Jane Austen and Charles Dickens actually lived, that would be great." For the Montgomery and Dostoevsky rooms she could pull descriptions from the novels. "And then anything general about Victorian-era furnishings. In England, that is, not here."

Ben sat down and pecked at the keyboard while mysterious pictures came and went on the screen. Within minutes he'd found everything she was looking for and placed orders for them. "Should be here within a week. They always say up to two, but usually it's a lot quicker."

"Thanks, Ben. Just give me a call when they come in." The reluctant, traitorous thought snuck into her head that online seemed to be a pretty convenient way to buy books when one was outside the sphere of influence of Powell's. But why should she bother getting a computer and learning how to do it herself when she could always have Ben order for her, and give him a needed commission in the process?

Luke had not yet reappeared—this had been a remarkably brief bookstore visit, after all—so Emily left word with Ben where she'd be, ducked her head to the wind, and dashed down the street to Laccy Luxuries, the antique accessories shop owned by her friend and kindred Victorian spirit, Veronica Lacey. Veronica's shop was rarely open in the winter, which she spent mostly on buying trips to restock. But today Emily got lucky and found her in.

"Veronica, I need your help. It's time to start planning how to redecorate the author rooms, and I don't even know where to begin."

They had a nice long powwow about rugs and wallpapers, curtains and bed linens. Veronica's stock contained little in the way of heavy furniture, however. "You're going to have to con sult Devon and Hilary down at Remembrance of Things Past. They're into serious furniture there, and they really know their stuff. If they don't have what you need, they can find it."

Emily had met Devon Penhallow and Hilary Carmichael back in August when they rented the one empty space in her storefront properties. They'd remodeled the shop to look as if it belonged on the Portobello Road in London rather than on Highway 101 in Stony Beach, which thrilled Emily no end. But the shop had yet to open formally.

"Are they in town? I figured they'd be off on a buying trip now the remodeling's done."

"Hilary's in England, but Devon's here. They like a break from each other now and then. Being life partners as well as business partners can get a little suffocating, I imagine."

"I suppose so." Emily wondered if she would ever find it possible to have too much of Luke. Their adventure in solving Beatrice's murder together had only made them love each other more. Even if she did make her move to Stony Beach permanent, it was hardly probable she and Luke would ever find themselves in each other's company 24/7. No, getting an overdose of Luke wasn't likely to be a problem.

After he dropped Emily at the bookstore, Luke couldn't get his mind off what she'd said about Jake Newhouse. The thought of that bastard anywhere near Katie made Luke's chowder churn in his stomach.

Katie was the kind of girl whose sweet wholesomeness brought out one of two things in a man: either the desire to protect it or the impulse to destroy it. She could be a threshing fork to separate the wheat from the chaff in the male population. Whether Jake had made a play for Katie in the past or not, he was as chaff as chaff could get, and he was sure to go after her the first chance he got. If only Luke could get hold of something solid against him.

Jake had worked for the other local contractor, Charlie Cartwright, back in the summer on the remodeling at the new antique shop—and was notably not working for him now. Maybe Charlie could dish some dirt on Jake. Luke made a quick U-turn and stopped his SUV in front of the new clinic location, where Charlie was working now.

Charlie was sitting on the floor in one of the back rooms, finishing his thermos of coffee. "Hey, Luke, what's up?"

Luke shook Charlie's hand—one of the few hands he knew to match his own for size and strength. They had a squeezing

contest every time they met. This time Luke let Charlie win—
he wanted him in a good mood.

He pulled his hand away and rubbed it. "Man, that grip of
yours gets stronger every day. Comes of swinging a hammer
while I'm stuck at my desk pounding a keyboard, I guess."

Charlie smirked. "Soft job you got there, Sheriff. Gonna put
you in your grave at sixty. I'll be hammering till I turn a hundred, just like my old man."

"I bet you will." Luke eased himself down on the floor next
to Charlie, waved away his offer of the thermos. "They don't
make 'em like you anymore, Charlie. These young guys—"

That was all it took. Charlie snorted out a snootful of coffee.
"Those young guys don't know one end of a hammer from the
other. And work? Hell, they go for an hour if you're lucky, then
they're whipping out their phones to see what their twitterpated
friends are up to. I wouldn't hire anybody under forty if I could
find guys that age. But most of 'em have moved on to soft desk
jobs. Like you." He elbowed Luke in the ribs.

"I noticed you didn't keep on the youngsters who were working for you last summer."

"That bunch? No way. You know what that Jake Newhouse
did to me?" Charlie leaned forward and banged his thermos on
the bare cement floor. "He cost me an arm and a leg, that's what.
You know I had him on that antique shop job?"

Luke nodded.

"Damn young idiot practically ruined a whole truckload of
fancy furniture moving it in. Scratches, dings, knocked a foot off
some bureau thing. I had to pay for the whole kit 'n' caboodle."

Luke's pulse sped up. Negligence like that should've kept
Jake from getting another job in the industry. "Why didn't you
take it out of his wages?"

Charlie made a disgusted *puh*. "He didn't make that much. Besides, I couldn't prove it was him. He claimed one of the other guys, Zach Campbell, was responsible—they moved the stuff in together. Zach swore up and down it was Jake. I wouldn't trust Jake as far as I could throw him; I'd trust Zach at least to Seaside and back. But it was just one of them's word against the other. In the end I let the insurance take care of it. Shot my premiums through the roof, though."

"You didn't have anything else on Jake? Other than general laziness?"

"That and an attitude you could cut with a knife and spread on toast. But no, nothing I could pin on him. All I could do was make sure never to hire him again."

"You didn't spread the word to the other contractors? Edwards, for instance? I understand he's working for Edwards now."

Charlie upended the thermos over his cup. Nothing. He set the mug down with a snort. "Edwards and me, we don't see eye to eye these days. Not since what he said about my boy."

"About Eli? What could he say against Eli?" Charlie's son Eli was about twenty, unusually polite and hardworking for his age, with a steady girlfriend since high school. Luke couldn't picture him in any kind of trouble.

"Claimed Eli had made 'improper advances' to his girl, Rachel. Seems Rachel came home from some party in tears, wouldn't tell Edwards what happened. Eli'd been at the party, and for some reason Edwards fastened on him as the troublemaker."

"Why would he do that?"

Charlie shrugged. "Probably 'cause Eli quit going to that so-called church of his. In Edwards's book, anybody who leaves his flock is headed straight for the devil. But hell, it's not like

Eli became an atheist or a Muslim or something. He just got tired of Edwards being so damn legalistic and went over to Jenny's Baptist church instead."

Charlie stood up and dusted his hands on his jeans. "Better get back to work. Good to see you, Luke."

"Take care, Charlie." Luke frowned his way back to his car. He still had nothing he could use to get Jake off Emily's job without risking a lawsuit. And nothing worth bothering Emily about. But he certainly had some food for thought.

When Luke dropped Emily off after her errands were done, Katie waved to her from the window above the carriage house and gestured to her to come up. She dashed up the stairs and shook herself off under the sheltered entry before stepping inside onto the drop cloth that covered the living room carpet.

"Almost finished," Katie said with a proud smile. She had a right to be proud: she'd created a marblelike effect on the three window walls in a soft beige with peach undertones and veins of dark brown, while a solid, rich reddish brown framed the windows and accented the fourth, unbroken wall.

"It's gorgeous," Emily said. "I can't wait to see what you'll do with our author rooms. Where did you learn to do this?"

Katie shrugged. "Oh, I just picked it up. Watched some YouTube videos, helped a couple friends with their rooms. It's not that hard."

"Not hard if you have talent dripping out your fingertips with energy to match. I couldn't do this in a million years."

Katie blushed prettily. A faint cry sounded from the baby monitor on the adjoining kitchen counter. "Oh, shoot, I was hoping she'd take a good nap so I could get this done."

"No worries, I'll get her." Emily had proven herself adept at soothing Lizzie back to sleep when she woke prematurely.

Emily hurried down the stairs, across the gravel drive to her front door, and into Katie's bedroom. Lizzie was sitting up in her cradle, grasping the sides and rocking the cradle gently back and forth.

"You are an independent spirit, aren't you? Rocking yourself back to sleep." Emily picked Lizzie up. "A real modern woman. But don't get too independent, okay? Your mommy and I enjoy taking care of you."

Lizzie cooed and made a grab at a stray strand of Emily's hair. Emily gave her the stuffed lamb from the cradle instead. "It's a good thing you two are moving into that apartment. You need a real crib before you tip yourself right out of this cradle."

Lizzie was clearly not interested in going back to sleep, so Emily took her into the library and played with her for an hour until she started to make hungry noises. They went to the kitchen in search of arrowroot biscuits, which Lizzie loved to mouth to death, although Emily was convinced she never swallowed a morsel of them. Strapping Lizzie into her high chair, Emily glanced out the window and saw Katie in her polka-dot rain boots slogging across the swampy lawn from the carriage house. The dark, intense new worker, Roman, was heading from the front door toward Jeremiah's truck.

Roman turned, spotted Katie, and stopped in midstride. He hesitated, then pivoted and went to meet her. Katie paused with a pleasant smile, which soon turned to a look of confusion and then discomfort as the conversation progressed. Just when Emily was thinking she might need to intervene, Roman abruptly turned and strode back toward the truck.

Katie came in the kitchen door, her brow puckered, chewing her bottom lip.

"Are you all right?" Emily asked. "I saw Roman stop you. He's not making a nuisance of himself, is he?"

She slowly shook her head. "Not exactly. He says we know each other. Apparently he went to school here in seventh grade. He says I was the only one in the whole school who was nice to him. He's never forgotten me. But I don't remember him at all." Mechanically she wet a washcloth and wiped Lizzie's face and hands, already thoroughly sticky with biscuit. "I feel bad I don't remember him. But the way he looked at me—like he wanted to absorb me or something. Kind of creepy." She gave herself a shake.

Emily touched her arm. "Katie—I don't like this situation. Both these new guys are making you uncomfortable. I think I should ask Jeremiah to replace them."

"No, no, I can deal with it. Honestly. I don't want to cause trouble and hang up the work."

"Well, if you're sure. But if things get out of hand, you just say the word and they're gone."

Katie nodded. She lifted Lizzie out of the high chair, not meeting Emily's eyes. "I'd better get to cleaning. The dust is getting all the way down from the attic."

Oh my stars. As if it weren't enough having him on the property, now this Roman guy is getting on my case. Well, not getting on my case exactly, but he says he knows me. From seventh grade, of all things. And the way he looks at me—like he wants to devour me. Like there's something he wants from me that there's no way I can give.

Okay, so I was nice to him when he was the new kid and everybody else was mean. So what? I'm nice to everybody. Or try to be. And nobody else has come back after seven years trying to eat me up.

Now there are two guys I have to try to avoid. Right in my own home. What is it with me and guys? I'm just an ordinary girl from the wrong side of town. Nothing special. Why can't they leave me alone?

Emily returned to the library, steeling herself for an afternoon of construction noise. The wind and rain, as if feeling the need to compete for her attention, were making plenty of noise of their own. Emily, again reminded of the Brontës, pulled *Wuthering Heights* off the library shelf. She felt an obscure loyalty to the book, even though it wasn't fully to her taste, simply because she'd been named for its author. The opening chapters were slow going—she always found the story within a story confusing with its Gordian knot of family relationships. The reading required all her concentration, and she actually managed to filter out the cacophony for a while.

When the workday was over, she caught Jeremiah on his way out. "Come into the library for a minute, would you? There's something I want to talk to you about."

Jeremiah followed her, stooping to get through the doorway. "Any problem with the work, ma'am?"

"No, no, the work seems to be going fine. I haven't been upstairs yet, but the carriage house looks great. It's about those two new guys, Jake and Roman. They both seem a little too interested in Katie."

Jeremiah's bristly brows drew together and his lantern jaw

set. "The Lord abhors a lustful man. I'll get rid of them right away."

Emily drew back a step. "I don't think we need go that far—they haven't actually done anything. I just wanted to ask you to keep a close eye on them. See they're not downstairs on their own, that kind of thing. Maybe have a word, tell them to keep out of her way."

His frown deepened. "Words aren't much use with that kind. A fool only listens to his own counsel."

Emily was afraid he might be right. "Is their work satisfactory? Of course, if they weren't good workers, we could dismiss them on that ground."

"No big beef there. Roman's a hard worker, knows his stuff. Jake's a fool, but no worse than most his age. Tough to find young guys who know how to work these days."

"All right. Well, like I say, keep an eye and we'll see how it goes."

He gave a nod that was almost a bow and left.

In the blessed silence that descended when the workers were gone, Emily went up to the second floor and began the long-delayed task of sorting through Beatrice's belongings. Beatrice had been a sensible dresser; her clothes were of the highest quality, but classic and few. They wouldn't fit Emily's figure or her personal style, so she folded them carefully into boxes to take to the charity thrift store in Garibaldi. But she paused when she came to the mink coat encased in a cotton bag with cedar chips at the back of the closet. She'd never be comfortable wearing such a coat herself, yet giving it to a thrift store didn't seem right. She couldn't leave it here indefinitely, though.

She draped the garment bag over her arm and trudged up the stairs to the third-floor storage room. There she found space for the coat in an old cedar wardrobe, smiling to herself at the thought that one day, six or eight years from now, Lizzie might find it there and pretend she'd discovered the gateway to Narnia. This house was ideal for a child's fanciful explorations—it even had a secret staircase that led from Beatrice's room down to the library.

Heading back toward the stairs, Emily paused to survey the scene of lath-and-plaster carnage the front attic had become. Two poky storage rooms were being combined to make her new sitting room; the remains of the wall between them now littered the floor. Plumes of dust rose around her feet as she picked her way across the rubble to the large south-facing window that looked out over the front porch. No ocean view from here, but the row of poplars that lined the drive would make a nice view in themselves. Barely visible now by porch light in the stormy darkness, they put on a fine show of burnished orange foliage on a sunny day. This room would be cozy and light when it was finished. She approved her own decision.

She peeked into her tower bedroom just to assure herself that all was well and that the builders hadn't disturbed anything there. This room would not be altered—it was sacred to the adolescent dreams of Luke that had visited her as she slept in the canopied bed or mused on the ocean-facing window seat. In a peculiar way those dreams had been even sweeter than the actual time they spent together.

Perhaps that was what she feared about a future with Luke— that the mature, mundane reality of their love ultimately would not measure up to those poignant adolescent dreams. Dreams she'd carried with her all through her marriage to Philip, whose love had been more companionable than passionate. Dreams that had sustained her whenever she felt she'd drown in the tedium of her professorial days.

You're a grown-up now, Emily, she told herself sternly. *Time to put away childish dreams.* She turned from the tower and went downstairs. Only sensible dreams could ever come to her sleeping in Beatrice's bed.

· four ·

"Diana said they would both consider themselves rich with a thousand pounds, so with five thousand, they will do very well."

—Jane to St. John Rivers, *Jane Eyre*

The next morning, Dr. Sam Griffiths called. Emily heard her voice with dread but tried to act as though she didn't know what was coming.

"Hi, Sam, what's up?"

"Come down to the new place. Something to show you."

Emily sighed. Whatever Sam had to show her would surely translate into a request for more funds. The new Stony Beach clinic had been funded initially by a bequest in Beatrice's will, augmented by another large donation from Emily herself. But either Sam was a poor prognosticator or she had deliberately lowballed what she needed in the beginning, thinking it would be easier to extort the money from Emily in stages. Since the remodeling work began, Emily felt she was being nickel-and-dimed to death.

Still, she'd begun this, and she'd better see it through. "I'll be down in an hour or so."

She took her time, not wanting to give Sam the impression she was at her beck and call. The weather had cleared, so she took Beatrice's vintage Vespa into town and pulled up in front of the new clinic location around eleven o'clock. Beatrice had deeded the clinic a piece of prime real estate, right next to City Hall in the middle of downtown.

Sam met her at the door with her usual gracious charm. "Charlie says it's going to take another ten grand."

Emily fell back a step. "Another ten thousand just for the remodeling? When is this going to end?"

"Come back." Sam led the way into what would become the X-ray room. Charlie Cartwright stood in the middle of the floor, scratching his cropped head with his cap in his hand.

"Hi, Charlie. What's this about another ten thousand?"

"See that?" He pointed to the lone standard electrical outlet in the outside wall. "Gonna need a heckuva lot more power than that to run an X-ray machine. Have to rewire the whole place, top to bottom. And listen to this." He stomped on the floor. It trembled and gave back a hollow sound. "This floor'll have to be reinforced. Those machines weigh a ton."

He pushed past Emily toward the door. "And lookit here." He led the way into the tiny restroom crowded into the back corner beside a broom closet. "This here's the only plumbing in the whole damn place. Gonna need a sink in every exam room, minimum, plus a john that'll take a wheelchair."

"But, Charlie—I can see all this is necessary, but surely you must have known about it when you gave your original estimate. Why didn't you factor all this in?"

Charlie glared at Sam, who flushed purple. "I, uh—sorta forgot to mention the X-ray machine in the plans. And the sinks were kind of an afterthought, too."

Emily dug her nails into her palms. Luke had warned her she ought to bring in a professional with experience in medical facilities to draw up the plans for the remodeling, but Sam had been adamant she and Charlie could handle it between them, and Emily had not been unwilling to save a little money. Beatrice would never have been so foolish. "Never scrimp on quality," she'd always told Emily on their annual clothes-shopping trips to Portland. "You'll only pay for it in the end."

But this mistake was going to cost her a lot more than the price of a poorly made dress. "The thing is, Sam, I have my own remodeling going on. I can't spend my whole capital all at once."

"Can't go on without that ten grand," Charlie growled. Sam shot Emily a mute puppy-dog entreaty that was all the more heart-wrenching for being ridiculous on her broad, mannish face.

Emily was beginning to feel like a walking checkbook. "The whole town's going to benefit from this clinic. Wouldn't it be better if they all had a chance to contribute? Give them a sense of ownership."

Sam's eyes widened like a cornered rabbit's. "You want me to go hat in hand to every house in town? No time for that. Still have a practice to run."

"I was thinking more along the lines of holding a fund-raiser."

"Even worse. Wouldn't know where to start."

"I'll take care of it." Emily quailed internally. She knew nothing about running fundraisers. But she could find someone who did.

From the clinic she puttered around the corner to Luke's office. He was just leaving.

"Hey there, beautiful, want to join me for lunch?"

"Sure, but I have a question for you. Who in this town would be good at running a fundraiser?"

"Huh. That's a tough one. Beatrice always did that kind of thing in the past. What do you want a fundraiser for?"

She told him about the clinic. "And before you say 'I told you so,' I've already given myself that lecture, so don't bother."

He grinned. "Y'know, I bet Katie'd have some good ideas."

"I bet she would." And it would take her mind off the situation with Jake and Roman. "I'll start there."

Over lunch he told her he would be going to Portland for a few days toward the end of the month. "Firearms certification. Have to do it every year." He gave her a wistful look. "Why don't you come with me?"

"To Portland?" She'd lived in Portland for thirty years, and it was only a two-hour drive away. But somehow, coming from Luke, traveling to Portland sounded like trekking to the South Pole.

"Sure. You could say hi to Marguerite, check on your renters, hang out at that bookstore you like. Powell's, right? And when I'm done for the day, we can do—whatever you used to do in Portland. Restaurants, symphony, whatever."

It should have been the perfect plan. Combining everything she loved and missed about her old life with her new life—Luke. But instead it appealed to her about as much as garlic-flavored ice cream.

"I don't know, Luke. It doesn't seem like a good time to be away, you know? With the remodeling, and now a fundraiser to plan. I feel like I need to be here to keep things running smoothly."

"You don't think Katie can handle it? That girl's got compe-tence oozing out her pores."

"Normally, yes, but right now she also has Jake to contend with. And the other worker, Roman—he seems to have some weird thing for her, too. That's another reason I can't leave. I need to keep an eye on Katie."

He sighed and dropped the subject, leaving her to chew over her own feelings along with her sandwich. Why should Luke and Portland seem like such a bad combination? Was it because Philip's ghost haunted Portland for her? But surely he was laid to rest by now; he hadn't spoken to her in months, and the last feeling she'd had from him was a blessing on her relationship with Luke.

No, it was just that she couldn't picture Luke at Reed or at the symphony or even at Powell's. He was too big for those places—not in physical dimensions, but in presence. He needed the open air, miles of beach and infinite expanse of ocean, with only enough people to keep life interesting. Morally and emo-tionally he was nothing like Heathcliff, but they had that one quality in common—they needed *space*.

A relationship in which she and Luke split their time be-tween Stony Beach and Portland—an idea Luke had floated when they first got back together—would never work. Luke and Stony Beach were a package deal. Was she really ready to take them on for life?

After lunch, Emily found Katie painting the kitchen of her new apartment. Her younger sisters Abby and Erin called greetings from the bathroom and bedroom, respectively.

"Wow, you have a whole crew working here!"

Katie dimpled. "Yeah, it goes faster with help. Besides, the three of us used to do everything together. The Three Muske-teers."

From the other rooms came the cry, "All for one and one for all!"

"It's been tougher since I've been living here. So I rope them in whenever I can."

"That's good news, actually, because I have an idea that I think we're going to need a lot of help with." Emily related her thoughts about putting on a fundraiser for the clinic. Abby and Erin, paint rollers in hand, crept closer as she talked.

"Hmm . . ." Katie pondered as she brushed on a sunny yellow between the backsplash and the upper cabinets. "My high school drama class did a murder mystery dinner once for a fundraiser. I bet I could get them to do one here."

Emily grimaced. "This house has seen two real murders. I'm not sure I could get into the spirit of a pretend one."

"Yeah, I know what you mean. But people love that stuff. We charged a hundred bucks a head and made ten thousand dollars."

"Lots of people would pay just to get a good close look at Windy Corner," Erin chimed in. "And if we did it on Halloween, that would really go over big. We could even make it a period costume thing."

Emily did some quick mental arithmetic. "Ten thousand at a hundred a head—that's a hundred people. We couldn't seat a hundred people for dinner at Windy Corner. Could we?"

Katie brushed a stray hair out of her eyes, leaving a smear of yellow paint on her temple. "I bet we could. Four tables of six each in the dining room, the parlor, and the library. And we could use the downstairs bedroom, too—Lizzie and I'll be out of it way before Halloween. That's almost a hundred—make a couple of the tables seat eight and you'll have it."

The thought of all those people in her home made Emily's palms sweat. And the ticket price made her cringe. Not so long ago it would have been painful even for her.

"I want this to be a way the whole town can participate in the new clinic. Lots of people can't afford a hundred dollars."

"You could raffle off a couple tickets—five bucks a go. Probably get more than the regular price of the tickets that way."

"That's a thought." *Deep breath, Emily. You can do this.* "What would we have to do on our end?"

"Well, the food, of course. Unless you want to have that catered?"

Emily winced, remembering the bill for the catering of Beatrice's funeral reception. "Catering would really cut into the profits. But dinner for a hundred—I couldn't ask you to handle that on your own."

Abby spoke, so quietly Emily almost didn't hear. "I work at Gifts from the Sea. They do catering. I think they'd give you a discount for a fundraiser."

"And I can do the publicity!" Erin cut in, bouncing on her toes in excitement. "I'm awesome at graphic design."

Katie nodded. "She really is. Even people who aren't related to her think so." She flashed a grin at Erin.

"But where would they stage the whole mystery thing?" Emily was still doubtful. "Downstairs would be too crowded."

"Yeah, we'd have to use the second floor for that. That would mean putting off redecorating the author rooms, unless you think we could finish in time."

"No, we'd better wait on anything big. I can use the time to finish planning. Then we can jump in after the fundraiser."

Katie's eyes lit up. "Ooh, and the secret stairway would come in handy."

"I'm not sure I want to give away that secret to the whole town."

"I know. But it's part of the romance of the place, y'know? It would add a lot." Erin and Abby nodded their agreement.

"I'll think about it. So you really think we can pull this off?"

"Sure we can. I'll call the drama teacher tonight." The three Parker girls leaned in for a high-fifteen. "All for one and one for all!"

Emily kissed Katie's cheek and beamed at her sisters. "You are a treasure, Katie Parker. I don't know what I'd do without you."

five

The red-room was a square chamber, very seldom slept in, . . . the carpet was red; the table at the foot of the bed was covered with a crimson cloth; . . . the wardrobe, the toilet-table, the chairs were of darkly polished old mahogany.

—*Jane Eyre*

Within a few days, Emily's period decor books arrived, and she spent a pleasant morning paging through them and making notes for her redecoration. In the afternoon she invited Veronica Lacey and Devon Penhallow to tea in order to show them the rooms and get the benefit of their expertise.

Veronica had seen Windy Corner before, but Devon had not. He could hardly settle down to his tea, he was so fascinated with the library—both the room itself and its contents.

"I've rarely seen workmanship like this in America," he said, running his small, smooth hand along the molding surrounding the curved bookcase that concealed the secret stairway. "Or such beautifully bound books. I could almost believe I was in an English manor house."

"I take that as the highest compliment," said Emily. "Or would, if I were in any way personally responsible for them. But

I'm only a steward. Do sit down and have some tea before it gets cold."

"Of course. I beg your pardon." Devon hitched up the knees of his custom-tailored wool trousers and perched his diminutive form on a straight chair. "Milk and two sugars, please."

Emily poured milk into one of Beatrice's bone china teacups, then added tea and used the silver tongs to drop in two cubes of sugar. With Devon here, she was glad to have the necessary accoutrements to serve a proper English tea. Katie had provided a luscious array of finger sandwiches, cakes, and scones to complete the effect.

"What do you hear from Hilary?" she asked.

"Oh, he's having a high old time scouring the country for antiques. It isn't easy these days to find good pieces that people are willing to part with—not like in my grandfather's time, when everyone was eager to modernize. But Hilary said he picked up some excellent eighteenth-century bargains at an estate sale in Wales. He'll be shipping them over next month. He and his finds should all be home by Christmas."

"Good. I plan to have a real Dickensian Christmas this year, and you must all join me."

"What fun! I'll tell Hilary to bring home some party crackers—I doubt you can get them round here."

Veronica said, "I make a mean plum pudding, believe it or not. That can be my contribution."

"And I'll lead the singing, if you like," Devon put in. "I was a choirboy, you know."

"Goodness, between you, you'll leave nothing for Katie and me to do. But thank you—it'll be more fun as a group effort."

They finished their tea, and Emily led them through the

bedrooms. Devon and Veronica approved the Brontë room as it stood. The heavy mahogany furniture and the dark red drapes and bed hangings evoked the red-room that had struck such terror into the heart of the young Jane Eyre. "I have a silhouette of Charlotte Brontë in the shop," Veronica said. "That will make the perfect finishing touch."

In the similar room next to it, the planned Montgomery room, Devon examined the massive four-poster bed and tallboy dresser. "If I were you, I'd move these down to the Dickens room. They'd be just right there. You'll have to add a writing desk, of course. I think we have one that would harmonize."

"And I have all kinds of things that will work for Montgomery," Veronica said. "A lovely white wrought-iron bed frame, plenty of old quilts, a braided rug, some lace curtains—all you need is a cherry tree outside the window. Anne Shirley would be right at home."

Beatrice's old room, with its semicircular bay echoing that of the library beneath, was to become the Forster room—*A Room with a View*. It was pronounced nearly perfect as it was. "If you want to be really clever," Veronica said with a twinkle in her eye, "you could draw a big question mark on the back of one of the pictures."

Emily smiled. "I'd thought about that."

The east room, destined to be the Austen room, had the visitors temporarily stumped. "Oh, dear," said Devon.

"I know," Emily replied. "Oh, dear." This room was the only one in the house with the proper Georgian proportions, unbroken by bay or dormer. But its furniture was dark, heavy, and unappealing—except for the carved headboard with its secret compartment. "It wouldn't be hard to make it allude to *Northanger Abbey*—to Catherine's preconceptions about the place, that is. But I rather wanted it to be a room Jane herself would have been comfortable in."

Veronica nodded. "Light, airy, elegant, simple. That's what Jane would want, I think."

"You know," said Devon, "some of those eighteenth-century pieces Hilary picked up in Wales might be perfect in here. Shall I have him look out for some period linens as well? Period imitations, that is—actual period linens wouldn't have survived in proper condition for everyday use." He turned to Veronica. "I don't want to trespass on your department, though."

"No, no, that's fine. It's difficult to find anything pre-Victorian in this part of the world."

Finally they turned to the small bedroom at the end of the hall that would become the Dostoevsky room—evoking Raskolnikov's garret. This room had been neither used nor much cared for since Emily's brother Geoff slept there on vacations thirty-five years before. The furniture looked like leftovers from a rummage sale held in the 1950s. Stained and peeling wallpaper covered the short dormer walls, while a threadbare rug failed to disguise the wood floor's desperate need of refinishing.

"The flavor isn't too far off, actually," Devon said. "All you need is some older furniture. I'm afraid you won't find anything sufficiently dilapidated in my shop. Perhaps an estate sale somewhere nearby?"

"You know, there might be some things in my attic. Katie and I ran across a few battered old pieces when we reorganized up there. But they'd have to be mended. The room might be meant to look shabby, but we can't have guests falling through the bed in the middle of the night."

"No." Veronica's mouth twitched. "Then you'd have to call it the Thurber room."

Emily laughed. "And get a big dog. Which the cats would never approve."

Devon looked baffled—having, presumably, never read James Thurber's story, "The Night the Bed Fell." "I could probably handle the mending for you. May I see the pieces you found?"

"The guys are still working up there. I don't want to get in their way." Emily turned at a clomping noise to see Jeremiah and his men descending the attic stairs, which faced the doorway they were standing in. "Oh, it looks like they're finishing for the day. I guess we can go up."

She greeted Jeremiah and asked about the day's progress. "Going fine, ma'am. Got the walls framed in. Should be safe if you want to go up and look around." He touched his cap brim to Emily, then stared past her at Devon, his nostrils flaring.

Emily smelled trouble. If Jeremiah had zero tolerance for lustful heterosexuals, how would he treat a gay man? Hurriedly she said, "Good night, Jeremiah," and he blinked, nodded, and moved on. Roman shuffled after his boss without raising his head, but Jake paused to give Devon the once-over with a contemptuous smirk. Then he sauntered off after the others, whistling.

Emily turned to see the usually even-tempered Devon red-faced, his jaw tight and his fists clenched. "Devon, what's wrong?"

"That young fellow worked on our shop remodel. He clearly thought Hilary and I were not fit for him to wipe his boots on. Several of our more valuable pieces were badly damaged in moving in. I'm morally certain he did it on purpose, but I can't prove it."

"Did you report it to Luke? Sheriff Richards?"

Devon stared at his patent-leather toes. "I'm ashamed to say we did not. We didn't want to cause trouble, make ourselves conspicuous. And besides—well, small-town lawmen aren't always the most sympathetic to—people like us."

Emily felt her own face flame. "Luke isn't like that. A citizen is a citizen, and his job is to protect us all. Promise me you won't let yourselves be bullied that way in the future."

Devon looked up at her and managed a smile in which his eyes did not participate. He gave an unconvincing nod.

Emily led the way up the stairs and into the main attic, where all the stored items were crowded together. The broken furniture was not too deeply buried. The three of them managed to unearth a single bed frame, a dresser, an end table, and a small desk—mismatched and in poor repair, but all of an old enough style to pass for a late-nineteenth-century garret.

Devon examined the pieces and declared them all mendable. "I'll come back on a dry day with my truck and pick them up."

"Thanks, Devon. I really appreciate it."

"No problem. It'll give me something to do. I like to keep my hand in."

Emily showed Devon and Veronica to the door. "Thanks again, both of you. The Windy Corner Writers' Retreat Center is well on its way."

On Saturday, when the workers weren't there, Emily and Katie began the process of moving unwanted knickknacks and linens from the second-floor bedrooms to the attic. After about the fifth trip up the attic stairs, Emily flopped on the top step, feeling certain her lungs would burst and her legs cramp permanently from all that climbing.

"I think I'm going to need an elevator up here," she said to Katie. "I'm getting too old for all these stairs. And once the retreat center is going, I'll need to be up and down them a lot more frequently."

Katie looked bemused as only the young can in the face of elderly weakness. "I guess an elevator could be handy for the guests, too. But where would you put it?"

"Good question." She wouldn't want to replace the attic stairway or she could be trapped in an emergency. The back stairway was already marked for sacrifice to make way for an extra bathroom on the second floor and an expanded pantry below.

But there was one space that was almost never used, and it might be made to extend the full height of the house. "What about the secret stairway?"

"You wouldn't want to get rid of that, would you? It's so cool. What's a big old house like this without a secret passage?"

"I know. I'm not crazy about the idea myself, but I don't see another way. I won't rush into anything."

However, it couldn't do any harm to have Jeremiah check out whether the idea was even feasible. It would have to take last priority if she did decide to do it, so she had plenty of time to consider.

On Monday she caught Jeremiah on his way in and asked him to look over the space with her. He brought Roman along, and they entered through the curved bookcase in the library.

Jeremiah shone his powerful flashlight around the unlit stairwell. "No electricity in here, huh? Course, we'd have to wire it special for an elevator anyway." He took out his tape and had

Roman hold it against one side of the circular wall while he skirted the stairs to reach the opposite side. "It's big enough. But if you want it to go all the way up, I'll have to check the plans to see what's up there."

"Let's do that now." She led the way up the spiral stairs to the top landing that opened into Beatrice's room. Jeremiah and Roman both ran their hands over the solid cedar paneling. "Good wood here. Shame to waste it," Roman said.

"I know. But like I said, it's just an idea at this point. I haven't decided anything yet."

They went on up to the attic, where Jeremiah spread out the plans on his worktable and examined them. "Looks like the shaft would come out about here." He pointed to a spot between the existing stairs and Emily's tower bedroom, where currently there was only a hall leading to the back attic.

"So that could work?"

"Looks okay. Have to check the structural drawings."

"Sure thing. Let me know what you figure out."

Emily went back downstairs, realizing she'd faintly hoped her idea would prove to be impossible—at least it would have taken the difficult decision out of her hands. What would Aunt Beatrice have done? She'd valued the house at its full worth, but she was wholly practical, neither sentimental nor romantic. Obviously she hadn't felt the need of an elevator in her time—she'd been remarkably strong, even into her eighties—but if she'd needed it and it could be put in without doing great violence to the house, she'd have done it. Emily was almost certain of that.

six

"If he loved with all the puny powers of his being, he couldn't love as much in eighty years as I could in a day."
—Heathcliff to Nelly Dean, *Wuthering Heights*

A few days later, Emily received a call from Holly Carver in the Reed College development department.

"Hi, Emily. Just a nudge about that bequest of yours. You said you wanted to set it up as a trust for a scholarship fund, remember?"

Back in June, when she'd made her will shortly after receiving her inheritance, Emily had included a sizable bequest to Reed but had never formalized the terms of the trust. She wanted to be sure the scholarships would go to the kind of students she herself would choose—those with real creativity and a passion for literature, not just those with the highest SAT scores.

"Oh, right. Thanks for reminding me, Holly. I'll get my lawyer on that right away."

After briefly catching up with the goings-on at Reed, she hung up with Holly and called her young lawyer in Tillamook, Jamie

MacDougal. "It's time I set up that formal trust fund for Reed College. Can I come see you sometime in the next few days?"

"I'm free late this afternoon. But why don't I come up to Windy Corner? Your library's more comfortable than my office anyway."

Emily smiled to herself. She knew Windy Corner's true attraction for Jamie, and it had nothing to do with the comfort of the library. "Fine. Why don't you come for tea? Four o'clock?"

"I'll be there."

Jamie arrived five minutes early. Even though she knew Katie was busy preparing tea, Emily stayed in the library and waited for her to let him in. She watched through the crack of the hall door as Katie went to the front entrance with Lizzie on her hip.

She greeted Jamie with simple friendliness, but the tilt of her head suggested a self-consciousness that was probably bringing a blush to her unseen cheeks. Jamie, in contrast to previous encounters with Katie, managed to find his tongue. He pulled a grotesque face to make Lizzie laugh, then offered the usual remarks about how she had grown and how adorable she was— hardly original, but guaranteed to dispose a mother in his favor. Emboldened by Katie's response, he moved on to a question about the remodeling.

"It's going great. My new apartment's all done—I painted it myself. When you're done with Mrs. Cavanaugh, why don't you come up and have a look?"

Emily's surprise at this bold move from Katie was mirrored on Jamie's face. As he stuttered out a reply, Roman rounded the bend of the stairs, carrying a load of rubbish. Glowering in Jamie's direction, he pushed between him and Katie and out the front door without so much as an "excuse me." The two of them watched Roman out, gaping.

Katie recovered first. "Come on back. I'll have tea ready in a minute."

Emily hastily shut the door and scurried back to her chair, where she picked up her knitting. She was working on a sweet little ivory alpaca sweater, hat, and mittens for Lizzie—a nice break from the lengthy sweater project she'd recently finished for herself.

When Jamie came in, she set the knitting down and rose to shake his hand. "How are you? I haven't seen you for a while." At close range now, she noticed his fiery shock of hair had been trimmed and beaten into submission with some sort of goop that flattened it to his head. He had also acquired a navy pinstripe suit that actually fit him in place of the old one, which had looked like a hand-me-down from a big brother at least two sizes larger than he. Jamie looked more like a professional now, but Emily rather missed the little-boy image he was trying to leave behind.

He grinned, and the little boy was back. "Good. Busy. I really appreciate the clients you've sent my way." Emily had been talking up his services to anyone who would listen. An honest lawyer with moderate fees was a treasure she couldn't keep to herself.

She nodded at the briefcase he held. "Why don't you set that on the table. We'll have tea first and then get down to business."

They sat in the wing chairs before the fire. Katie brought in the tea on a large silver tray and set it on a low table between them.

"Join us, Katie. Bring Lizzie in, too."

Katie blushed and went out to return in a moment with Lizzie and a blanket, which she spread on the hearthrug before setting the baby down. She handed Lizzie a biscuit to gnaw on while Emily poured the tea.

"Tell Jamie about our fundraiser, Katie."

Katie's usual animation returned as she described the plans for the murder mystery dinner. "You'll come, won't you?"

"Oh! Sure! Sounds like fun. And I'll spread the word to my clients, too." He said "clients" as a new author might say "my book." "Do you have a flyer or something?"

"Not yet, but I'll send some along when I get them." Katie shot a look at Emily.

Emily knew what that look meant. She herself was the bottleneck on all the publicity. "I know, it's my job to write the copy. And I could do it in two minutes if I could just think of a name for the darn thing. I mean, really—we're hosting a fake murder for the benefit of a life-giving clinic. What do you do with that? 'Murder for Life'?"

Jamie grinned. "Kill for a Cure?"

"Healed by Death?" Katie put in.

They tossed around more impossible options, until finally Jamie said, "You could just ignore the problem and go with a classic, like 'The Game Is Afoot.' Everybody knows what that means."

"Good idea. All right, Katie, I'll get that copy done tonight."

They finished tea, and Katie rose to clear the dishes away. Jamie followed her with his eyes, sheer adoration shining there now that she wasn't looking at him. When she closed the door behind her after returning to retrieve Lizzie, he gave a sigh that summed up the hopelessness of generations of would-be lovers.

"I'm pretty sure she likes you," Emily said. "I wouldn't rush her, but I think you can allow yourself to hope."

Jamie jumped and blushed purple. "Oh, gosh, is it that obvious?"

"I'm afraid it is. But I don't think that's a problem. She seems to like it."

"And you—don't mind?"

"I don't know anyone I'd rather lose her to. She needs a good man in her life, if only to keep the wolves away."

"You mean like that dude who went by when I came in? I thought he was going to stab me with that broken board he was carrying."

"He's one of them, yes. Though probably not the most dangerous."

Jamie whistled. "I'd better get back to karate class."

Emily laughed. "Let's hope it won't come to an actual fight."

Okay, so maybe I don't have to give up on the entire male sex. 'Cause there is at least one guy in the world like Jamie.

It's funny—Jamie looks at me like he can't get enough of me, too, but it's totally different from Roman. And TOTALLY different from him. With Jamie I feel like any little thing I do makes him so happy, so grateful, so surprised I'd pay him any attention at all—which makes me want to pay him more. With Roman it's more like he's demanding something, though I don't know exactly what, and he's mad that he's not getting it. Which, of course, makes me want to have nothing to do with him.

And the way he looked at Jamie today—if looks could kill! Ugh. I hope Mrs. C warned Jamie to stay out of Roman's way.

The next morning, Emily was showering in the second-floor bathroom when the water suddenly went cold. She rinsed off hurriedly, threw on her robe, and went to check the water heater.

It was set as usual, and she wasn't aware of any extraordinary hot water use so early in the day. She'd have to get Billy Beech, her part-time gardener and handyman, to look at it when he came in.

But Billy called in sick, even though it was the first day in weeks that was dry enough for him to have done some gardening. Billy was zealous enough in the summertime, but Emily suspected he preferred to regard the rainy season as one long vacation. No matter, she had a whole crew of skilled workers on the spot—though the plumbing work wouldn't begin for a while.

She caught Jeremiah Edwards when he came in. "Jeremiah, do you have a competent plumber here at this point? I think there's something wrong with the hot water in the upstairs bathroom."

He nodded solemnly. "Roman said he'd done some plumbing. I'll send him down when he gets here."

Explaining the problem to Roman might give Emily a chance to find out more about him. "All right. The sooner the better, please."

She'd barely dipped into *Wuthering Heights* when Roman knocked on the library door. "Boss said you had a plumbing problem."

"Yes. I lost hot water halfway through my shower this morning, and I can't figure out why."

She led him up the stairs, treading slowly despite his obvious impatience. "So, Roman, Katie tells me you and she have met before."

He made an affirmative-sounding grunt. "Seventh grade."

"You were only in the school for that one year?"

He nodded. "Moved around a lot."

"Was your father in the military?"

This time the grunt was negative.

"Transferred for his work?"

Derisive snort. "Could say that."

Emily didn't want Roman to feel she was interrogating him—even though she was. "My own father could never keep a job for more than a year. He had—shall we say, issues. With alcohol, mainly. Maybe your situation was similar?"

Roman stopped on the stair, and she turned to face him. "My father was a migrant worker. Along with all the rest of my family. My parents worked themselves to death. I got a lucky break and learned building work. Now I'm back here to stay. Satisfied?" He clamped his mouth shut as if angry with himself for letting so many words escape at one time. He pushed past her and continued up the flight.

Emily followed, somewhat taken aback. "Why choose Stony Beach of all the places you've been? It isn't exactly a builder's paradise."

He stopped and faced her again. "Because of Katie. I've loved her since seventh grade. She's the reason for everything I do."

He stared at her fiercely from under his shaggy bangs as if daring her to object. "You think I'm not good enough for her. But I will be. I'll have my own company by the time I'm twenty-five. I'll be a solid citizen. She'll have no reason to say no to me then."

Emily felt as if someone had filled her inner ear with water, throwing her sense of balance into a tailspin. Surely he hadn't said all this to Katie herself. "And it doesn't matter to you that she has a baby? Some other man's child?"

"That baby belongs to Katie, period. And anything that belongs to Katie belongs to me."

That was surely an odd way of putting it. And the ferocious light in Roman's black eyes looked to Emily not like love but like obsession. It made her think of Heathcliff's obsession with Cathy. Roman could easily be the kind of lover who would kill the object of his passion rather than let her love another man. Or kill the man. Or both.

Dumbfounded, she passed him at the top of the stairs and led him in silence to the cupboard that held the water heater. He tapped and prodded, turned this knob and that, and at last pronounced her water heater dead. She would have to get a new one.

A new water heater, and perhaps a new remodeling crew. This one was making her very nervous indeed.

Luke had an invitation to Windy Corner for dinner the night before he was to leave for Portland. He figured this was a good sign. Lunches at the Crab Pot were all well and good, but they were public and had a definite end point, since he always had to get back to work. Dinner at Windy Corner, on the other hand, could theoretically lead to just about anything.

He arrived a little early. The construction workers were just clearing out. Luke waved to Jeremiah Edwards and saw a young fellow climbing into the passenger side of his truck. Shady-looking type, shaggy-haired and scowling. Must be that other fellow Emily mentioned—what was his name?

Emily opened the door to him wearing his favorite dress— the same one she'd worn that night back in June when he took her to Gifts from the Sea and they figured out what went wrong all those years ago. She wouldn't have forgotten. That dress had to be a good sign.

She let their hello kiss linger longer than usual, too. He slipped his arm around her as they walked back to the dining room. All he wanted was her by his side like this for the rest of their lives. She seemed to enjoy it, too. The warmth of her body went all through him so that he almost forgot his question.

"By the way, that guy I saw outside, getting into Edwards's truck—dark, shaggy young guy, looked like he hated the world and everyone in it. That the other guy you mentioned who has a thing for Katie?"

"Yes, that sounds like Roman. Kind of startling-looking, isn't he?"

"You can say that again. If we could arrest people 'cause they looked likely to commit a crime, I'd have him locked up before you could say 'suspicious character.'"

Katie served their dinner—a steak so tender, he could have cut it with a butter knife. He savored a few bites before asking Emily, "So what have you been up to lately?"

"Let's see . . . Oh, I had Devon and Veronica over the other day to help me plan the redecorating. I won't be able to start on it until after the fundraiser, but I want to have some plans in place so we can get going once that's done."

"Devon . . . remind me who that is?"

"Devon Penhallow. From Remembrance of Things Past. The new antique shop? Devon's the small one."

"Oh, right. Stony Beach is really coming into the twenty-first century now, with a gay couple right downtown."

Emily frowned, and Luke wondered if she considered his little joke in poor taste. But she said, "Not all the residents of Stony Beach are living in this century, apparently. Jake passed us in the hall and gave Devon the rudest look I've ever seen. In fact, Devon suspects Jake of deliberately damaging some of their furniture when they were moving in."

"Come to think of it, Charlie Cartwright told me about that. Why didn't Devon report it?"

"He said he didn't have any proof, and he wasn't sure you'd be sympathetic. I told him you'd never discriminate—you protect all citizens equally."

"Course I do. I know what he means, though. I know fellas, right in my own department, can't put their personal feelings aside and do their duty. Not to mention nasty citizens. Can't understand what makes people behave that way."

Emily shook her head. "For that matter, the look Jeremiah Edwards gave Devon could have fried this steak. He doesn't seem too welcoming, either."

"You know he's a preacher, right? Part-time. Real hellfire and brimstone stuff."

"I'm not surprised. Why does he bother with construction? I'd think he'd be preaching full-time."

"He might like to, but his congregation's not big enough to support him. Doesn't have a real church, just a dozen or so hard-cores that meet in his living room. Not part of any recognized denomination, far as I know. Call themselves the Church of the Elect of the Almighty."

"Sounds about right."

When they retired to the library, he made sure they sat on the love seat instead of the wing chairs. She let him put his arm around her, but she wouldn't relax.

"Something wrong, beautiful?" he asked her. "I'm getting the feeling you're not all here."

She looked up at him, then laid her head on his shoulder.

"I'm sorry, Luke. I'm just worried, I guess." She dropped her voice. "About Katie."

"You mean about having Jake in the house?"

"Jake for sure, but Roman's starting to creep me out, too." She told him about their conversation that afternoon. "What do you think?"

"Sounds like stalker material to me." He frowned. Two bad eggs after Katie was two too many. "I'm starting to think you ladies might need some protection. Want me to stay over for a while?" It wouldn't be the first time he'd spent the night at Windy Corner to protect Emily from a possible assailant.

"What good would that do? You'd be here at night. Roman's only here during the day."

"For now he is. But if he decided to do something crazy, like as not he'd come back at night."

Emily shook her head. "Anyway, you're going to Portland tomorrow. Let's see how things stand when you get back."

seven.

She seemed desirous of getting away; to prevent it, he laid his hand on her arm. She averted her face, . . . supposing himself unseen, the scoundrel had the impudence to embrace her.

—*Wuthering Heights*

Katie's painting was finished and dry, and it was time for her and Lizzie to move into the apartment over the carriage house. The plan was to transfer the bedroom furniture from the room she was currently using—the future Dickens room—and to fill in the living area with odds and ends from the attic along with what had been in the apartment before.

Emily asked Jeremiah if he could spare a couple of guys to help move furniture. Only when Jake and Roman presented themselves in the main hall did it occur to her she had made a tactical error. Jake and Roman were the only guys on the job.

Katie was trundling boxes between the two buildings while Emily took care of Lizzie. But Emily couldn't take the chance that either of the young men might end up alone in the apartment with Katie. With Lizzie on her hip, Emily followed as they carried the dresser, end tables, and desk over to the carriage house and up the stairs, using the excuse of supervising where each piece was placed. Katie dropped her boxes in the living room and kept mostly out of the men's way; she avoided catching Roman's eye and flinched whenever Jake came within two yards of her. Jake kept whistling the same obnoxious, repetitive tune.

Finally the two young men disassembled the bed and carried it over piece by piece. They were nearly finished reassembling it when Emily heard an ominous sound from Lizzie and smelled an urgent need of a diaper change. She found the diapers and took the baby into the bathroom. Hearing footsteps pass through the hall behind her, she assumed both Jake and Roman had gone back to the house. But a minute later she heard voices from the bedroom—Katie's and a man's.

"Hey, not so fast there, girl. How come you've been avoiding me all this time?" His voice was smooth, insinuating, but with an intimidating edge.

"How can you ask such a thing? Isn't it obvious? I'd put half the Earth between us if I could."

"What, and keep that sweet little baby from ever knowing her daddy? I did the math, Katie. She's mine, isn't she?"

"It's none of your business whose she is. She's *mine*. I'm all the parent she needs."

"Every girl needs a man in her life. Including you. Especially you."

Emily heard scuffling and muffled protests. Hurriedly she taped up Lizzie's clean diaper and set her on the floor with a toy. "I'll be right back, sweetie." She ran into the bedroom.

Jake had a vise grip on both of Katie's arms and was pressing his mouth against hers. She struggled and squirmed but couldn't get free. Just as Emily was about to intervene, Katie shoved a knee up into Jake's groin. He released her, groaning. Katie sprang away from him and cowered in the corner, sobbing.

Emily spoke to Jake with more authority than she'd known she possessed. "Get out. Get off my property and do not come back. You're fired."

Crouched over and holding his crotch, Jake stared up at her, his face an ugly study in pain and frustrated lust. "Can't . . . move."

"You have thirty seconds." She stood back away from the door and saw that Roman had come up behind her.

He strode over to Jake and yanked him upright by his shirt with his left hand, shoving his right fist under Jake's nose. "If you—*ever*—touch her again—or so much as look at her—I will kill you."

Jake's head went back. He eyed Roman's fist in disbelief.

"You got that? I—*will*—kill you."

Emily believed him if Jake didn't. "That's enough, Roman. Let him go. Just make sure he leaves. Immediately."

Roman drove his point home a second longer with a glare that might have been lethal in itself, then reluctantly stepped back and dropped his fists. Jake shuffled out, still bent over, and Roman followed him like Nemesis.

Emily darted over to Katie, who was huddled in the fetal position, rocking. "Katie, honey, are you all right?" Stupid question—clearly she wasn't all right. Emily knelt beside her and folded her in her arms. "There, there, sweetheart. It's all over now." She stroked Katie's hair and murmured to her until her sobs subsided.

"Is he really Lizzie's father?" she asked, handing Katie a tissue.

Katie nodded as she blew her nose. "I never meant for it to happen."

"Did he—force you?"

"He'd been after me for weeks, but I wouldn't go out with him—I knew his reputation. Then I ran into him at a party. He brought me a drink—he must have put something in it, 'cause next thing I knew we were in a bedroom and he was—"

Suddenly Katie sprang to her feet and bolted to the bathroom. Emily rushed after her to see her vomiting into the toilet. Lizzie clung to her leg, whimpering.

Emily picked Lizzie up while Katie rinsed her mouth and composed herself. "So he raped you."

Katie nodded. "School was over, so I managed to avoid him after that. And then a few weeks later I found out I was pregnant."

"Why didn't you report him?"

Katie gave her a look. "Do you know who his father is?"

Emily remembered her conversation with Luke. "Oh, right. The hotshot lawyer."

"Girls have tried before. Never even gets to court."

"Lord, have mercy. There has to be some way he can be stopped."

Katie's face turned grim as death. "I think Roman's solution might be the only one that would work."

Emily's first impulse was to call Luke, but he was in Portland. He'd have his cell phone on him, no doubt, but wouldn't be able to talk in the middle of his training session. What a time for him to be out of town—his absence made her feel as if a swath of her clothing had been cut away at the back, leaving her unprotected and exposed. At least she'd had the prescience not to go with him. She shuddered to think what might have happened if she hadn't been here.

She made up the newly assembled bed, then persuaded Katie to lie down for a bit. "I'll take care of Lizzie. Do you want me to call Sam? Give you a sedative or something?"

"No, I think I'll sleep. I'm exhausted."

"Okay. The rest of the moving can wait till tomorrow."

She tucked Katie in, scooped up a confused and whimpering Lizzie and soothed her, and went in search of Jeremiah. She found him just coming out the back door on his way to lunch.

"Can I have a word?" All those British detective shows were rubbing off—the inspectors were always asking people if they could "have a word." Barnaby of the long-running *Midsomer Murders* must have acquired half the words in the English language by now.

Jeremiah pulled off his cap by way of assent.

"Come into the library." He followed her in. She grabbed a blanket and toy for Lizzie on their way through the kitchen and set her to play on the library hearthrug.

"You should know I've just fired Jake."

His eyebrows shot up. "What for?"

"He made a pass at Katie. Worse than that, actually—he was trying to force her. There's a—history between them, and it upset her pretty badly. I don't want her to have to look at him ever again."

His bushy brows drew down into a solid line over eyes sparking fire. "I'm with you, ma'am. I'd have fired him myself and given him a kick in the pants for good measure. The Lord hates a lustful man." His lantern jaw worked as if further words were fighting either to get out or to stay in. But all he said was, "I have a daughter myself."

"Good. I'm glad we understand each other. I didn't like going over your head, as it were, but it was a desperate situation."

"No problem with Roman, I hope?"

"No. In fact, he came to Katie's defense and escorted Jake off the property. I have to say I hope those two young men don't run into each other elsewhere, though. Roman was furious. I wouldn't answer for his behavior toward Jake in future."

"I'll keep an eye on him, ma'am. He's not a drinker, I'll say that for him. It's usually the demon drink that leads to trouble between my guys."

Emily willed her eyes away from the innocent bottle of sherry sitting on the bar shelf. "Well, anyway, Katie's resting now. We're going to wait till tomorrow to finish the moving. Can you get some different helpers? I still think it's best if Roman and Katie are kept apart."

He touched the brim of his cap. "Yes, ma'am."

Oh God, oh God, oh God. Here it is all over again, just like it had happened yesterday. I can smell him on me like I could then, he's all over me, I'll never be clean again. What is it about me that makes him do this? All I've ever said to him was no. No, no, a thousand times NO! How can he hear that as a "yes, please"?

Mrs. C sent him away, but how do I know he won't be back? I thought I was done with him before, and he turned up again like a bad penny. No, make that a bad million-dollar bill. No penny could be as bad as him. He's a billion filthy stinking counterfeit dollars' worth of bad. He ought to be locked up in a dark

dungeon full of mud and shit with all the filthy stinking crawl-
ing biting poisonous things ever invented. Forever.

And I can't even send him to a normal jail. His precious
daddy would just get him right out again. And make me look
like a slut in the process.

My poor Lizzie. She has to grow up in a world like this. With
that—thing—as her biological progenitor (I refuse to dignify
him with the usual word). But he'll never get his claws into her.
I'll make sure of that—or die trying.

After Emily had fed herself and Lizzie, she carried the baby and
Wuthering Heights back over to the carriage house to put Lizzie
down for her nap in her brand-new crib—new to her, at least; it
had come from the attic, and Luke had lovingly refinished it. In
the remodeling they'd carved out a tiny nursery adjacent to the
main bedroom, so she was hoping Katie wouldn't have to be disturbed. But Katie was in the shower when they came in.

Lizzie wasn't about to go straight to sleep—not with a brand-
new environment to explore. Emily had to use all her soothing
skills—singing, walking, bouncing, back-rubbing—to get the
baby to drop off before she laid her back down.

Once Lizzie was safely snoozing in the crib, Katie emerged
from the bathroom, pushing wet hair out of her dark-hollowed
eyes.

"Oh, Katie—couldn't you sleep?"

"I slept a little." She stumbled to a chair and dropped into it.

"You still look exhausted. Let me make you a cup of tea. If
I can find the necessary."

"I think that box is on the kitchen counter. Tea would be
great, thanks."

Emily rummaged among the boxes until she found a kettle, two mismatched mugs, and a box of herbal tea bags. It wouldn't be proper tea, but it would be soothing. She boiled the water, poured it, and carried the mugs back into the living room.

After the tea had cooled enough for Katie to sip a bit, Emily asked, "Are you up to talking about—things? I don't mean what happened today, but . . ."

"Yeah, all right. Probably better if I talk, it's been bottled up so long."

"I've just been wondering . . . What made you decide to keep the baby? A lot of girls in your situation would have wanted to— well, to get rid of it." Not that Emily could imagine herself wanting to get rid of a baby, no matter how it had come to be; but so many did these days.

"I wanted that at first, too. When I found out, the first few days, all I could think of was getting it out of me—I couldn't stand the thought that *his* cells were inside me, multiplying, taking over my body. I would've gone to the worst butcher, done anything to get rid of that alien thing in my womb."

Yes, that feeling Emily could imagine. "But—you didn't."

Katie shrugged. "I didn't have time. It's hours to the nearest Planned Parenthood. I was working full-time, plus running the house because Mom was on bed rest with my littlest brother. I didn't have one minute to myself, even to sleep—Abby and Erin were in the same room."

"So what changed your mind?"

A slow, sweet, teary smile spread across Katie's enervated face. "My baby brother. Actually more like my mom. She had him at home, like she did with all of us. Since I was about twelve, the midwife's been letting me help. I watched Mom go through agony—it was a really tough birth—thinking no way am I doing this for *his* baby. But then when it was over and the midwife put Stevie in her arms—all that pain just vanished like it had never been. I saw *joy* on her face. Pure joy."

Katie looked up at Emily, the tears flowing freely now. "He was her eighth baby, and half the time she didn't know where dinner was going to come from for the rest of us 'cause my dad drank up his paycheck before he could get it home. She was going to have to put the baby in a dresser drawer to sleep because number seven was still in the crib. But she looked at little Stevie as if he were the most wonderful thing that ever happened to her. She was just radiant.

"And then I knew. I knew I could have *my* baby and love her and think she was the most wonderful thing that ever happened to me. I was just sure she was a girl, and I knew she wouldn't be a bit like *him*. She'd be all mine, and I could raise her to be good and kind and respectful of other people." Her voice went hard and resolute. "And too damn smart to drink whatever some guy handed her at a party."

Emily reached over and squeezed her hand. "You couldn't have known."

Katie rolled her head from side to side on the back of the chair. "I was an idiot. I'd never been to a party like that, never drank at all because of my dad. But I'd turned eighteen and I thought, 'What the hey, one drink won't hurt.' And I was a virgin, too. I wanted to be like Lizzie Bennet, save myself for the man I loved. But it seems like there are a lot more Wickhams in the world than Darcys."

"Too true. But don't despair. I think Jamie's more of a Darcy, in his principles at least, and he's certainly crazy about you."

A little smile emerged through the tears. "Jamie. He is sweet, isn't he? I think I could almost feel safe with him." She sat up and looked Emily in the eye. "That's the worst of the whole thing. I've never felt *safe* since that night. Never felt clean or whole or like I could ever possibly have a normal relationship. I feel— polluted, defiled, unfit for any decent man."

At that moment Emily could have murdered Jake herself. She took Katie's hands and held them hard, as if thus she could impart her own conviction. "Katie, what happened to you was *not your fault*. Even if you might have avoided it by refusing that drink, you didn't make Jake the kind of person who would do such a thing. You didn't encourage him in any way—not that *that* would even excuse him. But you are *innocent*. Completely innocent. You can put this behind you and be whole again—so you can accept a good man's love."

Katie gave a sigh that seemed to come from the Earth itself. "I hope you're right, Mrs. C. I hope you're right."

Emily heard a knock at Katie's front door—a timid, tentative knock, as if the knocker knew he or she was interrupting something. She gave Katie's hands a last squeeze and went to the door. Jeremiah stood there, hat in hand. His expression— eyes full of apology, jaw clenched as if holding in rage—made Emily wonder how long he'd been standing there. This place didn't have foot-thick walls like the main house. How much might he have heard?

His jaw unclenched. "Sorry to interrupt, ma'am, but I need you to decide something before we can go on."

"Oh, certainly. What is it?"

"Hard to describe. Can you come up?"

Emily glanced over at Katie, who nodded. "Go ahead, we're fine."

Jeremiah led Emily over to the main house and up to the third floor. On the inside wall of what would become her sitting room, a section of paneled wall interrupted the plaster. "This isn't on the original plans," Jeremiah said. "They show the wall two feet further back. You want us to leave it in or take it out?"

"What's on the other side?"

"Flat wall straight across, right where the plans show it. No plumbing or anything else to account for it. Best guess, it was a closet at some point, but I don't know why they'd close it off."

Emily laid her hand against the wood and felt the slightest vibration under her palm. The wall was strangely cold. She had a sudden vision of bodies walled up to rot, like in "The Cask of Amontillado."

She jerked her hand back. "I'm inclined to leave it alone. What do you think?"

Jeremiah shrugged. "You're the boss."

"Leave it, then. The paneling is nice, and a couple of feet less space won't matter." She hoped she wouldn't live to regret that decision.

· eight ·

Marguerite, Reed French professor and Emily's closest friend, called that evening from Portland. "*Chérie*, why have you not called me? For weeks I do not hear one word. You are not having more murders, I hope?"

"No real ones, thank God. We are planning a fake one on Saturday." Emily told her about the upcoming fundraiser.

"*Mais chérie, c'est très amusant! Il faut que je ce vois.* You will invite me down for the weekend, *non*?"

Oh, dear. She should have seen this coming. "I would, Margot, of course, but between the remodeling and getting ready for the party, the house is in chaos. We wouldn't have a minute's peace."

"Peace I have plenty of at home. A little excitement is just what I need. I will see you on Friday night. Besides, you need my special touch in the arrangements, *non*?"

Marguerite did have an amazing knack for table settings and

centerpieces. "True. But it is a fundraiser—a hundred dollars a head. You'll have to pay for your ticket like anyone else."

"*Mon dieu, cent?* *Alors,* it is the price of a night in a hotel. You will not charge me for the room, I hope?"

"Of course not. You may have to put up with people traipsing through your room during the party, though. I think they're going to want to use the whole second floor."

"Then I will leave my diamonds at home." Marguerite trilled a laugh. As Emily well knew, a Reed professor's salary didn't run to much in the way of diamonds. "*À bientôt.*"

Emily put down the phone with a sigh. Whatever the coming weekend might be, it certainly wouldn't be boring.

The drama teacher who was orchestrating the mystery game came by a couple of days later to scope out the house. Katie let her in and brought her back to the library, where Emily was immersed in *Wuthering Heights*. If ever there was an antihero, Heathcliff was it. On this reading, it struck her with great force how much hatred was contained within that house, and all focused into the person of Heathcliff. Even his passion for Cathy looked more like hatred, a good part of the time, than love. Emily felt as if she were drowning in a Yorkshire bog of envy, resentment, and bitterness. She was happy to be interrupted.

The drama teacher bounced into the room, brightly colored garments trailing after her. A cloud of frizzy dark hair stood out a foot from her head, and her eyes were as wide as a child's on her first sight of a Christmas tree. "What a house!" she exclaimed, standing in the middle of the room with her hands raised and turning to take it all in. "The *energy*! This place was absolutely *made* for a mystery play!"

Emily stood. Katie said, "Mrs. Cavanaugh, this is Cordelia Fitzgerald, the drama teacher."

Emily's eyebrows rose. Who was the Montgomery fan, this woman's mother or she herself? She suspected the latter—the name of Anne Shirley's imaginary alter ego was a bit rich for common use.

"Pleased to meet you." Emily put out her hand.

Cordelia clasped it in both of her own. Emily was nearly overcome by the waves of heavy floral scent that emanated from the woman. "I can't thank you enough for giving us this opportunity. It'll be a godsend to my students—the chance to expand, to stretch themselves in this environment. We have a sweet little mystery all worked out, and I'm using only my best students—including a few alumni. We need some people with *experience* to do this place justice."

"So what's the plot?"

Cordelia wagged a finger under Emily's nose. "Ah, ah, ah— mustn't peek until the curtain goes up. That would be cheating."

"Oh—but I wasn't planning to participate in the game. As the hostess, I need to know what's going on. Make sure every- thing is—well, in order. It is my house, after all." *And I want to know what a bunch of strangers are planning to do in it.*

Cordelia closed her eyes and shook her head. "Absolutely not. I'll take care of everything. If you knew, you might give something away. Inadvertently, of course." She smiled brightly at Katie. "Now, Katie dear, if you'll just show me around all the rooms that will be open. Including that secret passageway."

Emily made a snap decision. "I'm afraid the passageway is off-limits. It comes out in my bedroom, and I don't want that room used."

"Oh, but we must!" Emily had rarely seen a grown woman

pout. It wasn't pretty. "I was counting on that. In fact I've built the plot around it. The secret passageway is absolutely essential!"

Cordelia clasped her hands, almost under Emily's chin. Emily's head filled with floral perfume till she could hardly breathe, let alone think. After all, the Beatrice-Forster room wasn't really her own bedroom. She could move her personal things back upstairs for one night.

"All right, you can use the passageway. But please don't use that bedroom any more than you can help."

A summer garden enveloped her in a smothering hug. "You're a darling. We'll be so careful, you won't even know we've been in the house. Now come along, Katie dear. Let's case the joint."

After that invasion, returning to the stark, cheerless, aggressively masculine world of *Wuthering Heights* was almost a relief.

The murder party was only a few days away, and Katie flung herself into preparations with the fever of someone striving to drown out unwelcome thoughts. Emily felt *de trop* in her own home. The little outfit she was knitting for Lizzie was almost finished—time to go yarn shopping for her next project.

The weather was cloudy but not actually rainy, so she went to the garage to get out the Vespa. Billy Beech was raking leaves under the poplars on the far side of the lawn, his spherical form bobbing like an apple in a barrel of water. He straightened and hailed her.

"A lovely good morning to you, dear lady. At last, you see, the sky has abated its flooding in beneficence so that I may prepare our grounds for the coming festivities." Billy puffed his way through his ponderous sentence and paused to wipe a bandanna over his sweaty brow. Emily wondered, not for the first time, whether Billy deliberately mugged up on Victorian literature to fuel his flowery speech patterns or whether by some bizarre genetic fluke they came naturally to him.

"Yes, thank God for that. I'm sorry you have to deal with all these wet leaves, though."

Billy flourished his bandanna in resignation. "It is the lot of my kind, dear lady. To grumble would only make the work more onerous. Is everything in order indoors?"

"Yes, thanks. The remodeling crew has the work under control, and Katie's getting the whole place even more spotless than usual for Saturday."

Billy gazed a bit wistfully at the attic windows. Emily guessed he was missing the indoor portion of his usual work, which would likely be a little easier on his stout, aging frame than was his current task.

"Don't worry, Billy—we'll all be back to normal in a few weeks."

He bowed his acquiescence and pocketed his kerchief with a final flourish, then returned to work.

Emily puttered into town on the Vespa and pulled up in front of the yarn shop, Sheep to Knits. Beanie, the young proprietor, hailed her from her perch behind the back counter. "Hey, Mrs. C! I was just thinking it was about time I saw you again."

"Yes, Lizzie's sweater is done and I'll finish the hat tonight. She's moved into her big-girl crib now—she needs a bigger blanket."

"I got a new cotton-acrylic blend in—so soft you wouldn't believe it. Come feel."

Beanie held out her knitting—a strip about twelve inches wide, the top few inches of which consisted of a sort of roaming seed stitch in a cheery yellow. Below that were cables in a nub-bly deep purple tweed, then a dropped-stitch pattern in a green-and-black eyelash yarn, then a few inches of intricate lace in a fine pale blue mohair. Beyond that the strip became Beanie's garment, winding around and around her body with a random-ness that would have baffled the most accomplished sari wrap-per. A black tank and leggings made sure she was decent, while tattoos covered what could be seen of her arms.

Emily rubbed the yellow yarn between her fingers—it was indeed soft as pure cashmere. "Washable, I presume?"

"Machine wash and dry. Only thing for a baby. It's over there." She pointed to a table heaped with all the colors of an Easter basket full of eggs. Beanie's shop never reflected the season outside her windows but always anticipated the next one.

Emily picked up an aqua, a salmon, and a spring green in turn, but finally settled on the same yellow Beanie was knitting with. Yellow was a good color for Lizzie and would harmonize with Katie's decor.

As she was filling her basket with enough skeins to make a crib-sized blanket, the outside door tinkled open and a tall manly form ducked in. Emily did a double take as she recognized the bookstore owner. "Ben! I didn't expect to see you here. Are you taking up knitting?"

He wouldn't meet her eyes. "Uh, no, I, uh . . ." He ended his nonsentence with a nervous smile and headed to the back of the shop, where he held an inaudible conference with Beanie. Emily immersed herself in pattern booklets, smiling. Months ago, when she first came to Stony Beach, she'd detected a wistful-ness in Ben where Beanie was concerned and had dropped a hint or two in Beanie's ear. Apparently the hints had been effective.

When Ben turned to go, both his face and Beanie's were subtly radiant. "See you later then," he said, and with a nod to Emily strode out of the shop. Emily noticed a new bounce in his step.

She took her selections to the counter. "Everything okay with you, Beanie?" She tried to keep her tone neutral but suspected she wasn't managing to keep the twinkle out of her eye.

"Absolutely fabulous, Mrs. C." Beanie dropped her voice to a whisper. "Aren't Ben's dreads to die for?"

Emily made an affirmative noise. Her deduction about the dreads had apparently been correct.

"He just invited me to go to your murder party with him. Way cool, 'cause I couldn't afford a ticket on my own."

"Wonderful! I hope you'll enjoy it. Katie's knocking herself out, and I think most of the tickets have been sold."

"Hey, Windy Corner? Murder mystery? Costumes? Bound to be epic. What could go wrong?"

At Beanie's last words, a finger of ice crept up Emily's spine. What indeed?

Luke stood up at his desk, stretched his back, cracked his neck. Must be lunchtime—he'd been sitting too long. What he needed was a good crime to get him out of the office. Problem was, any crime that happened on his beat would have to happen to somebody he knew. That was the side of being a small-town sheriff they didn't talk about on *Andy Griffith*.

Granted, he'd just had a break from his desk. He'd gotten back late last night from the firearms training in Portland. And he'd missed Emily something fierce. If only she'd agreed to come along—he wanted to take her out to fancy restaurants, maybe the symphony or something, show her he wasn't just a country bumpkin with no culture. But she wouldn't come. And anyway, he'd been so bone tired at the end of each day, all he wanted to do was lie on his hotel bed, eat room service food, and watch the tube. He hated to admit it, but he wasn't getting any younger.

But he was home now, and at least he could take her to lunch. He pulled out his cell phone and called Windy Corner. Katie told him Emily was out, so he called her cell. It rang once and went to message. Figured. Either she didn't have it on her, or the battery was dead, or she'd never bothered to turn it on in the first place. He'd talked her into getting the cell back in the summer when her life was in danger. Now that danger was past, he couldn't get her to see carrying a working cell phone was a good idea.

Oh, well, he'd walk down to the Crab Pot and maybe run into her along the way. But when he opened the front door of the one-story cottage that housed the sheriff's office, there she was, just pulling up on her Vespa. His heart did a little flip, as it always did whenever he saw her. How had he survived all those years without her?

"Hey, beautiful. I just tried to call you to invite you to lunch. You running around without your cell phone again?"

Emily felt around her skirt and jacket where pockets should be but weren't. Why did women put up with clothes with no pockets? "I must have left it at home. It doesn't seem like an appendage to me yet. But here I am anyway, appetite and all. Want to hop on?" She waved at the seat behind her.

Luke eyed the Vespa. He trusted that machine about as much as he would a giant version of the wasp it was named for. Good stiff breeze could blow it right off the road. He didn't like to see Emily riding it, although he had to admit she made quite a picture with her long full skirt and ladylike jacket topped by that funky green helmet—like two centuries mashed into one. "I can't be seen around town riding shotgun on that thing. Bad for my image."

"So drive then." She scooted back on the seat.

"No license. Can't we just walk?"

"Oh, all right." She turned off the Vespa, set the kickstand, and took off her helmet. Her braid came loose from its pins and tumbled down her back. She used to wear it like that when they were kids—when he first fell in love with her. He could remember the very first time he undid that braid.

He moved up close to her and fingered the little curls that escaped along her hairline. "I like your hair like that. Reminds me of the old days." He put his arms around her waist, pinning her to the bike, and kissed her like he was making up for lost time. Which he was.

When he gave her the chance, Emily murmured, "Isn't this bad for your image, too?"

"Heck no. Kissing the most beautiful woman in town? I get all kinds of sheriff points for that."

Emily smiled and slid off the seat. "Let's go eat. I'm starved."

As they ate, she filled him in on what had been going on while he was away. When she told him about Jake attacking Katie—and the history behind it—he felt the blood go straight to his head. He'd asked for a crime, but he sure as hell hadn't wanted Katie of all people to be the victim.

"That bastard. She could just charge him with assault, you know. No need to bring up the past."

"But don't you suppose the defense would use their previous relationship against her? Make it look like she was consenting all along?"

"Yeah, you're probably right. Man, it burns me up. I'd like to round up that whole damn family and send them off to Siberia or something. Upstate Alaska maybe. Times I wish we didn't live in a free country."

"Coming from you, that's quite a statement." He'd flown the biggest Stars and Stripes in town on the Fourth of July—one at the office and one at home.

"I love my country. Doesn't mean I think it's perfect. You say you fired Jake?"

"On the spot. When I told Jeremiah Edwards, he said he would've done the same."

"Let's just hope he stays away. If he shows up again, let me know and I'll get a restraining order out on him." It wasn't much, but it was something, and all he could legally do unless Katie pressed charges.

"He doesn't strike me as the type to be that persistent. Seems more likely he'd just find some new prey to go after."

"Probably right." He lifted his burger to his mouth, but his stomach rebelled. He put it down again. "That's put me off my feed, dagnabbit. Give me some good news so I can finish my lunch."

She pondered, chewing a bite of crab melt. "Good news . . . Well, everything's in order for our murder party. And Marguerite's coming down for the weekend." She made a face like she wasn't sure that was all good news, either. "You are coming, right? I have to admit I'm a little nervous about the whole thing. That drama teacher is something else—she wouldn't even let me in on the plot. And murder doesn't seem like something to play around with, you know?"

It sure as hell wasn't—especially not with all the people he cared about most in the world right there in the house. "I'm with you there. Would've chosen something else if it was me. But it's not likely anything'll go too far wrong. And I will definitely be there just to make sure. Nobody'd be stupid enough to commit a real crime with the sheriff on the premises. I hope."

nine

Merry days were these at Thornfield Hall; and busy days too. . . . All sad feelings seemed now driven from the house, all gloomy associations forgotten: there was life everywhere, movement all day long.

—*Jane Eyre*

Marguerite blew in late Friday night on the back of a gale-force wind. She stood in the entrance hall, finger combing her short dark hair back into a semblance of order. "*Mon dieu,* I am lucky to be alive! My poor little car does not know what to make of your winter weather."

Emily grimaced. "That's why I didn't invite you down for fall break. This is pretty much the norm for this time of year."

"*Ce n'est rien,* it will make good atmosphere for your murder party." She bent down to greet Levin and Kitty, who were sniffing around her bag. "*Ah, oui, mes petits,* Tante Marguerite has brought you a little something." She fumbled in the bag and brought out three catnip mice. "But where is Bustopher Jones? He must not be left out."

"He's probably asleep in front of the fire. He's become terribly lazy of late. Must be getting old."

Marguerite dangled two of the mice until Levin and Kitty

pounced, then carried the third into the library. Bustopher raised his head and blinked languorously. When Marguerite dangled the mouse in front of his nose, he sniffed once, put out a lackadaisical paw, then returned to his nap.

Marguerite shook her head. "As you say, he must be getting old."

Katie brought in some coffee laced with brandy. "Marguerite wants to help out with the decorations for tomorrow night, Katie. If you don't mind."

"Mind? I'd love it. I'm a little stuck, frankly, for how to make it look spooky without being cliché Halloween."

In no time the two of them were deep in talk of candles, fall foliage, and draped organza. Emily sat back and stared into the fire, listening to the wind rattling the windows and imagining she could hear Cathy Earnshaw scratching there, begging to be let in.

The day of the fundraiser must have dawned, but the dawn was hardly noticeable, so thick and black were the clouds that loomed menacingly over the frothing sea. As Emily peered anxiously from the library windows, the first fat drops slammed against the pane.

"Perfect day for a murder mystery, wouldn't you say?" Katie said cheerfully as she brought Emily's coffee in and set it on the table by the fire. Marguerite had not yet appeared.

"I suppose it is that. Provided people are willing to come out in a storm. And provided the house doesn't blow away."

"Oh, don't you worry about that. Windy Corner's as sound as the Twin Rocks, and Stony Beach people are used to this weather. It won't faze them."

"What do I need to do to help get ready?"

Katie pondered a moment, readjusting her ponytail. "Honestly? I think between Marguerite and the caterers and the drama troupe, we have it covered. All we need you to do is— sorry—" She grimaced. "Write the checks and stay out of the way?"

"Stay out of the way? With the decorating on this floor, the drama troupe upstairs, and the construction crew in the attic, how am I supposed to stay out of everybody's way?" Though the crew didn't normally work Saturdays, Jeremiah and Roman had come in today to make everything as safe and tidy as possible before the party. Guests were not supposed to venture as far as the third floor, but the door to the attic stairs did not lock and Emily was not prepared to count on everyone's discretion.

"You could go over to my place. And actually, if you could watch Lizzie for me, that would be super."

Lizzie-duty sounded like a soft job compared to anything the others would be doing. "Deal. Oh, but before everybody gets going, I need to move a few things back up to the tower."

She climbed the main flight to the second floor, chiding herself for not having been more firm with Cordelia Fitzgerald about not using her room and the secret stairs. But it couldn't be helped at this point.

She gathered onto the bed the things she would need for the night, then swept her other personal things off the surfaces of the desk, dressing table, and tallboy into the drawers, locking as many drawers as could be locked. She made sure all closet and cupboard doors were firmly shut; surely people wouldn't go snooping in the midst of a murder party, would they? Well, most people wouldn't. She'd have to check the guest list—if Rita

Spenser, the local paparazzi, was on it, Emily would need to lock down every drawer, door, and cubbyhole in the house.

She gathered her night things and climbed up to the attic, where she picked her way around the construction detritus to get to the locked door of her own tower room. Balancing her load on her left arm, she fished the key out of her pocket and unlocked the door, then stepped in—into a pool of water that instantly soaked through the soles of her fuzzy slippers.

She jumped back. "Jeremiah!"

A shuffle behind her, then Jeremiah said, "Yes, ma'am?" sounding as if he'd just swallowed a mouthful of gravel. Emily wondered if he had a cold.

She pointed to the puddle. "Looks like we have a leak."

He came up beside her, and she looked sideways at him. He certainly didn't look well—his eyes were sunken and his cheeks gray.

He cleared his throat and spoke in something closer to his normal voice. "Sure does. Hadn't noticed it, that door being locked."

"I was planning to sleep here tonight. They need the whole second floor for the murder." That sounded odd. "The play, I mean."

"Yes, ma'am. I'll get somebody on it right away." He squinted up to where the drip was coming through the vaulted ceiling. "Looks like the join between the tower and the main roof. Always the first to go." He called out the door. "Roman!"

"Yeah?" Roman's voice preceded his shaggy dark head around the corner from the soon-to-be sitting room.

"Get up on the roof and put a tarp over that join." Jeremiah pointed upward.

Roman ducked in and craned his neck up. "Got it."

Emily followed him out with her eyes. "Will he be all right? It's pretty wet out there, and that roof is steep."

"That boy's like a mountain goat. He can handle it. Meanwhile, I'll clean up this water." He scanned the rest of the room, paying particular attention to the ceiling. "Looks to be just that one spot, thank the Lord."

Emily instinctively crossed herself, but Jeremiah didn't follow suit. Of course, he was a Protestant.

She stepped around the puddle to lay her burden on the bed, a safe distance from the leak. She'd put things away later, after the tarp was up, when she wouldn't be half expecting to see Roman's foot come through the ceiling at any moment.

She and Lizzie spent a pleasant morning in Katie's apartment, but by naptime Emily understood why baby care wasn't universally considered a relaxing occupation. Lizzie was just beginning to creep on her elbows, and Emily didn't dare take her eyes off her for a second lest some inappropriate object find its way into her mouth. On top of that were endless games of peekaboo and patty-cake, half-a-dozen stories, two diaper changes, lunch followed by a complete outfit change, and then a bottle to soothe Lizzie to sleep.

Once the baby was safely quiet in her crib, Emily put her feet up on the couch and snoozed for half an hour. She was getting a bit old for this kind of thing.

When she woke, she thought she'd better check on things back at the main house—especially her bedroom. After peeking in on Lizzie and making sure the baby monitor was on, she bundled up in her mackintosh and went around to the front of the house so she could get a look at the tower roof. She was surprised to see a dark figure clinging spiderlike to a huge blue tarp. Surely Roman should have finished that job hours ago.

She cupped her hands around her mouth and called up to him. "Roman? You okay?"

He lifted his head at the sound, looked around, and finally saw her. "Tarp blew off." The wind blew his words out to sea, but she thought he was saying, "Have to weight it back down."

Oh, dear. That didn't bode well for the night. She might have to sleep in Beatrice's room after all.

At five o'clock, Emily handed Lizzie over to Erin, who was baby-sitting for the evening, and went back to the house to dress. Her tower room was dry, but Jeremiah and Roman were still working in the sitting room. She poked her head in. "How's that tarp holding?"

Jeremiah shook his head. "Don't trust it, not in this wind. We'll stay and make sure it holds through the party."

"Good. I'll send you up some dinner." Surely the caterers would have enough extra for that.

Emily had planned her outfit days ago: an 1890s-style dress in deep red-brown satin dripping in handmade lace, with a sweeping train and puffed sleeves that would have made Anne Shirley swoon. At her throat she pinned her precious antique cameo, her only inheritance from her mother. Over her shoulders went the shawl she'd knitted when she first came to Stony Beach, intricate lace of the finest cashmere in a russet a shade lighter than the dress. She took extra care with her hair, achieving a few extra dips and swirls around her usual high bun. By the time she poked in the last hairpin, she understood why ladies of earlier eras needed personal maids.

Luke was the first guest to arrive. "Thought I'd come early and get the lay of the land. Just in case."

Emily surveyed his white tie and tails, which she'd persuaded him with some difficulty to rent for the occasion so the two of them would look like they belonged to the same era. While he was clearly not in his natural element, the suit accented his shoulders and the brilliant white shirt brightened his gray eyes. "You clean up pretty good," she teased.

"And you look like you stepped out of a painting. Is it safe to touch you?"

For answer she stood on tiptoe and kissed him. "Come on, I'll show you around."

It was Emily's own first glimpse of the completed decorations. In all the rooms to be used for dinner, Marguerite and Katie had created a cross between an autumn forest and a Victorian medium's séance parlor. Swaths of russet and gold organza festooned the windows and arches and draped the backs of the rented chairs. Matching sateen tablecloths fell to the floor, topped by seemingly random but perfect arrangements of tea lights, fall foliage, gold sparkles, and wide organza ribbons in colors from pale gold to deep orange. Chargers from Beatrice's best Haviland china, a simple ivory with a gold rim, graced each place, accompanied by Waterford crystal goblets and wineglasses and genuine silver utensils. A gold linen napkin folded into a fan lay atop each plate, a single oak leaf tucked into each bronze napkin ring. Huge candelabra stood on sideboards and mantelpieces, replacing the electric lights and bathing the rooms in a golden glow. The corners were alive with shadows from which one could easily believe a ghost might emerge at any moment.

"Is that real silver?" Luke asked. "I'll have to keep my eyes peeled to see none of that goes home in anybody's pocket."

Emily nodded. "Aunt Beatrice would only have the best. Let's hope anyone who can afford a hundred-dollar ticket will be above pilfering the silver."

The doorbell rang, and Katie went to answer it, looking charming in her long black parlormaid's dress with lacy white apron and cap. She and all the caterers were costumed as Victorian servants. Emily took up her position in the hall to welcome the guests and direct them to the appropriate room and table. Many of the faces were familiar. All her business tenants were there, including a giggling Beanie—dressed steampunk from head to toe—clinging to Ben's arm, and Veronica, resplendent in an authentic Edwardian lace shirtwaist, with Devon in knee breeches and a tall cravat. Jamie came with one of his sisters and gazed wistfully at Katie. Sam arrived in a black business pantsuit, looking as if the suit were full of pins that stuck into her whenever she moved. Not even a fundraiser for her own clinic could get Sam into a dress.

But there were a number of guests Emily had not seen before. Some had made an effort at period dress while others wore ordinary dinner clothes. All the guests' faces came alive with curiosity and excitement as they took in the scene.

Half the crowd had assembled before Marguerite made her appearance. She descended the broad staircase looking like Lady Mary from the first season of *Downton Abbey*. Her high-waisted black dress was a mere wisp of chiffon over a silk sheath, dripping with beaded embroidery. Black gloves covered her arms to the elbow. Her hair was too short to style authentically, but it was crowned with a glittering rhinestone tiara.

"Margot!" Emily exclaimed. "Where in the world did you find that dress? It must have cost the earth!"

"Only most of Paris. I found it in a consignment store. *Très élégant, n'est-ce pas?*" She gave a little twirl.

"*Oui.* Go and mingle. You add tone to the place."

Luke, who had left Emily's side to go on a deceptively casual patrol of the rooms, came back to report. "Looking good so far. Everybody seems impressed."

Emily nodded. The atmosphere was electric. "Can you tell who the actors are?"

"Only by their youth." Cordelia had her cast members dress upstairs, then go down the back stairway and come in the front door a couple at a time, mingling unobtrusively with the guests. "And they have better costumes."

Just then a blond young man in a dinner suit emerged from the crowd, whistling. Emily gasped. "Jake Newhouse! What on earth is *he* doing here?" She scanned the crowd around the door for Katie. She was greeting a guest, apparently calm. Jake must have slipped past without her seeing him. He was sauntering toward the parlor door when Emily stepped in front of him. Luke was right behind her.

"Jake Newhouse, you are not welcome in my home. If you paid for a ticket, I'll refund your money. I want you out of here *now.*"

He smirked, hands in his trouser pockets. "Can't. Cordelia needs me." He leaned close, and Emily drew back from the beer on his breath. He whispered, "I'm the corpse."

Emily ran through the evening's program in her mind. Katie would be occupied in the kitchen throughout dinner, so there was a decent chance she wouldn't have to run into Jake. And of course she wouldn't be participating in the mystery game. "Don't let him out of your sight," she whispered to Luke as Jake passed into the parlor. Luke nodded and followed him.

When the flow of guests had subsided to a trickle of latecomers, Emily found her own seat at a corner table in the parlor, whence she had a fair view of all the tables in that room and most in the library beyond. Luke was on her left and Marguerite on her right. Several of the young actors, including Jake, were seated together at a table near the open double doors between the two rooms. Emily guessed this was where the drama would begin to unfold.

Even before the mock turtle soup was served, the air around the actors' table vibrated with tension. Jake flirted openly with a girl who was supposed to be another boy's wife, while simultaneously dropping hints of blackmail to a couple of other actors and deftly fielding veiled accusations of fraud from a third. A plethora of motives for fictional murder. Emily had to admit Jake had been well cast for his role.

All through the salmon *en croûte*, the rib roast with Yorkshire pudding, the steamed asparagus with Hollandaise sauce, and the Waldorf salad, the bickering and innuendo at the actors' table escalated. From time to time someone from another table would come up and add a log to the fire in the form of another accusation against Jake's character. Finally, while the diners were enjoying their charlotte russe, the simmering tension boiled over. The supposed husband of Jake's flirting partner leapt to his feet, threw down his napkin, and shouted, "I'll get you for this, Alan Conroy, if it's the last thing I do!" Clearly original dialogue was not Cordelia's strong suit.

One of the other actors—Emily recognized him as Matthew

Sweet, whose father owned a local candy shop—said to Jake, sternly but not in anger, "Conroy, I think you'd better leave." Jake smirked to the audience, lifting his hands in a "What can you do?" gesture. With deliberate slowness he pushed his chair back, dropped his napkin onto the tablecloth, and sauntered out, hands in his pockets, whistling. From her seat Emily could see him head up the main staircase.

The remaining actors finished their desserts in silence, then left the room one or two at a time. The other tables, largely quiet till now, erupted in speculation about what would happen next. "That blond guy has to be the victim, don't you think?" "When's the murder going to be?" "What do we do now, just sit around and wait?"

After a few minutes, Cordelia Fitzgerald appeared in the hall doorway, looking like the madam of a brothel in a turn-of-the-century evening gown so low cut and tightly laced, so beaded, befeathered, and bedazzled, Emily wondered how she could move. "Ladies and gentlemen!" Cordelia proclaimed in a voice that projected through all the rooms. "You are now free to explore the second floor of the house. Only be on your guard—this is a night of mystery. Who knows what horrors may lurk in the dark corners above?"

The guests crowded toward the doorways, buzzing excitedly. Luke and Marguerite joined the crowd, but Emily stayed put. She had no desire to participate in the murder game; after all, she might find the culprit, and for the hostess to win the game would be unsporting. She signaled a waiter to refill her coffee, then took it to a sofa and sipped it at her leisure, enjoying her solitude. Around her, the costumed caterers began to clear the tables. Emily laid her head back and closed her eyes.

It couldn't have been more than a minute or two before she heard a scream. Someone must have found the "corpse" already. Quick work. But the scream continued, escalating in volume and terror, until Emily realized it wasn't a stagy scream; it was real. And it sounded horribly like Katie.

ten

I recognized in his pale and seemingly lifeless face—the stranger, Mason: I saw too that his linen on one side, and one arm, was almost soaked in blood.

—Jane Eyre

Luke was in the back bedroom looking for Jake when he heard the scream. It sounded like it was coming from Beatrice's old bedroom. Instinctively he checked his watch—8:29—then pushed past the startled throng of guests in the hallway and bedroom and found the door to the secret stairway standing ajar. The scream was coming from there.

"Sheriff here, let me through!" he commanded, and the onlookers melted to each side. He stood in the opening, his eyes adjusting to the dim light. He pulled out his mini LED flashlight, switched it on, and swept it around the upper landing.

Cowering against the wall behind the door was a boy in a tuxedo. Luke squinted and recognized Matthew Sweet. "Matthew? What's going on?"

The boy swallowed, wide-eyed. "I—don't know. I was supposed to meet Jake here, but he didn't show. Then I heard—" He gestured downward.

Luke leaned over the banister and trained his flashlight toward the bottom of the spiral stairs, where a glimmer of white caught his eye. He rounded the first bend of the stairs and saw that the glimmer was Katie's apron. She stood over a sprawled form in a tux, and in her hand was a glint of something metal— dripping blood.

He whipped out his phone and called for backup as he sprinted down the remaining stairs. Katie was still screaming as he took her by the shoulders and turned her to face him. He took a second to glance down at the body on the floor. Jake Newhouse. And he looked very dead.

Luke held Katie's eyes. "Katie, look at me. Calm down, now. I've got this. It's going to be all right." Well, not for Jake, and maybe not for Katie, either, given the situation; but he had to say something. "Take a deep breath. 'Atta girl."

Katie's fear-crazed eyes fastened on his and gradually calmed as she appeared to realize who he was and that she was no longer alone with a horror. She blinked a few times, then sagged against his chest. "Dead—he's dead—"

"What's that in your hand, Katie?"

She straightened and raised her right hand, staring at what it held as if she had no idea how it had gotten there. "I—don't know—I must have—" Her whole body shuddered under Luke's hands as if it would fly apart. She opened her fist and the metal thing clattered to the floor. She stared at her bloody hand, and a high, thin wail emerged from her throat.

Emily appeared in the doorway from the library. "Luke, what's going on?"

He pushed the hysterical girl into Emily's arms. "Get her out of here. Wash her hands, but leave her clothes alone. Get her a blanket and a hot drink, or brandy if you have it. She's a wreck."

Emily turned to lead Katie out, then looked back over her shoulder and down to the floor. "Oh my God . . . Is that Jake?"

Luke nodded. "Don't say anything. Just tell them there's been an accident, but don't let anybody leave." As an afterthought, "Get Marguerite to shoo everybody out of the library and close the doors."

He knelt over the body, checked the pulse just to be sure, although the glazed, blank eyes and the line of blood trickling from the corner of the gaping mouth had already told him all he needed to know. He pulled a handkerchief out of his pocket and picked up the weapon from where Katie had let it fall. An ordinary pocketknife, like anyone might carry—he had a similar one himself, though he hadn't transferred it to his suit. A slit in Jake's once-white tucked shirtfront appeared to match the width of the blade.

Luke stood and considered the position of the body. Mostly on its back, head down—some blood on the head, too—with the feet on the last couple of steps of the staircase. Luke trained his flashlight up the spiral stairs from step to step, cursing the lack of electric light in this stairwell. A trail of red drops confirmed it: Jake had been stabbed at the top of the stairs and then fallen, or been pushed, to the bottom.

Somebody leaned over the banister from the landing above. A male voice—more mature than Matthew's—called, "Sheriff? What's going on? You need any help?"

Luke pulled the library door shut, then sprinted up the stairs. Curious faces crowded the landing and the doorway. "There's been an accident. Everybody stay back. Find Dr. Griffiths and send her down there. The rest of you, out of the room but stay upstairs." As he spoke, he herded the sensation-seekers out of the stairwell. Oh, hell, what a mess the fingerprints up here would be—people leaning on the banister and the edges of the door. He'd have to discount all of those.

Matthew still stood pressed against the wall as if trying to melt into it. Luke took his arm and led him, limp as a sleeping puppy, into the bedroom, where he pushed him down onto a chair. "You stay right there till I come for you." Luke herded the rest of the crowd out into the hall and locked the bedroom door behind them. He needed his deputies, Pete and Heather, here stat, if only for crowd control.

Back at the bottom of the stairs, he heard a knock from the library side. "Sheriff? It's me, Sam."

That was fast. He pulled the release lever to open the door just wide enough to let Sam in. She was a deputy medical examiner and the only doctor for miles.

He stepped aside so she could see the body. "He's dead. This is a forensics job."

"I can see that." She set down her medical bag, pulled on a pair of latex gloves, and knelt over the body. Careful not to alter its position, she prodded gingerly at the chest and parted the blond hair where it was matted with blood. "Can't be sure if it was the puncture wound that killed him or the head trauma. Got a weapon?"

He displayed the pocketknife where it rested on his handkerchief.

Sam squinted at it, held her fingers up to measure without touching it. "Blade about three inches long. Have to know what you're doing to hit the heart with that. Probably punctured a lung, maybe cut an artery, judging from the amount of blood. Would've bled to death eventually, but I'm guessing it was the head wound that finished him off. Know more when they do the autopsy."

"But you'd agree it's murder?"

Sam pulled off her gloves. "Interesting technicality there. If he was stabbed but then fell of his own accord, so to speak, and if it was the head wound that killed him, might only count as attempted murder." She cocked an eyebrow at him. "That'll be your job, Mr. Super Detective. Did he fall or was he pushed? Only the murderer knows for sure." She gave a macabre grin.

Emily led the trembling Katie into the bathroom, where she scrubbed her hands, then into the dining room. The caterers had nearly finished clearing in here; the room held a fire and a brandy decanter, and most importantly, did not have a view of the concealed staircase. She sat Katie in an easy chair by the fire, unfolded the blanket she'd found providentially left behind in the bathroom closet, and draped it around the girl's shoulders, then poured her a snifter of brandy, followed by a cup of steaming coffee from the urn the caterers had yet to take away. Gradually a little color returned to Katie's cheeks and her trembling stilled.

Marguerite slid silently into the room. She'd rushed downstairs to Emily's side as soon as she realized the scream was real. "The library is clear," she said just above a whisper. "How is *la pauvre* Katie?"

"I think she'll be all right. I'm not sure if I should try to get her to talk, or if it would only make things worse."

Just then the door opened and Sam Griffiths marched in. "Sheriff sent me to take a look at her." Gruff and full volume. With that wonderful bedside manner, Emily wondered how Sam kept any of her patients alive. Yet she seemed to manage it.

The doctor knelt in front of Katie, took her pulse, looked in her eyes, felt her forehead. "She'll do. Keep her quiet and warm for now, and get her to bed as soon as possible."

Luke poked his head in. "Okay for me to talk to her?"

Sam frowned. "Can't it wait?"

"Not really. She's key to this whole thing. No point talking to anyone else till I've heard what Katie has to say."

Katie spoke in a thread of a voice. "I'm all right now. I can talk."

"What about—?" Emily cocked her head toward the library.

"Pete and Heather have it secured. Crime scene people are on the way. I have all I need for now."

Emily stood and let Luke have her chair next to Katie.

"All right, Katie, just tell me in your own words what happened. Take your time."

Katie drew a deep, ragged breath. "I—needed to go upstairs for something. People were all over the main stairs and—that was the quickest way."

Emily saw her own confusion reflected on Luke's face. Surely the back stairs would have been more logical? Katie knew the mystery play would involve the secret staircase.

"Why didn't you use the back stairs?"

Katie got a deer-in-the-headlights look—exactly as if she'd been making up a story and hadn't thought of that wrinkle. But Katie? Lie? Unthinkable.

"I don't know—I was in the library and the secret stairs were right there."

"Hmm." Luke frowned, clearly—and unsurprisingly—not convinced. "So then what?"

"I opened the door and—" She started shaking again. At a nod from Luke, Emily refilled the snifter and held it to Katie's lips.

"What did you see when you opened the door?" Luke's voice was soft and patient.

"I—don't remember. One minute I was opening the door, and the next—you had hold of me. In between it's all—just blank." She stared into the fire, her brow creased. "I think I heard somebody screaming."

"You. You were screaming." Luke stood and faced the fire, kicked a log back into position. He turned to Sam. "Anything we can do to help her remember?"

Sam shook her head. "Time. Might come back with time, might not. Needs rest, away from here."

Luke ran his hands over his cropped gray hair and blew out a long breath through puffed cheeks. "All right. Emily, take her over to her apartment and put her to bed. Maybe she can tell us more tomorrow." He started to turn away, then stopped himself. "Oh, and save her clothes just like they are." Katie's apron and white cuffs were spattered with blood.

Emily helped Katie to her feet and wrapped the blanket more tightly around her, as if the blanket itself could protect her from whatever had happened tonight—and its consequences.

"One more thing," Luke said to Katie. "Do you own a pocketknife?"

Katie blinked. "Pocketknife? No. That's a guy thing, isn't it?"

Emily opened her mouth. She was sure she'd seen Katie using the corkscrew of a Swiss Army knife to open a bottle of wine just the other day. Then she glanced at Luke and clamped her mouth shut again. She didn't like the set of his jaw, not one little bit.

Jake. On the floor. Bleeding. Knife in my hand. All my worst nightmares lying there on the floor. Dead.

Did I kill him?

I can't remember. I. Can't. Remember.

I sure as heck wanted him dead. When I saw he was here tonight, I just about died myself. If I came up against him in the dark with a knife in my hand—

Are all my worst nightmares just about to begin?

eleven

What crime was this, that lived incarnate in this seques-
tered mansion, and could neither be expelled nor subdued by
the owner?—What mystery, that broke out, now in fire and
now in blood, at the deadest hours of night?

—*Jane Eyre*

Luke's brain had snapped into detective mode as soon as he
saw the body. Katie'd become almost like a daughter to him
over the last few months, but he had no time or brain-space to
spare for the emotions that might have been stirred up by finding her like he did and hearing her Swiss-cheese story. "Just the
facts, ma'am" had to be his motto now.

He strode through the hall and parlor, checking that no
guests were lurking where they had no business to be, then entered the library and saw the back of a tropical tent topped by a
porcupine pelt of bright fuchsia hair peering through the crack
of the stairwell door. Just what he needed. Rita Spenser, aspir-
ing paparazzi and scourge of Tillamook County. How had she
gotten in here?

He cleared his throat and she jumped, sending shock waves
through her muumuu. "Sheriff! You startled me, you naughty

boy." She wagged a sausagelike finger flirtatiously in his face. "What's going on? The *Wave* reader wants to know."

"The *Wave* reader will have to wait until I know something myself. Ms. Spenser, the public is not allowed in this room. This is a crime scene." Swallowing his revulsion, he reached for her elbow to escort her out.

"Oh, but I'm not the public, I'm the press! You can't throw me out."

"Actually I can." Legally he could; physically he wasn't so sure. She must be twice his weight. He stepped around her and called through the crack of the doorway. "Pete? I need you out here."

His deputy Pete hauled his six-foot-four frame and two-hundred-plus pounds of muscle out into the room. "What's up, boss?"

"I need you to escort Ms. Spenser home. You can interview her on the way."

Rita opened her mouth to protest, then took a good look at Pete's handsome face, sleek blond hair, and impressive physique. Her protest gave way to a coquettish grin. "Well, fancy that, the interviewer being interviewed. I guess I can settle for that. For now." She shot Luke a look that said "This isn't over" and allowed Pete to lead her out.

Luke poked his head into the secret stairwell and saw the crime scene people already busy about the body. Rita must have snuck in on their heels.

He spoke to his other deputy, a petite redhead who looked like she ought to be teaching kindergarten instead of investigating a crime scene; but she knew her job, and Luke respected her for that. "Heather, I need you to take statements from the guests and the caterers—where they were when they heard the scream, whether they saw anyone in or near either end of these stairs or anyone who wasn't where he was supposed to be. You know the drill. Pete'll help you when he gets back. But leave the cast members to me."

Luke took the main stairs two at a time. At the top landing he put on his loudspeaker voice.

"Folks, there's been an accident. Jake Newhouse is dead." The crowd broke into a buzz of shock and speculation. He held up his palm until they quieted down. "We're looking into how it happened. I need you all to stay in the house, but stay out of that bedroom"—he pointed to Beatrice's door—"and the library. I'll get the caterers to put on more coffee in the dining room. My deputies will ask some of you to come talk to me in the library, and the rest of you they'll interview themselves. As soon as you've been interviewed, you can go."

He turned to Heather. "You set up in the back bedroom up here. Get the cast members to stay in easy call. Send Matthew Sweet down first, then I'll want to see Cordelia Fitzgerald after that. When Pete gets back, he can start with the caterers, then help you with the guests."

The library held the forlorn look of the aftermath of a party—the tables half cleared, dirty dishes piled on the side table, discarded napkins littering the floor. All the horror was hidden behind the curved bookcase door.

Luke caught one of the waiters in the hall and asked him to bring coffee. "We'll need a pot in the library with a dozen or so cups. It's going be a long night."

Matthew appeared in the doorway, looking like a frightened sheep.

"Come on in, Matthew. I won't bite." Luke waved him to a chair and took out his phone to record the conversation, taking his own notes as a backup in case the battery died. He hated being out of his element like this, without his usual tools, but the advantages of interviewing people on the scene with no time lag, catching their reactions raw, outweighed the inconveniences.

The waiter brought in the coffee, and Luke gestured for him to pour two cups. He used his knuckles to push one of them toward the boy. "Have some coffee, you're still white as a bleached shell."

Matthew took a sip and made a face. Probably a soda drinker by choice. But he kept his hands wrapped around the cup. A half inch of pure white cuff showed below his coat sleeves. His starched shirtfront held a splotch of something, but it looked more like beef juice than human blood.

"Now tell me exactly what happened, from after you left the dining room till I met you in the stairwell."

Matthew sat on the edge of his chair, his right foot jiggling. "I was the last to leave. I was supposed to be the 'killer.'" He made air quotes around the word with shaking fingers. "Jake was supposed to go up first and wait for me in the secret stairwell. Then I was supposed to go up and 'stab' him with this."

He stuck his hand in his trouser pocket and pulled out what looked like a jackknife. He pressed a button and a blade sprang out. "It's plastic, see?" He positioned the blade against his opposite palm and pushed, and the blade slid back into the handle. "Completely harmless. Just enough pressure to burst the capsule of fake blood under his shirt."

Luke held his hand out for the knife and ran his thumb over the point and edge. No way that prop could hurt anyone. He made a mental note to tell the ME to look out for fake blood mixed in with the real stuff.

"Gotcha. So that's what was supposed to happen. What actually did happen?"

Matthew slumped back in his chair. "I went upstairs like I was supposed to. The kids that went before me were heading into different rooms like the script said. But this other guy was coming out of the main bedroom—some dude I'd never seen before."

Luke sat up straighter. "Can you describe him?"

"Kinda short, dark, shaggy hair. Had on jeans and a rain poncho."

"Young?"

"Maybe twenty or so? Older than me, but not old."

That sounded like Roman. What business would he have on the second floor? "Did you speak to him?"

"No, he just pushed past me and headed for the attic stairs."

"Okay, what then?"

"I went on into the bedroom. There was nobody there. Ms. Fitzgerald had shown me how to open the door to the secret stairs, but it was already open, just a crack. I went in there, thinking Jake would be waiting. But he wasn't there."

"Anyone else there?"

"I didn't see anybody. It was dark, but I think I would've seen them if they were there."

"Hear anything?"

Matthew shook his head.

"So then what did you do?"

"Nothing. I just waited there for Jake. Then I heard somebody scream. Made my hair stand on end. Couldn't think. I just froze. Like you found me."

Luke drummed his fingers against the table. "All right. Let's back up. Did you know Jake apart from the play?"

"A little. Knew of him, that is. He was kind of a legend around school. But a few years ahead of me, so I didn't run into him much. Since he graduated I haven't seen him at all, till we started working on the play."

"Any run-ins with him? Any conflict, say over a girl?"

Matthew barely shook his head, but his whole face and neck went as red as the tablecloth.

Luke put on his sympathetic-uncle voice. "I'd be surprised if there was a guy in this county who hadn't run up against Jake over a girl."

Matthew mumbled into his chest. "Well, there was this one girl I liked. But she liked Jake better."

Luke sat back and waited. The boy needed to tell someone. It would come.

"It was a while ago." Matthew bit at his thumbnail. "Last summer. I went to this party where I knew I'd see her. She did dance with me once, but then she went off for a Coke and started acting crazy. I mean, she was all over the place, not like herself at all. Later I saw her go upstairs. With Jake." He looked up at Luke, his eyes suddenly fierce. "Jake was a real dick, if you want to know the truth. I didn't kill him, but I'm not sorry he's dead."

Luke found himself believing the boy. "Just one more thing. Do you carry a pocketknife?"

"A pocketknife? Sure, who doesn't?"

"May I see it?"

"It's at home. I had that prop knife and I didn't want to load down my pockets too much—it would look bad in this suit." He spoke simply, naturally, his eyes steady on Luke's.

Luke stood. "All right, Matthew, you can go. But I'm gonna need that shirt. You got something else to wear?"

"Yeah, we all came in our regular clothes and changed upstairs."

"Leave the shirt with the officer at the door. Not planning to leave town anytime soon, are you?"

"No, sir."

"Send Ms. Fitzgerald in before you go."

As soon as Matthew was out of the room, Luke used a napkin to pick up the boy's cup by the handle. He emptied the leftover coffee into a dirty cup and dropped Matthew's into an evidence bag—one of several he'd snagged from the crime scene team. He labeled the bag, then poured coffee into a fresh cup and set it on the table in front of the empty chair.

Cordelia Fitzgerald posed in the doorway, one hand clinging to the jamb, the other at her forehead. Her dress, dark red trimmed in black, blended with the party hangings. "I am shattered, Lieutenant Richards. Absolutely shattered. Who could have dreamed my innocent little play would end so tragically? I blame myself entirely. How can I ever face that poor boy's parents? So young, so charming, so talented. Such a dreadful loss."

Luke raised one eyebrow. First time he'd heard Jake described that way. He'd have expected most who knew him to agree with Matthew's "real dick."

He waved toward the empty chair. "Sit down and have some coffee." He looked her over, then picked up a bottle of brandy and gestured with it. "Maybe a drop of this?"

Cordelia floated toward the table, one hand at her tightly corseted side. "Thank you. A little reviver would be most welcome." She sank gracefully into the chair, head back and arm dangling.

Luke tipped a tablespoon of brandy into her cup and sat down. "You blame yourself? Now why would that be?"

Cordelia sat up straight and gripped the edge of the table with both hands. "Why, because I cast him as the victim, of course. What else could you think I meant?"

"I think his role as the victim was probably just a coincidence, don't you?"

"How can I know what to think?" She fluttered her hands, rings flashing. At some point she'd ditched the elbow-length black gloves she'd had on before dinner. "I don't even know what happened. Only that he died in the secret stairway, where the stage murder was supposed to take place. Did he lose his way in the dark and fall down the stairs? Oh, I knew I should have arranged for more light in there! You see, it is my fault after all!"

Luke clenched his jaw. Give him a dead body over a drama queen any day. "No reason at all for you to count yourself responsible, ma'am. We're just trying to nail down exactly what happened. Now, if you'll tell me how the pretend murder was supposed to play out, we can start to figure out where it went wrong."

"Very well." Cordelia took her cup of spiked coffee daintily by the handle and drank deeply. "Everything went according to plan up through the actors leaving the table. You saw all that, I suppose?"

"Yes, ma'am."

"Jake was supposed to go straight to the top of the secret stairway and wait there for Matthew. Matthew was to leave the table after the others and go directly to the stairway as well. Then he would pretend to stab Jake, go down the stairs, and leave by the library entrance. The guests would have been dismissed upstairs by then, so no one would see him. Jake, poor soul, would just have to lie there, quite still, until the game was solved."

"He was supposed to stay at the top of the stairs?"

She nodded, dabbing her eyes again.

"All right." That squared with Matthew's account. "Now tell me what you did yourself."

"*Moi?*" Her heavily made-up eyes widened till she looked like a porcelain doll. "Well, yes, all right. I arrived about three o'clock—"

"I don't need the whole day, ma'am. Just from when you left the dinner table."

"Oh! Oh, I see. Yes. I was seated in here—at that table, between my players and the hall door, so I could keep an eye on things. Give a little prompt if necessary. They are dear children, so enthusiastic, but when you're improvising, you know, it's easy for things to get a little off track now and then."

Like her story. But she was the kind you had to let talk—up to a point, anyway.

"Everything went smoothly, I must say. I was quite proud of my little cast. Jake left at the perfect dramatic moment, and the others timed their exits appropriately. After Matthew left the room, I waited exactly ninety seconds. We had that part timed precisely." She put her hand into her beaded handbag and pulled out a small watch of the type meant to be pinned to the chest. "I kept my watch in here to be inconspicuous. At any rate, ninety seconds, and then I went out into the hall and made my announcement to the different rooms. You heard that, I suppose?"

"Yes, ma'am."

"Then I went upstairs as planned. I checked on everyone's position; all the actors were in the various bedrooms where they were supposed to be. I didn't check on Matthew and Jake, though; guests were coming up behind me, it would have been too obvious."

"Anyone supposed to be in the master bedroom besides Jake and Matthew?"

"No, only those two."

"Did you see anyone upstairs besides the cast members? Before the guests began to arrive, that is?"

"Not another soul."

Luke frowned. He didn't much care for the way the field was narrowing down. "Exactly where were you when you heard the scream?"

"In the hall outside the master bedroom. I'd just opened the door—surreptitiously, you understand—so the guests could begin to investigate there."

"Any of the guests behave suspiciously in any way?"

"Not that I could see. They all seemed excited, anticipating, just as they ought to be." Cordelia drooped back in her chair, one hand to her forehead again. "If you're finished with me, Lieutenant—I'm feeling a trifle faint. All this has been terribly upsetting. I'd like to go home."

"One more thing. Did anyone other than the cast know exactly how the game would go?"

"Not a soul. At least, they didn't hear it from me."

"All right. I think we're done here. Just leave me your contact info in case we need to clear anything up later." He pushed his notebook and pen toward her across the table and noted that she wrote with her left hand. He hadn't been able to tell from the wound which hand the killer had used, but the postmortem would no doubt reveal all.

"Oh, and I'll need your gloves."

"My gloves! Whatever for?"

"Just routine." Whoever invented that phrase deserved a medal.

"Oh, very well." She opened her handbag again and pulled out a folded pair of black gloves. "But I'll need them back. They're rented, like all the costumes."

"Leave them with the officer at the door and he'll give you a receipt. If they're clean, you'll get them back in a few days." And if they weren't—well, then he'd have his murderer. But he highly doubted it would be that simple.

S am gave Katie a sedative, and Marguerite accompanied Emily and Katie to the garage apartment. "I would only be in the way *à la maison*," she said. "Besides, *les chats* will need me." They'd brought the three cats over earlier in the afternoon to be out of the way. "Cats are like bees—they know when things are not right. You have to explain to them."

Emily had never heard that about cats before, but it couldn't hurt. Marguerite certainly had a way with the beasts, that much was undeniable.

Erin was in the living room, watching TV with her earbuds on. She looked up when the three women came in, Katie's arms draped over Emily's and Marguerite's shoulders, and her eyes went wide.

"What's wrong with Katie?" She jumped up, dislodging the earbuds from her ears, and ran to her sister. "What happened?"

Marguerite slid out from under Katie's arm and let Erin take her place.

"Someone's been killed," Emily said. "For real. Katie found the body."

"Oh my God!" Erin's face drained of blood. She stood paralyzed.

"We need to get Katie to bed. Then you can go home. I'll stay here. Is Lizzie asleep?"

Erin nodded and matched pace with Emily toward the bedroom. They maneuvered Katie out of her costume and into bed, piling on every blanket they could find. She was asleep before they finished.

Marguerite, having explained the situation to the cats' apparent satisfaction—they had barely raised their heads in all the commotion—volunteered to drive Erin home. Emily made herself a cup of Katie's cocoa and settled in to wait for word from Luke.

She saw again the set of his jaw when she'd left him. Surely he couldn't be thinking Katie had anything to do with Jake's death? She had motive, undeniably, and she appeared to be hiding something. But Emily was sure there was no violence in her. She certainly wasn't the type to let hatred fester for more than a year before acting on it. Now, if Jake had attacked her again—but she would have had to go looking for him in the secret stairwell, which was unthinkable, and had a pocketknife on her, which was surely unlikely under the circumstances. Her maid's costume didn't even have a pocket, as far as Emily knew.

But if not Katie, who? Useless to speculate, since she knew nothing of the situation and little of the people. Jake was the kind to make enemies of men and women alike, but she knew of no one else specifically who had a grievance against him. Except herself, of course. If she were the murdering kind, she would have marked Jake for disposal the moment she heard of his history with Katie.

Emily had brought *Wuthering Heights* with her, expecting a long vigil. She shrugged off speculation and pulled the volume out of her bag. The frontispiece showed Heathcliff in profile against a wild, stormy moor—weather just like they were having tonight. And this Heathcliff looked intriguingly like Roman.

Roman. He had a grudge against Jake.

As far as she knew, Roman had never left the house this evening. He'd stuck around to make sure the roof tarp held. And if he had caught Jake making another pass at Katie—he surely would have had a knife on him, and almost as surely would have used it. He shared Heathcliff's wild appearance, passionate nature, and a chip on his shoulder the size of a blasted Yorkshire tree. Not much of a stretch to assume he shared that character's vengeful inclinations as well—especially since he had threatened Jake in no uncertain terms.

She had to tell Luke right away. She rushed to the door—then stopped. She couldn't leave Katie and Lizzie, not with Katie in a drugged stupor, and besides, Luke would be busy taking statements. If there was any evidence of Roman being on the scene, Luke would find it and would know what to do with it.

Back to waiting. Patience on a monument, that was Emily Cavanaugh.

She opened the book but couldn't settle to reading it. She had little tolerance for these people anyway. Cathy was a spoiled brat, Isabella delusional; Edward was weak, Hindley a bully, and Heathcliff should have been left in the back alley where old Earnshaw found him.

If only she'd brought her knitting.

She was too tired to pace, too nervous to sit still. When the door opened, she jumped, spilling cocoa all over her beautiful russet satin dress. But it was only Marguerite.

"Oh, Margot, look what you've made me do! This will never come out." She dabbed ineffectually at the cocoa with her lace handkerchief, then realized she was ruining that, too.

"*Désolée, chérie, mais ne désespère pas.* I know just what to do. Take off the dress."

"Take it off? But—I don't exactly have on the proper Victorian undergarments. I'll freeze."

Marguerite shrugged. "Put on your coat. *Enfin,* go back to the house and change, *non?* I will be the watchdog while you are gone."

"Well—all right." She turned her back so Marguerite could undo the dress's many hooks. The satin slid to the floor, and Emily sprang for her coat before the chill could get to her in her thin slip. "I'll be right back."

Clutching her coat tightly about her and praying her umbrella would hold against the wind, Emily ran the short distance across the sopping lawn, her delicate evening shoes squelching in the mud. The shoes would no doubt be ruined as well.

She ducked into the kitchen and up the back stairs, hoping to escape notice. The back stairs came out just across the hall from the attic stairs. People were milling about, but no one looked her way as she dashed across.

At the top of the attic stairs she paused, panting as if she'd run a marathon. She'd have to either get more exercise or put in that elevator.

With no warning, a tall, thin figure emerged from the

construction area ahead of her. Hard to say which of them was more startled. Emily gasped and clutched the railing behind her; Jeremiah fell back a pace and clonked his head against the lintel of the doorway he'd just emerged from. He looked, if anything, even more ill than he had that afternoon.

"Jeremiah! I didn't expect you to be here still."

He rubbed the back of his head, looking slightly dazed. "Couldn't leave Roman here alone to look after that roof. Dangerous job, specially in this weather."

"How's the roof holding so far?"

"Had to reposition the tarp a couple times, but I think we've kept most of the water out. Don't recommend sleeping in that room tonight, though." He jerked his head toward her tower room, then winced and rubbed his head again.

"No, I suppose not. I just came up to change clothes and grab a few things. I'll wait till everyone leaves and sleep in—" She was about to say "Beatrice's room," until she thought of what lay behind the secret door. "In one of the guest rooms." She moved to the tower room door and stopped with her hand on the knob. "I can't expect you and Roman to stick around all night. Once Lieutenant Richards has finished questioning everyone, you may as well go home. With any luck the storm will have died down by then."

"Questioning?"

"You know, taking statements." She cocked her head at him. "Have you been up here all this time? Don't you know what's happened?"

He started to shake his head, winced, and said, "No."

"Good heavens, I thought Katie's scream would've been heard all the way to Seaside. Jake Newhouse is dead. Katie found his body at the bottom of the secret stairwell."

Jeremiah swayed on his feet. That clonk on his head must have been harder than it looked. He put out a hand to the wall for support. "No. No idea. Heard a commotion, thought it was just the game."

Emily didn't like the look of him. "I think you'd better sit down, Jeremiah. Let me get you an ice pack for that head. And have you had anything to eat? I'm sure there must be some food left over."

He clutched his head and sank to the floor, back against the wall. "I ate. Be all right in a minute."

"Well, if you're sure." With a last concerned glance she slipped into her room and, after a moment's hesitation, locked the door behind her.

Luke had finished interviewing the last of the clueless cast members and was staring at his unenlightening notes when Pete came in. "Chief, I think we might have something."

"Something's better'n the nothing I've got so far. Shoot."

"One of the waiters saw another one go up the back stairs a few minutes before Katie screamed. Abby Parker." Pete flipped through his notes. "Is that Katie's sister?"

"Probably. Big family, don't know all their names. This waiter see anything else?"

"Saw Abby later in the kitchen, crying. Katie was comforting her."

"Huh. Katie didn't mention that. All right, send Abby in."

Luke poured yet another cup of coffee and topped off his own, though his stomach warned him he'd had enough. The hall door opened a crack and half of a blond head appeared.

"Abby? Come on in." He put on his favorite-uncle voice again.

This one was going to need some encouragement. "I bet you could use a break. Been a busy night."

"Yessir." She crept up to the table, keeping as much distance as possible between herself and Luke.

"Have a seat." He pushed the cup of coffee toward her, but she kept her arms wrapped around her body. Like all the waitresses, she was dressed in a Victorian maid's uniform a little plainer than Katie's. Her white cuffs were spotted like a painter's palette—could be all food and wine, or some of the spots could be blood.

"Now suppose you tell me what you did from the time the actors started to leave the table."

"I was just going around the library, clearing dessert plates and pouring coffee."

"The whole time? Up until Katie screamed?"

The girl gave a little gasp. "Well, after the guests went up, I started clearing the rest of the stuff."

"Sure you didn't go upstairs at some point? One of your coworkers says he saw you."

Abby's pale blue eyes widened. "I—uh—oh, that's right, I—I forgot." She unfolded her arms and clasped her hands until the knuckles went white. "I went up to use the restroom."

Luke raised one eyebrow. "There's a restroom right next to the kitchen."

"Yes, but—it was occupied." She wouldn't meet his eyes.

This girl was lying, that was obvious. And she didn't seem to have a lot of practice at it, either. She was hiding something—but not necessarily murder.

"Did you know Jake Newhouse?"

Her eyes went round, then she blinked and lowered them. "A little. By sight, you know. Everybody knows—knew Jake."

"He never asked you out? Pretty girl like you? We all know Jake had a weakness for pretty girls." He kept his voice neutral—didn't want to suggest he shared that weakness.

She shook her head. Could be technically true, but he'd bet his badge something had gone on between the two of them.

"So you went to the restroom. What happened up there to make you cry?"

"Cry?" He wouldn't have thought her eyes could get any wider, but they did. "I w-wasn't crying."

"Somebody saw you crying in the kitchen. With Katie. Katie's your big sister, that right?"

"Oh . . . yeah. Katie and I—we were both upset. About—about Erin. She's having trouble with our folks right now."

Luke gave her his I'm-gonna-sit-here-till-you-tell-me-the-truth look. She dropped her eyes and let her hands fall to her lap. He gave her a minute, but she didn't budge. Her breath came quick and shallow, her color high.

Finally she looked up. "Can I go?"

She wasn't going to tell him the truth—not tonight, anyway. But she was no hardened liar. The pressure of all she was hiding would build inside her, and finally she'd blow. He could afford to wait.

Luke let Abby go, and Heather came in. "Got something you might want to follow up on, Chief."

"What's up?"

"Veronica Lacey says Devon Penhallow left the parlor soon after Jake went out. She didn't see which way he went."

"Devon Penhallow." Oh, right, the antique store guy. "You interview him?"

"No, I thought you'd want to talk to him yourself."

"Right. Send him in."

Luke added a bit of hot coffee to Abby's untouched cup for Devon. So far Abby was the only one he'd interviewed who hadn't left him a nice set of fingerprints on a coffee cup. He'd have to get hers the official way.

The door creaked ajar. A short, slender man, dressed like one of Emily's favorite Jane Austen heroes, stood in the gap. "You wished to see me, Inspector?"

For a second Luke thought he'd been transported into one of those British detective shows Emily loved so much. "It's 'Lieutenant.' We don't have inspectors in the sheriff's department." He waved to the chair across from him. "Take a seat."

Devon moved to the chair as if walking on hot coals. He was sure skittish enough to be guilty. But this guy take a knife to somebody? Luke surveyed his pristine white shirtfront and perfectly tied cravat with a skeptical eye.

"We're just following up on everybody's movements around the time of the accident." They weren't telling everyone it was murder yet. "Where were you seated for dinner?"

"I was in the parlor, the table nearest the hall door."

"Did you go up with the others when Ms. Fitzgerald dismissed you?"

"No, I went out before that. Right after—Newhouse left." He seemed to be reluctant to pronounce Jake's name.

Luke raised an eyebrow. "What for?"

Devon's smooth skin went pink. "Call of nature."

"So you used that one back there?" Luke jerked a thumb toward the ground-floor bathroom.

"I tried there first, but it was occupied. So I went up the back stairs to the second floor."

"Back stairs?" The back stairs were enclosed and hidden away, not something a casual guest would be likely to stumble upon. "How'd you even know there were back stairs? Snooping around?"

Devon's cheeks went from pink to crimson. "I've been helping Emily with her redecorating project. She showed Veronica and me over the entire house. Those stairs were the closest route, and I—well, I was a bit desperate."

Luke held his pen between two fingers and drummed the clicker end against the table. "See anybody?"

"The waitstaff were coming and going from the kitchen. All on their lawful pursuits, as far as I could tell."

"How about upstairs?"

"I believe there were people in the hallway—cast members, probably—but I was focused on getting to the loo. I didn't really look around."

"The upstairs bath was free when you got up there?" It wouldn't have been if Abby were telling the truth.

"Yes."

No surprise there. But now he had a needle to poke a hole in her story with. "How long were you in there?"

"I really couldn't say. Some minutes, I suppose. I had to— you know. I was just washing my hands when I heard the scream."

"Uh-huh. And did you come out right away?"

"Yes, of course. By that time there were crowds of people everywhere. You passed right in front of me yourself, Lieutenant."

That fit—the bathroom door was between the back bedroom, where Luke had been when he heard the scream, and the door to Beatrice's room. No reason to think Penhallow was lying—and probably no way to verify he was telling the truth.

Time to change tacks. "Did you know Jake Newhouse?" Luke knew the answer to this question, but he wanted to see how Penhallow would react.

Devon's elegant hands tightened around his coffee cup, knuckles whitening. "Not to say *knew*."

"But you'd run into him?"

"He was on the crew that remodeled our shop." The crisp British accent positively crackled on the words.

"What was your impression of him?"

Devon's jaw clenched. "Not particularly good. In fact, I believe him to be responsible for several of our best pieces being damaged when we were moving in." He looked up at Luke, his gray eyes darkening like this afternoon's sky kicking up for a gale. "Purposefully responsible."

Luke weighed his words. He was pretty sure of Jake's motive for the vandalism—not hard to guess what a guy like that would think of a fellow like Devon. But he wanted to hear the words from Devon's own mouth.

"And why do you suppose he'd do a thing like that? Wouldn't he know he'd get in trouble? Have to pay for the damage?"

Devon's nostrils flared as he took in air. "He evidently didn't care for people like Hilary and me."

"Did you confront him? You must not have sued for damages or I'd've heard about it."

"We had no real evidence he was involved, or that he had done it on purpose. The contractor compensated us for the damages."

"I see." Luke looked at Devon's hands, still clutching the cup. One of his white cuffs, the right-hand one, was stained with a smear of red.

"What's that on your cuff?"

Devon started, raised his left wrist toward his eyes and turned it around, then raised the right one. He fingered the spot and frowned. "I must have dipped it in the juice when I was helping myself to the roast beef. Blast, that'll be difficult to get out now it's set."

"Uh-huh." Luke moved to the hall door and called to Pete. "Pete, would you escort Mr. Penhallow home and take custody of his shirt?" He turned back to Devon. "We're going to have to have that analyzed."

Devon's face drained to a pasty white. "You surely—don't think—didn't you say Newhouse had an accident?"

"Jake Newhouse was stabbed. On somebody's clothes somewhere, we're going to find his blood."

thirteen

"Now for the hitch in Jane's character," he said at last . . .
"The reel of silk has run smoothly enough so far; but I always knew there would come a knot and a puzzle: here it is.
Now for vexation, and exasperation, and endless trouble!"
—Mr. Rochester to Jane, *Jane Eyre*

Emily emerged from the tower room a few minutes later, bundled in a fisherman's sweater, wool tweed slacks, and stout ankle boots, knitting bag in hand. Jeremiah was nowhere to be seen. She hoped he'd gone into the other room to lie down and nurse his sore head. She made her way down by the main stairs, looking around for Sam—despite Jeremiah's protests, she was sure he needed a doctor's attention.

By this time about half the guests had been interviewed and gone home. Emily passed the closed library door and hesitated. She still hadn't found Sam, so she knocked softly and cracked open the door. Luke sat alone at a corner table. He waved her in.

"Katie okay?"

"Sleeping." Emily sat next to him. "I left Marguerite with her and came back to change. Spilled cocoa all over my beautiful dress."

Luke tsked. "Too bad. That was some dress. I was looking forward to seeing more of it."

"Margot thinks she can rescue it. So how's it going? Are you done?"

He leaned back in his chair and stretched his arms up over his head until his back popped. "Done with the cast. Pete's interviewed all the caterers. Nobody saw anybody except Katie go into the stairwell from this end, but somebody saw Abby go up the back stairs when Jake went up the front. She claims she was just going to the bathroom, but what she's *not* saying is as loud as the Fourth of July."

"Abby? That little mouse? Surely you can't imagine she'd kill anyone. And why?"

"I don't know, but I've never seen anybody in all my years of sheriffing more obviously lying than she was. Could be she's just protecting Katie."

Emily bridled. "Katie doesn't need protecting! She's as innocent as you or I."

"That may be, but Abby may not know it. Look, Em, the things we don't know about this case would fill the Library of Congress. All I have at this point is pure speculation."

"Well, you must have some more likely suspect than either of the Parker girls."

"How about Matthew Sweet? He was on the scene. And then there's Devon Penhallow—he can't prove he wasn't in the stairwell, and he has a bloodstain on his cuff."

"I can't imagine a less likely murderer than either of them. Except for Katie and Abby, of course."

"Frankly, neither can I, but we've got to follow it up. Nothing else to go on."

"Don't you have *anything* more promising?"

"Just one thing. Matthew saw Roman coming out of Beatrice's room when he went up. I was just about to go looking for him."

"I *knew* it!" Emily sat forward and slapped her palms against the table. "That boy is a Heathcliff if ever I saw one. He has *murderer* written all over him."

Luke cocked an eyebrow at her. "I haven't read that book since high school, but as I recall it, Heathcliff never actually killed anyone, did he?"

"Only because he could get more fun out of tormenting them while they were still alive. He had the killer instinct, no question."

"Em, we've been down this road before. Just because somebody reminds you of a nasty character doesn't make him a murderer."

"I suppose not, but it's worth pursuing, isn't it?"

"Course it is, given he was in the right place at the right time. But so were Matthew and Katie."

Emily waved a dismissive hand. "Purely coincidental. They couldn't have had anything to do with it."

Luke looked sideways at her. "You seem awful sure about that."

"Aren't you?"

He stared into the dregs of his coffee. Not a good sign. Luke never hesitated to speak unless he knew she wouldn't like what he was going to say.

"Luke, you don't seriously suspect Katie? That girl doesn't even kill spiders. She traps them and carries them outside."

He looked up at her, and she saw the weariness etched in the lines around his eyes. Weariness and something deeper. Revulsion? She knew murder was not what Luke thought he was signing up for when he joined the sheriff's department in this quiet backwater town. Especially not murder involving people he cared about.

She almost relented, then thought of Katie, shaking and near senseless at witnessing the death of the one man in the world she had most reason to wish dead. "She was devastated, Luke. She hated Jake, but she was still devastated. No way could she have actually used that knife."

He passed a hand over his brow, dug thumb and fingertip into the corners of his eyes. "She was in shock. If she had killed him, don't you think she would've reacted the same way?" Emily opened her mouth to retort, but he held up a silencing palm. "I know as well as you she'd never kill in cold blood. But what if he attacked her? What if it was self-defense?"

Emily refused to admit she'd had the same thought. "Where would she have gotten the knife? She didn't even have a pocket, for pity's sake." She crossed her fingers under the table and hoped that was true.

"Maybe Jake had the knife and she got it away from him." Luke put his palms on the table and leaned toward Emily. "Look. I'm not saying Katie's my number-one suspect. But I did find her first on the scene, standing over the body with the murder weapon in her hand. And she can't account for her actions. I *cannot* rule her out. Not without more evidence than I have right now."

Emily fumed. He might have reason on his side, but affection trumped reason in her book. For a minute she wished she and Luke were sleeping together so she could deny him her bed as punishment.

She pushed away from the table and stood. "It's Roman. It

has to be Roman. You'll see." She marched out of the room without a backward glance.

Luke watched Emily out the door, silently cursing this case that had shoved a wedge between them when all he wanted in the world was to draw her as close as could be. Why couldn't she understand he had to do his job? But then, if she weren't going all mother hen over Katie, she wouldn't be the warmhearted, loyal woman he loved.

Nothing for it but to find Jake's real killer, and fast. And pray that blank in Katie's memory held nothing more than picking up a knife.

Feeling every second of his fifty-four years, Luke pushed himself out of the chair, drained the last swig of his coffee, and plodded upstairs in search of Roman. At the top of the attic stairs he paused and looked around. The door of Emily's bedroom opened and Roman came out.

Luke scowled at him. "What were you doing in Mrs. Cavanaugh's room?"

Roman's eyes widened, but he returned Luke's gaze full-on. "Had to climb out that window to get to the roof. Tarp keeps blowing off."

Luke scrutinized the boy's dripping orange poncho. If it had ever been stained with blood, the blood would have washed off in the downpour on the roof. How convenient.

"Need to ask you a few questions."

"About what?" Roman looked sincerely puzzled. Not a bad actor, but overdoing it to pretend he didn't even know.

"About the murder."

"Oh, the game?" Roman's scowl picked up where Luke's left off. "Not in on that. Just the help, here to keep out the rain."

"The *real* murder."

Roman's start seemed genuine. Luke made a mental note to check whether he had a background in drama. "*Real* murder?"

"Jake Newhouse was killed about an hour ago, downstairs. For real. He was supposed to play the victim, but somebody took the game a little too seriously."

Roman's dark features worked in a mix of emotions. Shock? Curiosity? And somewhere deep in those secretive black eyes, surely a glint of satisfied glee.

"You were seen on the second floor right about the time of the murder. I need an account of your movements from eight fifteen to eight thirty-five."

Roman scratched his head. "Don't wear a watch. Knock off when boss lets me go. Just the help, like I said."

Lord, give me strength. "Then tell me about any time you weren't either here on the third floor, or on the roof."

"Went up to check on the roof last time, tarp had blown off. Couple hours ago, maybe? More water on the floor in there." He jerked his head toward Emily's room. "Went downstairs to see if it was leaking through. Checked both bedrooms on this side of the house, just in case. Front one first, then the one with the big bay window out to sea."

"See anybody?"

"Not that time."

"Not that time? So you went back?"

"Yeah, went back to get my knife."

Luke's ears pricked up. "Your knife?"

"Used it to test the ceiling, make sure it was dry."

"Wouldn't you just use your hand for that?" As soon as he said it, Luke realized his mistake. Luke himself, if he stood on a chair, could easily put up an arm and touch those high ceilings; but Roman only came up to his shoulder.

Roman flushed and mumbled, "Couldn't reach."

"So you left the knife in that bedroom?"

"That's what I thought. Dropped it, then by the time I got off the chair and put it back, I forgot about the knife."

"Uh-huh. Left it right there on the floor for anybody in the house to find."

"Yeah." Roman's face went an ugly purple. "Look, I know how it sounds, but I didn't know somebody was gonna be murdered, all right?"

That was plausible. Like everything else Roman had said. So damn plausible, it just might be the truth.

"So you went back. How much later?"

"Ten minutes, maybe? Finished mopping up the water in the tower, then realized I didn't have the knife."

"What happened then?"

"Went down, looked in the room, no knife. Figured one of those rich kids must've swiped it."

"Rich kids?"

"Bunch of jokers wandering around, dressed up in penguin suits and long dresses."

"What about Jake? You see him?"

"Nope. Last I saw of him was when Mrs. Cavanaugh fired him." Roman's swarthy face darkened further. "And good riddance."

"Anybody in the bedroom?"

"Some kid went in as I came out. Didn't recognize him."

"What'd he look like?"

"Tall, skinny. Zitface. Looked stupid in that monkey suit."

Matthew. "Did you notice the secret passage? Was it open or shut?"

Roman squinted over Luke's shoulder. "Barely ajar. I think."

"How long were you in there?"

"Couple seconds."

"Then what?"

"Came back up here."

"Hear anything?"

"Only the storm. Pretty loud up here, in case you hadn't noticed."

With only a roof between them and the rain, with wind howling past the windows and in through the cracks, the din was pretty fierce. Luke could almost believe Roman might not have heard Katie's scream—or at least not have recognized it as produced by genuine horror.

Luke pouched his lips and tapped his pencil against his notepad. "What's your knife look like?"

"Black wood handle, spring catch, one three-inch blade. No fancy stuff."

That sounded like the murder weapon, all right. "Come downstairs with me."

Roman scowled but followed Luke down the two flights to the library. Luke poked his head into the stairwell and asked one of the technicians to hand him the knife Katie had been holding, now encased in a plastic evidence bag.

He held up the bag so Roman could get a good look. "That your knife?"

"Looks like it." Roman leaned in, and his skin went an ugly gray. "No blood on it when I saw it last."

Luke was tempted to arrest him on the spot. But ownership

of the murder weapon wasn't technically enough evidence for that.

There was one potential group of people in the house he hadn't accounted for yet. "Any other workers besides you stay behind after the party started?"

"Just me and the boss."

"Where's the boss now?"

Roman shrugged. "Last time I saw him was before I went up on the roof last time. In the front room."

Luke huffed. This house had way too many stairs. "All right. You can go. But stay where I can reach you. That knife's going to have be accounted for, one way or another."

Luke dragged himself back up the main stairs, then the attic stairs. If only Emily were waiting for him at the top instead of yet another witness. Emily in nothing but a lacy silk negligée with a single hairpin holding that coppery mass on top of her head, ready for him to release it to ripple down her back. That would have put a spring in his step. But if Emily was waiting for him anywhere, it was probably in the kitchen with a rolling pin.

At the top of the stairs he paused for breath, hitched up his slacks, and eased the stiff collar around his neck. He'd give a lot to be in uniform right now. Funny thing to say, but his uniform had become like second skin. He felt like at least two-thirds of his authority was imbedded in that khaki twill. He might as well be naked in this "penguin suit," as Roman called it. Very constrictedly naked.

He walked on through to the front room. The light was on, tools strewn around the half-finished room, even the remains of somebody's lunch on the windowsill. But no workers. No Jeremiah Edwards.

Funny he should take off so suddenly. Not like him to leave a mess behind. Maybe gone downstairs to take a leak?

Roman came into the room after him. "You seen Edwards?" Luke asked him.

"Looks like he went home. Left me to clean up, as usual."

Luke had a sudden flash of something inexplicable. "Leave it. I don't want anything in the house disturbed more than can be helped."

Roman shrugged. "You're the boss." He checked his tool belt, appeared to find all in order, and went out.

Luke peered around the room, wondering what had set off his sixth sense. This room was nowhere near the crime scene. What evidence could it possibly hold?

He made a circuit, examining the walls, the tools and debris, the floor. All was just as it ought to be, except for one place in front of the paneled back wall where a drop cloth was rucked up, exposing the wooden floor beneath. Luke knelt and examined the floor, tried the boards. No trapdoor here, though it wouldn't have much surprised him if there had been. This old house was full of secrets.

He gave up. If there was anything here, he was too tired to see it. Now to tell Emily her precious remodeling would have to be held up for a bit. One more thing for her to be mad about.

Emily sat at the kitchen table, nursing a glass of wine left over from dinner. Not the most comfortable seat in the house, but all the other rooms were subject to intrusion by wandering guests, any of whom might ambush her with questions she either couldn't or shouldn't answer. The caterers still came and went through the back door, removing the last of their gear, but at least they kept their whispering among themselves.

Luke paused in the doorway as if unsure of his welcome. She nodded him in and held up the bottle of wine with a question in her eyes.

"Better not. Still have to inform the next of kin." He pulled up a chair and looked at her sideways from under his brows. "You still mad at me?"

How could she be mad at that look? But on the other hand, how could she not be mad at the man who suspected Katie of murder? "Depends on whether you've amended your suspect list."

He sighed. "Yeah. I've decided there's nobody who could've done it. Well, Roman's the best fit—it was his knife, apparently—but if he's guilty, he's the best darned actor I've ever come across. And finding his prints or DNA on the knife won't prove a damn thing."

"But if you found someone else's?" She didn't know why she said that; it was obvious Roman was guilty, good actor or not.

"Besides Katie's, you mean? Then we might be getting somewhere. I'm not going to stake my badge on it, though." He passed a hand over his eyes. "I'm beat. Body's gone, crime scene's done. Pete and Heather are just rounding up the ghouls and sending them home. Listen, this is up to you, but I'd strongly recommend you get a professional crime-scene cleanup team in here. We can't have Katie cleaning that stairwell."

"Because she's a suspect?" Emily was shocked at the waspish way that came out.

Luke started and widened his eyes at her. "Because she's been traumatized." Then his eyes dropped. "Well, yeah, and because she's a suspect, too. At least until she remembers what happened."

Emily set her jaw. And to think she'd begun to soften. "I suppose you know some such people." As if they were the worst sort of lowlifes that only a cruel and clueless sheriff's lieutenant would know. She must be channeling Beatrice's old housekeeper, Agnes Beech.

He winced at her tone. "Yeah." He pulled out his wallet and dug around in it, then handed her a business card.

The address was in Portland. Of course there wouldn't be enough work for a firm like that around here. "Do they work weekends?"

"Yeah. If they're free." He looked at her solicitously. "You'll have to live with—that—in the stairwell for tonight at least. You be okay here?"

Emily honestly wasn't sure, but having Luke stay over wouldn't help. Not the way things stood between them. "I'll be fine. Probably go back over to Katie's and sleep on her couch in case Lizzie wakes up. Marguerite won't mind sleeping in the house, she's not squeamish."

"That reminds me. I better go over there with you. Need to take Katie's maid costume."

Why hadn't she washed that, or burned it, when she had the chance? No, that was crazy talk. Katie was innocent, must be innocent. Her clothes could only prove that.

Luke walked with Emily across the dark lawn, the grass squelching under their feet. At least the rain had stopped and the wind abated. She lost her footing at one point, and he shot out a hand to steady her, but she shook it off.

They mounted the stairs to the apartment in silence. Marguerite was dozing on the couch. Luke stood just inside the front door while Emily got a trash bag from the kitchen, went into the bedroom, and returned with the black dress and white apron and cap shoved unfolded into the bag. At least he trusted her that much.

He stood awkwardly with the white garbage bag in his arms. "Guess I'll get going then. If you're sure you'll be all right."

She stood with her arms crossed, a good two feet between them. "Good night." They hadn't parted without a kiss since they first came to an understanding back in June. But she would not kiss a man who thought her Katie capable of murder.

· fourteen ·

By the time Luke had finished at Windy Corner Saturday
night, it was past midnight. But he still had to inform Jake's
next of kin—his parents. He stopped off at home for a quick
change of clothes—he needed the moral support of his uniform
for this.

Carter Newhouse's office was in Tillamook, but his house
stood high on the hill above Stony Beach—almost as big and
grand as Windy Corner but modern, the front mostly windows
to get the best view of the sea. Emily would hate it. Luke knew
nothing about architecture and cared less, but even he felt intimidated and shut out by the three stories of reflective glass and
gleaming metal that loomed above him as he ducked under the
low bit of roof over the double ebony doors. He felt like he was
asking admittance to a prison.

He knocked, rang the bell, and knocked again before he

heard somebody at the door. A young, sleepy female voice asked, "Who is it?"

Luke identified himself, and the door was opened by a stunning young girl in a bathrobe. Did Jake have a sister?

"Everyone's in bed, Lieutenant. What's this about?" The girl didn't seem fazed by his uniform; as a criminal lawyer, Newhouse probably got visits from law enforcement all the time.

"Are you the daughter of the house?"

She snorted. "Me? No. Just the hired help." Newhouse himself must do the hiring; no wife with any sense would allow a girl who looked like that under her roof. Especially not if father was anything like son.

"I need to speak to Mr. and Mrs. Newhouse."

She blinked and widened her eyes. "*Mrs.* Newhouse?" she repeated.

"That's right. I have something very important to tell them both."

"Important enough to wake them up for? 'Cause if not, my job's on the line."

Luke nodded. "I guarantee it."

"All right. It'll be a few minutes."

She showed him into a small reception room—small for the scale of the house, anyway, though it was bigger than his living room. The black leather club chairs looked comfortable, but looks were as far as it went; the leather didn't yield an inch when he sat on it.

His hosts didn't show up right away, so he flipped through his notes to refresh his memory. After a few pages he checked his watch. He'd been waiting ten minutes. What were they doing, getting their hair done?

Five more minutes went by before the door opened and Carter Newhouse came in by himself, freshly shaved, wearing a crisp dress shirt and slacks. At least he'd left off the tie and coat.

Luke stood to meet him. Even if he hadn't already known Newhouse by sight, he would have recognized him by his resemblance to his son—the same sleazy good looks, though older and starting to sag around the jowls; the same arrogant strut, lifted chin, lip ever ready to curl into a sneer.

"What's this about—" He glanced at the business card Luke had handed to the maid. "Lieutenant? The maid assured me it was important enough to get me out of bed. I hope she was right."

"I need to speak to you and your wife together, sir. Didn't the maid tell you?"

"My wife will be here shortly. Though I can't imagine what you think could concern *her*."

The door opened again and a middle-aged woman scurried in, fully dressed and made up as if she were going out to bridge or a fancy lunch. Even Luke, fashion-blind as he was, could tell her outfit was pricey. It stood out from her shrinking body like it was held in shape by wires. She didn't so much wear her clothing as visit it, like a scared kid in a china shop who'd been warned not to touch. She shot a glance at her husband before putting out a hand to meet Luke's, then barely touched his fingers and snatched her hand away. Luke tried to look into her eyes, but she wouldn't meet his. Under the careful makeup he thought he could see a shadow on one thin, pale cheek. But maybe it was just a trick of the light.

He hated the errand he'd come on even more now, and was almost sorry he'd insisted on seeing Jake's mother. This fragile woman might break apart before his eyes at what he had to tell her.

"I'm afraid I have some bad news for you both. You might want to sit down."

Mrs. Newhouse gave a little gasp and groped for the chair behind her. Newhouse stayed on his feet, braced like a sailor against the swell. "Out with it, Lieutenant. I've taken bad news before."

I, not we. Luke fixed his eyes on the wife and put into them all the compassion he could drum up. Jake might have been a prime candidate for Shithead of the Year, but he was this woman's son. She must have loved him if anyone did.

"I'm very sorry to have to tell you your son Jake was found dead earlier this evening. During the party at Windy Corner."

Mrs. Newhouse did in fact come as close as flesh and blood could to breaking up before his eyes. She shrank into her chair, clutching her hands to her mouth, her face all eyes. A mouse-like squeak came from her throat.

Newhouse just stared at Luke, frowning. "Found dead? What does that mean? Did he have an accident?"

Luke chose his words carefully for the mother's sake. "He was found at the bottom of an enclosed spiral staircase." He cleared his throat, hoping Mrs. Newhouse's shock would keep her from taking in his next words. "We're treating it as a suspicious death."

No such luck. Her squeaking rose to a moan, and she rocked herself in the chair. "My boy . . . my beautiful, foolish boy . . ."

Newhouse frowned at her and strode to the door. "Amy. Mrs. Newhouse has had a shock. Get her back to bed." The maid helped Mrs. Newhouse to her feet, more gently than Luke would have expected, and led her out of the room, bearing most of her weight. Seeing his wife could hardly move her own feet, Newhouse added, "And better call Dr. Tomlinson."

So Newhouse had a tame Tillamook doctor at his beck and call. Luke wasn't surprised; Sam Griffiths would be way too much "of the people" for Newhouse's taste.

He shut the door and turned back to Luke. "Now tell me the rest. What happened to him?"

Luke had no qualms about spelling out the details now. "He was stabbed in the chest. It looks like he subsequently either fell or was pushed down the stairs. The autopsy will tell us whether it was the knife wound or the head trauma from the fall that killed him."

"So it's murder."

"Looks like it."

Newhouse's nostrils flared. "I knew that so-called fundraiser was a damned fool idea. Putting the idea of murder in people's heads. I'm surprised Beatrice's niece would be so irresponsible. Beatrice would never have allowed it."

Luke bridled for Emily's sake, though he'd questioned the plan's wisdom himself. "People have murder mystery parties all the time without anybody getting killed for real. If a person has reason enough to kill somebody, he's not gonna wait for a setting like that to do it in. Just made it a little handier, is all."

"You say 'he.' Do you have the killer in custody?"

"Just a form of speech. We have half-a-dozen suspects, male and female. Just need to narrow them down."

"I trust you'll do that speedily. I want my son's killer brought to justice without delay."

"We'll do our best, Mr. Newhouse. These things can take a little time. You could expedite the process yourself by answering a few questions." Luke took out his notebook and sat down.

Newhouse remained standing, his face like an old Roman

statue. "What questions? You can't suspect me. I was nowhere near the place."

Odd that he didn't say *you can't suspect me of killing my own son.* Most parents would. "No, sir. I mean about Jake. Anything that might shed light on who'd want to kill him and why."

"No one. Jake was a law-abiding young man, respected by his peers. I can't imagine who would dare to do this to him."

"There are some indications it might have been a crime of passion, as they say. Either a girl he—didn't treat too well, or a jealous guy."

Something like a smile cracked the stone of Newhouse's face. "He was one for the ladies, my Jake." He waved a hand. "But murder? You don't kill a boy for sowing his wild oats."

Luke swallowed the revulsion that rose in his gullet. Was Newhouse in denial about the true nature of Jake's "wild oats," or did he know and genuinely consider it trivial? Either way, it was clear Jake's attitude toward women didn't come out of nowhere.

"You'd be surprised what some people will kill over. But if there's anything else you can tell me—was Jake involved in drugs? Have a falling out with a friend? Anything that might not be obvious on the surface?"

Newhouse walked to the window and stared toward the sea, though all he'd be able to see in the dark was his own reflection. "No drugs. I told you he was law-abiding. But Jake has—had—been living on his own since he finished high school. I don't really know that much about his life."

"Did he have any close friends? Any brothers or sisters?"

"One brother, but he's much older, practicing law in Portland. He and Jake have never been particularly close. As for friends—" He turned to face Luke, the Roman statue lost in a childlike bewilderment that looked ridiculous on his middle-aged face. "I simply have no idea."

"Maybe your wife could tell me."

He gave a small snort. "As you've seen, she's in no condition to tell anyone anything."

"Not now, of course. Maybe when she's had a little time to recover."

Newhouse turned back to the window. "She isn't good for much at the best of times. But by all means waste your time with her if you like."

Luke took his leave. Mrs. Newhouse was so easily intimidated, he doubted he'd get much out of her himself—but that didn't mean there was nothing to be gotten. Emily would be more likely to get her to talk.

Emily awoke next morning with every joint feeling as if it were encased in an iron cast. She was positive she'd never be able to move a millimeter. But then she realized what had awakened her was Lizzie whimpering, gearing up for a full-scale cry—accompanied by the sound of the shower running.

And Katie's voice, incredibly, rising above the water's roar in a gleeful rendition of "Oh, What a Beautiful Morning."

Propelled by necessity, Emily pushed herself up to a sitting position on Katie's couch. She ran her hands over her face and hair—oh, dear, that elaborate turn-of-the-century coiffure that she'd never brushed out last night—and dug the sleep out of the corners of her eyes. Then she summoned every ounce of strength and willpower she possessed and stood.

She could do this. She could walk into the nursery, pick up

Lizzie, change her diaper, get her a bottle. She might be getting old, but she wasn't dead yet.

But Jake Newhouse was.

And that must be why Katie was singing.

The weight that had been hanging around Katie's neck since Lizzie's conception—and with renewed dragging heaviness since Jake reappeared in her life—had been lifted, completely and permanently. The man who had violated her, destroyed her self-esteem, and changed the direction of her life could never disturb her peace again.

The realization dazed Emily. She herself had reason aplenty to wish Jake out of existence, but his death had nevertheless left her feeling almost as violated as Katie had been by his rape of her. Jake had died at Windy Corner, polluting Emily's beloved home with hatred, violence, and blood.

At least the blood could be dealt with. She felt in her trouser pocket for the business card Luke had handed her last night. CLEAN SCENE—WE ERASE ALL TRACE. She'd call them as soon as she'd taken care of Lizzie.

Emily returned the card to her pocket and hurried to the nursery, where Lizzie's whimpering had escalated to a wail. She scooped up the baby and held her close, cooing to her and rubbing her back. In moments Lizzie was calm again.

Poor thing, she doesn't even know her father is dead. Even poorer thing for the fact that it's better for her that he is.

Jamie would make a great stepfather. Maybe now that Jake was out of the way, that relationship would have a chance to bloom.

Emily changed Lizzie's sopping diaper and took her to the kitchen, where she strapped her into the high chair and gave her an arrowroot biscuit to pacify her while she fixed a bottle. Meanwhile she heard the shower cut off, and a few minutes later Katie came into the kitchen in her bathrobe, toweling her long wet hair.

"Mrs. C! What are you doing here?" She scooped Lizzie out of the chair and nuzzled her biscuity cheek. "Good morning, babycakes. How's my girlie?"

"I slept on your couch. Dr. Griffiths had given you a sedative, so I thought someone should be here in case Lizzie woke up before you."

"A sedative? What for?" The light slowly dimmed from Katie's face. "Oh. Right. I remember now."

Emily put down the bottle and went to hug her. "It'll be all right," she said meaninglessly as she patted Katie's back.

Katie pulled away and put on a smile. "Of course it will. Everything will be all right now. Come on, Lizzie-lou, let's get you dressed. You can bring your ba-ba." She took the bottle from the counter and headed for the nursery.

Emily followed. "If you're okay then—I guess I'll go get cleaned up. My hair must look like Fright Night."

"Sure, no problem," Katie said over her shoulder as she laid Lizzie on the changing table. "We're good. Everything's ticketyboo." Katie was a fan of British television as well.

Emily's first action on entering her own house was to call Clean Scene. A chirpy female voice promised they would be there early afternoon. It was seven now—they must work 'round the clock.

After a long negotiation with her stiff and ratted hair, an even longer shower, and some clean clothes, Emily emerged to find Marguerite's bedroom door still firmly closed and Katie singing as she produced enticing odors in the kitchen. The library was back to its normal self, all trace of last night's frolics removed. The cats lifted their heads from the hearthrug and mewed in greeting as Emily sat in her favorite chair and took up her knitting. She could almost believe last night had been nothing worse than a dream.

But she couldn't bring herself to look at the curved section of bookshelf that led to the secret stairs. No, her house was not unaffected, her life wasn't normal, and she wasn't sure it ever would be again.

And it was all Jake Newhouse's fault. If he hadn't been such a lousy excuse for a human being, he wouldn't have gotten himself killed in her stairwell. She could kill him herself for that. But that would be redundant, and she had always exhorted her students to eschew redundancy.

Maybe she should go back to teaching. Since she'd come to Windy Corner, her life seemed to consist of one murder after another. Nothing like that ever happened at Reed. Well, the occasional student did commit suicide; last year it had been one of her own protégés, and that had cut deep. But at least suicide didn't leave a trail of hatred behind it.

Katie would be perfectly capable of running the writers' retreat on her own. Emily could simply pay the bills and visit once in a while. Marguerite and her other colleagues would be thrilled to have her back. Her little house would welcome her with open doors. And Luke—

Luke. The fly in the ointment, the flaw in the plan. The rub, as in "Aye, there's the rub." She might be furious with him at the moment, but to cut him out of her life—she couldn't even follow that thought to its logical conclusion.

She would have to stay and prove Katie's innocence. That—

and Clean Scene—would surely exorcise Jake Newhouse's spirit from Windy Corner once and for all.

Marguerite did not appear at breakfast, so Emily felt no compunction about leaving her guest to go to church. She didn't often attend St. Bede's, the little Anglican church on the hillside in whose cemetery Beatrice was buried, because the contrast between the comparatively bare clapboard building, with its off-key priest leading poorly attended services, and her own Russian Orthodox church in Portland, with its icon-covered, incense-saturated walls and richly sung liturgy, was too stark and painful. Instead she tried to get to St. Sergius once a month or so; but at this point she hadn't been for six weeks or more. Her spirit was parched, and she must give it whatever water she could find.

The choir stumbled through the first part of the service, more than half of them obviously the worse for last night's excitement. Emily was relieved when the time came for the sermon, but her relief was short-lived. Father Stephen was well-intentioned and at times achieved something like eloquence, as he had at Beatrice's funeral. Today, however, he seemed dumbfounded by last night's events. He could hardly eulogize a young man as notorious as Jake, nor refer to his death as a "tragedy" without coughing into his sleeve. Instead he spoke vaguely of the need for the community to pull together in this "difficult time."

Emily, sitting in Beatrice's customary front pew, snuck a few glances behind her to see what expressions met Father Stephen as he looked out on his unusually large congregation. Thinly veiled ghoulish curiosity predominated, with a sprinkling of guilty discomfort from some who felt they ought to regret Jake's death more strongly, and outright satisfaction from several who, like Katie, would find their lives much improved by his loss.

The communion portion of the service offered no comfort, either, since Emily, as an Orthodox Christian, could not partake in a church of a different tradition. So she withdrew into her own prayers, drawing on the fragile threads of a century of remembered piety that waved like broken cobwebs from the chipped stained-glass windows, the worn burgundy velveteen of the kneelers, the frayed fabric covering of the hymnals. People had genuinely prayed here at some time—prayed in joy, in hope, in anguish, in thanksgiving, or in desperate grief. Emily joined their prayers with hers now, imploring God for Jake's ghost to be exorcised from Windy Corner, for Katie and all innocent persons to be exonerated, and for the guilty—not to be punished, but to find peace. Peace was all she wanted, for herself, for her home, for all who had ever entered it or ever would.

After the service, the crowd milled around her, discreetly or overtly pumping her for information about the investigation. "I'm sorry, I'm not at liberty to comment," she said over and over. "Lieutenant Richards will make a statement when he's ready." Luke hadn't actually told her that, but she was pretty sure he would have if he'd thought of it, and it got her off the hook. She made it all the way down the aisle and out the front door, only to run smack into Rita Spenser. The reporter filled the porch, blocking Emily's way.

"So, Emily, got yourself another murder at Windy Corner? That house is starting to seem positively unhealthy." Rita grinned, showing crooked nicotine-stained teeth and exuding vapors to match.

Emily backed up a step and repeated her formula with added

conviction. "I'm sure Lieutenant Richards will contact you when he has anything to report."

Rita leaned closer. The combination of her halitosis and rank body odor made Emily gag. "But I want the scoop. Straight from the horse's mouth."

Emily held her handkerchief to her face and pretended to sneeze. "I assure you, I know far less than the sheriff does. Practically nothing, in fact. Please excuse me. I really need to get home."

Rita planted her feet, arms akimbo. This wasn't going to be easy.

Emily heard a voice behind her. "Is this egregious individual discomfiting you, Mrs. Cavanaugh?"

She turned to see Billy Beech, a scowl disfiguring his normally jovial round face. Billy was Rita's cousin, though kin to her only in size, and perhaps the only person in Stony Beach who could intimidate her.

"Yes, Billy, she is." Emily flattened herself against the doorframe to let him pass.

He rushed Rita like a fullback, head down, leading with his shoulder. "Begone, you perfidious viper! Before I squash you like the crawling insect you are!" Billy's vocabulary exceeded his ability to stick to a single metaphor, but at the moment Emily was not inclined to critique his choice of words.

Rita, astonishingly, gave way and melted resentfully into the crowd, eyes smoldering. If only there were some way to pin Jake's murder on Rita—Stony Beach would be rid of two scourges with one blow.

fifteen

But the morning passed just as usual . . . only, soon after breakfast, I heard some bustle in the neighborhood of Mr. Rochester's chamber. . . . There were exclamations of "What a mercy master was not burnt in his bed!" . . .
To much confabulation succeeded a sound of scrubbing and setting to rights; and when I passed the room, in going down stairs to dinner, I saw through the open door that all was again restored to complete order.

—*Jane Eyre*

Emily arrived home just as Katie was putting lunch on the table for Marguerite.

"*Alors,* my wandering hostess returns at last," Marguerite said with some asperity. "Is my visit so long already that you tire of my company?"

"You were asleep, for pity's sake. And I really needed to go to church."

"Ah, church . . ." Marguerite shrugged. She had enough Catholic in her to make her respect others going to church, though not enough to make her enter one herself for anything but a wedding or a funeral.

"Your sheriff came by while you were gone."

"Luke? What for?" He'd better have come to apologize and assure her he'd stricken Katie from his suspect list.

"He wanted to, how you say, investigate the third floor. He

was too *fatigué, le pauvre,* to do it properly last night. But when I told him you were not here, he said he would come back later."

"The third floor? What does the third floor have to do with anything?" Luke's behavior was getting stranger by the minute.

Marguerite gave an eloquent shrug. "In me he did not confide. You will call him yourself, *non?*"

Non. He could call her if he had something to say. She tore at her bread as if it were responsible for the rift between her and Luke.

Marguerite regarded her impassively. "You know that I must leave this afternoon, *oui?*"

"Yes, of course." Clean Scene would be here in half an hour, and Emily did not care to linger in the house while they did their grisly work. "The weather's cleared. It's actually fairly nice outside. Want to walk on the beach after lunch and see what the storm blew in?"

Marguerite sipped her café au lait with a visible softening. "*Pourquois pas?* Your beach, it has always *quelque-chose amusante* to say."

When they'd finished their mock turtle soup, left over from last night's banquet, Emily changed into a sweater and chinos and made it back downstairs just in time to let the cleaners in. She'd sent Katie and Lizzie home to rest so they would be out of the way.

Clean Scene turned out to consist of a middle-aged man and a boy in his late teens, evidently father and son. They shared an unfortunate nose, but the boy's abundant blond hair had gone sparse and muddy brown on his father. The boy was tongue-tied—Emily guessed from shyness rather than sullenness—but his fair skin flushed purple as his father shook

Emily's hand with a heartiness that would have been more appropriate in an after-party cleaner than an after-murder one. "Clean Scene on the scene, 'We Erase All Trace.' Just point us in the right direction and we'll get that damned spot out in no time flat." He winked to be sure she caught his veiled Shakespearean reference. He might have been one of the Bard's buffoons himself, ready to bestow upon her all the tediousness of a king.

"This way." The Beatrice in her wished she'd stayed in her church clothes so she could look more the part of the grande dame and less like someone with whom liberties might be taken. She ushered the pair into the library and opened the door to the concealed stairway, then plugged in the extension cord for the floodlights the crime scene people had left behind.

"It's all contained in here. There's no need for you to do anything outside this stairwell, but you will need to address the whole area." She gestured to the brown stains that trailed up the wooden steps. "It's an old house and quite a showplace, so please be as gentle as you can. But thorough."

Clean Scene Senior clapped her on the back. She was glad she had on her thick Aran sweater to cushion the blow. "Don't you worry, ma'am. In like a lion, out like a lamb, that's our motto."

Emily did not find that metaphor greatly comforting, but she let it pass. "How long do you think it'll take?"

He shrugged. "Couple hours. This is a piece of cake. No carpet, no furniture, confined space—all our jobs should be so easy. Right, Fred Junior?" He elbowed his silent son, who managed a feeble grin, then rolled his eyes behind his father's back.

Emily caught Fred Junior's eye with a sympathetic quirk at the corner of her mouth. "I'll be back in a couple of hours to write you a check." She slipped out before Fred Senior could come up with a snappy reply.

Emily and Marguerite enjoyed a pleasant if breezy walk on the beach. Marguerite found several tiny but exquisite shells to take home, and Emily almost managed to forget what she'd be going back to. But return to the house was inevitable.

Freds Junior and Senior were lugging their equipment back out to their van as Emily and Marguerite approached across the lawn.

"Perfect timing," Fred Senior called out. He shoved a large wet-dry vac into the van and produced a small clipboard from one capacious pocket. He scribbled on it and presented it to Emily.

She took it without looking and proceeded into the hall, then into the tiny office next to the front stairs where she kept her checkbook. Fred Senior followed, prattling away.

"Real quaint old place you got here. Beautiful workmanship. Used to be a contractor, so I know. And all those secret passages—what a hoot! You could have a terrific Halloween party here."

Emily turned, check in hand. "Actually, we just did. A murder mystery party. Only the intended pretend victim got himself killed for real."

Fred Senior whistled through his teeth. "Is that what happened! Straight out of a book, ain't it?"

It could have been, actually, now that Emily thought about it—in fact, hadn't Ngaio Marsh written a story exactly like that? The first Roderick Alleyn, if she recalled correctly—*A Man Lay*

Dead. Maybe the murderer had read it, too. But no, Roman hardly seemed the reading type. Better stick with Brontë.

Emily waved Clean Scene off from the porch, then turned back to see Marguerite in the doorway, overnight bag in hand. "Margot, you're leaving already? I thought you'd at least stay to tea."

"*Merci,* but I wish to arrive in Portland before dark. I have papers to correct. *Hélas,* I am not yet a lady of leisure like yourself." Marguerite had not yet given up on her dream of marrying a wealthy man and spending the rest of her life on the Riviera.

She kissed Emily on both cheeks. "You should come and stay with me for a while, *chérie.* This house, it is too gloomy just now. You need a change."

Emily sighed. A change did sound wonderful. But how could she leave Katie? And the remodeling? And leave the investigation solely in Luke's hands, when he was being so wrongheaded about it?

"I don't know, Margot. I'll think about it. It does sound nice, but . . . maybe when all this is over."

Marguerite gave Emily one of her searching looks. She occasionally exhibited Miss Maud Silver's trick of appearing to find the human race—or at least Emily—glass-fronted. "As long as you take the weight of the world on your shoulders, *chérie,* 'all this' will never be over."

Emily swallowed, knowing Marguerite was right. "I will think about it. Really. I'll call you."

Marguerite nodded inscrutably and picked up her bag. "We will talk soon."

Emily went in to find Katie just laying out her tea. "How are you, Katie?"

"Just fine, Mrs. C. Aren't we, Lizzie-lou?" She turned her head to address the baby, who was perched in a backpack on her mother's back, attempting to catch and eat Katie's swinging ponytail. Lizzie gurgled in reply.

Emily scooped Levin off her favorite chair and planted him in her lap. He purred as she scratched his favorite spot behind his ear. Katie was fine; Lizzie was fine; the cats were fine. Why was she the only one who could not shake the feeling that an ill wind had blown into Windy Corner and was not giving any sign of blowing out?

She read the final pages of *Wuthering Heights* along with her tea, then carried the book over to the curved section of shelving that housed the fiction library—and opened onto the secret stairs. The door was firmly closed now, and Emily was resolved it should stay that way indefinitely. Yet she didn't feel Jake's shade had utterly departed. Perhaps he was waiting for justice. Though she would have said his death in itself had been justice, albeit carried out by an unofficial hand. Upon that thought she guiltily crossed herself. She should never rejoice in the death of a sinner who'd had no warning that death was upon him and hence no opportunity to repent.

She nerved herself and shoved *Wuthering Heights* back onto the shelf with a sense of relief. Maybe that book was partly responsible for the way she was feeling. Who could be cheerful in the presence of Heathcliff & Co.? She skimmed the lower shelves for something that might lift her mood. L. M. Montgomery? P. G. Wodehouse? But they seemed *too* cheerful. She wasn't ready for that dramatic a change.

She straightened and spotted *Jane Eyre* right next to *Wuthering Heights*. It stood out a bit from the row as if beckoning to her. *Jane Eyre* wasn't exactly cheery reading, but it did have glimmers of light—and a happy ending. Perhaps it could help her transition back to normal.

As she read the opening paragraph—*There was no possibility of taking a walk that day . . . the cold winter wind had brought with it clouds so sombre, and a rain so penetrating, that further outdoor exercise was now out of the question*—the weather outside her window took a turn and followed suit. Emily sank into the world of the forlorn, misunderstood little Jane, with whom she had identified so strongly as a child, and welcomed melancholy as an old friend.

After his abortive visit to Windy Corner—which he didn't dare invade in Emily's absence, given her current mood—Luke spent Sunday alone at the office, reading through last night's interview transcripts till he had them memorized, sifting through the crime scene reports, and staring at fingerprints until he could see them even in the texture of the paint on his office walls. Try as he might, the only clear prints he could match off the knife were Katie's and, somewhat surprisingly, Jake's. Some of the smudged partials looked consistent with Roman, but he couldn't be sure; none of them matched up with any of the cast or guests. Anyway, Roman's prints on the knife didn't prove anything; they already knew the knife was his.

The absence of anyone else's prints was more suggestive. That implied three possibilities for the culprit: Roman, Katie, or X wearing gloves. Luke played over the dinner scene in his mind: at least a third of the guests, including all the cast members, had come in wearing gloves as part of their costumes. They'd taken them off to eat but could easily have put them on again to kill. Holy cow, was he going to have to check for blood-stained gloves with every single one of the hundred guests? And the caterers had been wearing gloves, too. What were there, twenty of them?

No, no. *Pull it together, Richards.* He'd already ruled out most of those present due to their position at the time of the murder. Those unaccounted for included Abby, Matthew, and Devon—none of whom he could seriously imagine as a killer. But he didn't dare dismiss them yet—not till he'd looked at their gloves. And gotten the results from those spots on Matthew's shirtfront and Devon's cuff.

He'd better interview them all again. But first he made a quick call to Windy Corner to make sure Emily was in. He'd go by there on the same trip. And maybe he'd be able to tell Emily he'd found something that would point away from Katie. Emily's anger at him sat like a ten-pound rock in his gut. He had to get things right with her, and stat, or he'd never be able to gather his wits enough to solve this case.

He put on his hat and coat and opened the front door, only to see Jamie MacDougal standing on the doorstep, knuckles raised as if to knock. Jamie started back and his face went white under his freckles. "Lieutenant! I wasn't sure you'd be in on a Sunday."

"No such thing as a day off when there's a murder to solve." Luke backed up to let Jamie in, not sorry to be delayed in his current errand. "What can I do you for?"

Jamie took off his sou'wester and turned the brim in his hands. "I—think I may be able to help you with that mur—with your investigation." His hands clenched, crumpling the hat. "You see—I did it." He looked Luke full in the face. "I killed Jake Newhouse."

sixteen

Not a human being that ever lived could wish to be loved better than I was loved; and him who thus loved me I absolutely worshipped.

—*Jane Eyre*

Jamie came to see me today while Mrs. C was out with Ms. Grenier. For no other reason than to see how I was doing in the aftermath of—what happened. How sweet can you get?

We sat in my living room and talked while Lizzie was asleep. He was a perfect gentleman. A gentleman caller, just like Lizzie Bennet might have had. I can't say Jamie much resembles Mr. Darcy, but still I think Miss Austen would approve.

He asked me how I was taking it, finding the body. He didn't know at all what Jake's death meant to me—just his being dead, gone, out of my life forever finally. Not his being murdered, not the horrible thought I might possibly have done it myself. I guess Jamie didn't know about that part—that Lieutenant Richards thinks I did it. He does think that, I know he does. And part of me thinks it, too.

I ended up telling Jamie everything. I never would have believed I could do that, tell my worst secrets to a man of all

people. But he was so gentle, so kind, so understanding. So out-
raged at Jake. If Jake hadn't already been dead, I think Jamie
would have gone after him himself.

And then he got this look like I've never seen on him before.
A look like he was about to do something terrible. Or maybe
something heroic. He said good-bye like he wasn't sure he'd ever
see me again. I didn't want him to think that, so I kissed him.
Just a little kiss, but he stood about a foot taller after that. He
marched out of here like he was going off to war.

I hope he doesn't do something stupid. Though I don't know
what that could be, since Jake is already dead and I didn't say
a word about Roman. I need Jamie to stick around.

Luke stared at Jamie's bloodless and quivering lips. It took every
drop of courage the boy could muster to come in here and confess to murder; that much was obvious. What was less obvious
was whether he really meant it.

The chill wind blew rain into the outer office. "Come on in
and sit down." Luke shut the door, hung up his own coat and
hat, took Jamie's coat and hung it up, but the boy wouldn't let
go of that hat.

In his own office, Luke sat behind the desk, waving Jamie
to the other chair. He switched on the digital recorder. "Now
suppose you tell me exactly how it happened."

Jamie's Adam's apple bobbed. He opened his mouth, but no
sound came out. He licked his lips and whispered, "Could I have
a glass of water?"

Luke poured him a paper cupful from the cooler in the corner. Jamie downed it in one gulp, then tried again. "I—I don't
know where to start."

"Let's start with dinner. Where were you sitting?"

"In the library. The table in the window bay."

Luke rifled through Heather's notes until he found Jamie's statement from the night before. So far, so good. "And when did you leave your seat?"

"Not till after that lady—the director, I guess she was—said everyone could go upstairs. I stayed behind. . . ." Jamie consulted his hat as if for guidance. "I was hoping to see Katie."

"And did you see her?"

He nodded. "After everyone—all the guests, I mean—had gone upstairs, she came in and started helping the caterers clean up."

"Did you speak to her?"

"No. I don't think she even noticed I was there." Jamie's freckles disappeared in a flush of red. That part sounded true, anyhow.

"Then what happened?"

"The wall opened. I mean the door to the secret staircase, only I didn't know about it then. The wall opened and Jake came out."

"He came out? Was he hurt?"

"No, he was fine at that point. He snuck up on Katie from behind and grabbed her."

Luke raised one eyebrow. That didn't match Katie's story, but then he already knew she hadn't told him the absolute truth. "And you just sat there and watched?"

"No! I went over and dragged him off her."

"Uh-huh." Jake had about six inches on Jamie and probably twenty or thirty pounds of solid muscle. "He just let you do that?"

Jamie bit his lip. "Well, he struggled, of course. But Katie was pushing him off, too. It was two against one."

"I see. Then what?"

"He shrugged me off and—pulled out a knife. I was afraid he was going to hurt Katie, so I got the knife away from him and—and in the struggle I accidentally stabbed him."

"You got the knife away from him." Yeah, Luke was really buying that.

Jamie flushed again. "I have a brown belt in karate."

Okay, maybe one good chop to the wrist would do it. "And then what?"

"I dragged him into the stairwell and dumped him there. Then I ran out and went up the back stairs and melted into the crowd."

Luke drummed his pen against the desk. "And Katie? Did she help you?"

"No! She must have gone into the stairwell after I was gone."

"So you're telling me you stabbed a man to death in the library and dragged him into the stairwell, all without anybody hearing or seeing anything, and without getting a drop of blood on the library carpet—or on yourself—nor any drag marks, either. Then you hightailed it out of there, leaving the woman you love alone and terrified, and she—of her own accord and for no reason whatsoever—went into the stairwell with the body, pulled the knife out of him, and started screaming her head off. And all this happened in less than a minute, 'cause that's all the time there was between Ms. Fitzgerald going upstairs and Katie's scream."

Jamie's eyes darted around the room, his hands clenching and unclenching on his hat brim. "She—she must have been trying to protect me. You know, draw suspicion away from me. And as for the blood—sometimes stab wounds don't bleed all that much. I read about it somewhere. It depends on exactly where the knife goes in."

Luke leaned forward, then caught Jamie's gaze and held it the way he'd stare down a wild animal. "You seem to know an awful lot about this crime. So much, I think you must've been talking to Katie about it. But there are a couple of things you don't know." He paused, and Jamie's Adam's apple bobbed again. "What you don't know is that Jake's head was bashed in. That may even be what killed him. And there were spots of blood all the way down those stairs."

Luke sat back, watching as all the stiffness went out of Jamie's spine. "Jake was stabbed at the top of the stairs and fell, or was pushed, to the bottom. And your so-called confession is a pack of lies."

Jamie wilted. He put his face in his hands and shook. "I just wanted to protect Katie." He rubbed his hands down his face and looked Luke in the eye. "She didn't do it, Lieutenant. She couldn't have. Not Katie. I know she doesn't remember, but it's just the shock of finding him like that. All she did was pick up the knife. You'll see."

"If you're so sure she's innocent, why come in here and confess? Why not just trust me to work it out?"

Jamie threw up one hand. "I don't know. I'm sure you know your job, but it looks so bad for her on the face of it. She isn't even sure herself she didn't do it. I wanted to spare her from living with that fear."

Luke stood. "Look, Jamie, I don't want to believe Katie's guilty any more than you do. It's just that I have to get more evidence against whoever did do it before I can technically rule her out."

Relief flooded Jamie's face. "Really? Oh, Lieutenant, you made my day." Jamie stood and put on his hat, then took it off again. "You're not going to—arrest me?"

"What for?"

"For—you know. Wasting police time, or whatever you call it. With my false confession."

Luke clapped Jamie on the shoulder. "As one man in love to another—I'll let it pass. If it was Emily who was under suspicion, I'd be in here confessing to myself."

Luke tracked down Matthew Sweet at Sweets by the Sea. The shop stayed open at least on weekends through the winter, although customers were as scarce as unbroken seashells at this time of year.

"Couple more questions for you, Matthew." Matthew looked startled but led the way into the back room.

Luke leaned against a counter. "First off, were you wearing gloves last night?"

"I had some on when I came in. Took them off to eat and never put them back on."

"Can I see them?"

"We had to turn all our costumes back in to Ms. Fitzgerald last night."

Luke groaned inwardly. Like as not, all the gloves would be thrown in a pile with no indication of who had worn which pair.

"All right, we'll leave that for now. When you first went upstairs—think carefully now—are you sure you didn't see anybody who didn't belong there except that one guy you told me about?"

Matthew nodded. "Just him. The guy in the poncho."

"Now I want you to cast your mind back. Picture him just exactly as you saw him." Matthew squeezed his eyes shut. "Picture that poncho. Was it clean? Any spots on it?"

Matthew was still a minute, then shook his head. "I can't be sure. I don't remember noticing anything, but that's the best I can say."

"All right. That's all, thanks."

Luke headed up the street toward Remembrance of Things Past, thinking about Roman's poncho. Blood spots on orange nylon would show, but maybe not be too obvious to someone just brushing past. Wait a minute. That poncho was designed to shed liquid, and it would've been even slicker since Roman had just been out in the rain. If blood had gotten on it, it could've dripped right off. It would've dripped all the way across Beatrice's rug.

He tried to picture that rug. Not a wall-to-wall carpet—some kind of Turkish thing, maybe. Some design where a spot or two of blood wouldn't stand out. It could've been missed when crime scene looked at that room—they were concentrating on the stairwell, wouldn't have paid as much attention to the bedroom.

And Emily was going to call the cleaners today. They might've already come and gone. He'd better hightail it over there right now.

Emily was roused from Jane Eyre's tear-jerking farewell to Helen Burns by a knock on the front door. Katie would be busy preparing dinner about now, so Emily went to the door herself. She opened it to Luke with mixed emotions.

"Oh. Hello. Marguerite said you came by earlier."

Luke stepped in and took off his dripping coat and hat. "Yeah, I wanted another look at the construction area upstairs. But I thought of something else, too. Did you have the Clean Scene people here already?"

"They left a couple hours ago. Why?"

"They do anything outside the stairwell itself?"

"No, I didn't think there was any need."

"Whew. You may be wrong about that, but I'm glad that's what you thought. I need to look at the rug in Beatrice's room."

"The rug? Why?"

"If the murderer left that way, he could've dripped blood on it. Mind if I take a look?"

"Help yourself." If Luke found blood on the upstairs rug, that would surely rule Katie out.

She followed him up and stood in the doorway. He took out a spray bottle and sprayed something on the carpet, working carefully over a three-foot-wide strip from the stairway opening to the hall door.

"What is that stuff?" she asked.

"Luminol. Reacts with blood and makes it fluoresce."

Levin and Kitty appeared in the doorway, her sentinels, making sure nothing untoward happened with a visitor in the house. Levin took one sniff of the luminol and sprang away from it. Kitty rubbed against Emily's legs until she picked her up and sat down with her in Beatrice's vanity chair. Kitty circled twice and settled down for a nap as Emily stroked her absently.

When he had covered the area thoroughly, Luke checked that the curtains were closed, shut the hall door, and turned off the light. Emily saw only darkness.

He flipped the light on again. "No blood."

"What makes you so sure it would have dripped?"

"Didn't say I was sure. Just a possibility. Roman was wearing a wet rain poncho, pretty slick. Blood would've likely slid off it."

Emily's spirits fell along with her favorite suspect's position in the lineup. "Maybe no blood was on it to begin with."

Luke made a clucking sound. "Possible. Hard to say till we know the autopsy results. But there was a fair bit of blood on the stairs. I'd expect some to be on the murderer, too."

Emily's mind filled with a picture of Katie's white apron, dotted with blood around its hem. Surely that was consistent with her bending over the body—not with her doing the deed. But she didn't dare ask.

"You wanted to look at the third floor. Does that mean you're suspecting me now?"

Luke gave her a pained look. "Emily, for pity's sake! Come to think of it, though, I never did get a statement from you. You were too busy taking care of Katie."

"Good point." The thought crossed her mind that this was her chance. All she had to do was say she'd seen Katie enter the stairwell the very moment before she screamed—leaving her no time to mount the stairs, confront and kill Jake, follow him down, and pull out the knife. Luke would trust her word, and Katie would be in the clear.

And that lie would stand between her and Luke for the rest of their lives.

Emily's hand froze on Kitty's back. In an instant that stretched into eternity, she weighed Katie's life and freedom in the balance against her own relationship with Luke—a love it had taken her a lifetime to rediscover. She'd known Katie only a few months—and since she was undoubtedly innocent, surely the truth would come out on its own?

But what if the truth was not Katie's innocence after all? Jake deserved to die—under the Mosaic law, at least, if not under modern American law. And if Katie had killed, it could only have been in self-defense.

She opened her mouth to tell the lie. But Kitty raised her head, glared at Emily, dug her claws in, and launched herself off her lap. Levin, sitting at Luke's feet, made a low growling sound. What was this, a feline Greek chorus?

It was enough to tip the balance. "I stayed in the parlor until I heard Katie scream. I couldn't see the stairwell door from there. And in fact I didn't see anything at all—I was resting my eyes."

She'd done it. She'd lost her opportunity to clear the girl she loved as a daughter. The cat chorus's rebuke had been backed up by her lifetime of training in searching for the truth in everything she read. In the back of her mind echoed Christ's words, *You shall know the truth, and the truth will set you free.* O God, let that be so for Katie now.

"Right. I figured if you'd seen anything important, you would've told me." Luke gestured toward the attic. "I just want to look at the front room where they're working. When I was up there last night, I had a feeling about it, but I was too exhausted to pin it down."

"You don't look any too chipper now." He had shadows under his eyes, and his cheeks looked drawn, as if he hadn't slept the night before. Served him right for not exonerating Katie on the spot.

"Maybe not, but I'd like to give it another shot. You coming?"

She followed him up the attic stairs and into the soon-to-be sitting room. "Just looks like a construction site to me. A rather messy one at that."

"I told Roman not to clean up last night. Wanted to see it the way it was left." Luke made a slow circuit of the room, pausing when he came to the rucked-up drop cloth in front of the paneled wall. He frowned at it, scratched his head, then passed a hand over his eyes. "I must've been dreaming. There's nothing here."

He gazed at her wistfully as she stood in the doorway, arms crossed. "I better go. Got to see a man about some gloves." He paused significantly. If he was angling for a dinner invitation, he'd have to fish in another pool. "Unless I could talk to Katie first. See if she remembers anything more."

"She doesn't. I've asked."

He blew out a long breath. "Look, Em, I'm doing all I can to clear her. You've got to believe that. But it sure would help if she could remember what happened."

"Doesn't the law say 'innocent until proven guilty'? You seem to have it backward."

"That's for the courts. If cops assumed everyone was innocent, we'd never make an arrest."

"I'm not asking you to assume *everyone* is innocent. Only Katie." She felt the tears coming and did nothing to stop them. Tears might constitute fighting dirty, but at this point she didn't care. "She's the closest thing we'll ever have to a daughter, Luke. I thought you loved her as much as I do."

His face spasmed in pain. "I do, Em. Or nearly. But that doesn't exempt me from having to do my job. Feelings are one thing. Facts are something else. I *have* to look at the facts. Otherwise I might as well turn in my badge right here and now."

She was about to spit out, "Why don't you, then?" until it occurred to her that if someone else took over the investigation—

someone who had no prejudice in Katie's favor at all—her chances would be far worse.

"Well, get on with it, then. I won't be able to sleep until you've crossed her off your list." She set off down the stairs before he could reply. But she was pretty sure he'd heard the implication: "And I won't let you rest secure in my love till then, either."

· seventeen ·

Mr. Rochester was not to me what he had been; for he was
not what I had thought him. I would not ascribe vice to him;
I would not say he had betrayed me: but the attribute of
stainless truth was gone from his idea.

—*Jane Eyre*

Luke's steps dragged as he left Windy Corner. Once again
he'd parted from Emily with hardly a friendly word, let alone
the hug and kiss he'd grown to depend on more than his daily
bread. If he couldn't clear Katie soon, he'd go out of his mind.

Once again he drove to Remembrance of Things Past, where
he knew Devon Penhallow was living over the shop. The shop
door was locked—naturally, since it was Sunday night—but a
piece of white printer paper was taped to the window. Big let-
ters scrawled with a red crayon read, SODOMITES GO HOME.

Good grief. Just what he needed, some knucklehead going
postal over a gay couple in the middle of a murder investigation. He pulled out his phone and took pictures of the paper
in place—one close up, one far back enough to get the shop's
sign in—then put on a latex glove and pulled it carefully off the
window. He wished he didn't have to show it to Devon, but
those were the rules—the target had to be informed.

He rang the bell at the side door that led upstairs to Devon and Hilary's apartment. Light feet pattered down the stairs, and Devon opened the door. His greeting stopped in his throat as Luke held up the sign. "Found this on your shop window."

Devon put a hand up to his eyes. "Oh, my sainted aunt. It begins again."

"Again? You've had incidents like this before?"

"Not here. Other places. Places we've left, always hoping to find a home where we might be accepted as simply people rather than 'those people.' I suppose a small town in Oregon wasn't the wisest choice." Devon stepped back from the door and waved Luke in.

"Portland'd be a better bet, I'd think." Luke followed Devon up the stairs.

"In that sense, yes. But we wanted a community we could become part of. Not a gay community, but an average one, with people of all ages and orientations—not just young, hip, liberal people. We wanted to fit in, live a normal life." He opened the apartment door. "Have a seat, Lieutenant. Can I get you anything? Tea? Coffee? Wine?"

"No, thanks." Luke scanned the room, furnished with pieces he'd expect to see behind a red velvet rope in a museum. He sat on the one chair that looked like it might hold his weight. "I didn't actually come here about this sign—just found it on my way in. You want me to investigate this?"

Devon perched on a sofa with enough carved curlicues to make Luke's head spin. "No. I'd rather let it pass. We've made too much of an investment in this place—I don't want to stir up any more trouble than we can help."

"Your call. I do have to ask you one thing, though. When was the last time you looked at your front window and didn't see the sign?"

"Last night when I came home from the party. I'm sure it wasn't there then. I haven't gone out all day—last night was rather exhausting."

"Couldn't have been Jake, then. Would've been pretty convenient if your little problem had died with him."

Devon raised an eyebrow. "A bit too convenient. Is that what you're implying? I take it I'm still a suspect?"

"No more than a few others. I'm in the process of eliminating people now. Were you wearing gloves last night?"

"I was when I arrived. I took them off to eat, of course. As I recall I never put them back on."

"Do you have them here?"

"Certainly." He went into another room and came back holding a pair of white gloves. Luke expected fabric, but when Devon put them into his hand, he realized they were made of the finest, softest kid leather he'd ever seen. Way too soft to have been washed since last night. He turned them over, looking closely at the seams. No sign of blood anywhere.

"These look all right, but I'll have to have them analyzed. If the gloves and your shirt both come back clean, I should be able to strike your name off the list."

"Really? Well, that's a relief, although I must say being a suspect did inject a wee bit of romance into my humdrum existence. Almost a compliment, you know, to be thought capable of murder. Hilary would have been impressed." He gave a wry smile.

Luke found himself liking this fellow more than he would have expected. He stood. "I'd like to tell you I'll keep a discreet eye out for your vandal. But frankly, in the middle of a murder investigation, that's gonna be tough."

"Understood." Devon stood and shook Luke's hand. "I appreciate the thought." He dropped his voice confidentially. "My money's on Cordelia Fitzgerald. Such a drama queen! You know she was seated next to me last night. If her gown hadn't been cut so low, I'd have sworn she was a bloke in drag."

"Cordelia? But her movements are accounted for. She didn't leave the table till it was time to send everybody upstairs."

Devon drew back. "Is that what she told you? I'm afraid she was fibbing, Lieutenant. Cordelia left the table just before I did. Immediately after Newhouse went out."

Luke's view of the case stood on its head. "Why the hell didn't you say so?"

"The classic answer: You didn't ask. You only asked me about my own movements, not those of the people around me."

Served him right for not being thorough. "But Heather asked the other people at your table—Veronica Lacey, for instance. She didn't mention Cordelia leaving."

"I expect she assumed—as I did—that Cordelia was going about her lawful errands as director of the play. I'm sure you've noticed, Lieutenant—people tend not to remark on things they expect to happen."

"True enough." Luke amended his mental to-do list for tomorrow to put Cordelia smack at the top.

"Good night, Lieutenant. And I do hope you'll solve your case quickly—for Emily's sake."

Luke's "Me, too" in response was more heartfelt than Devon could know.

Monday morning, Luke went over the statements from Devon's tablemates one more time. Nope, not a word about Cordelia leaving early. You'd think there'd been a conspiracy to back up her story. Or—just possibly—Devon was putting the finger on her to take Luke's eyes off himself. But Luke doubted it. Devon just didn't smell like a murderer.

He checked Cordelia's statement again. Huh—she hadn't actually said she hadn't left the table after Jake; she just implied it. Sly little—well, he'd see what she had to say for herself. And pick up those gloves in the process.

He tracked her down at the high school, sorting costumes in a back room behind the stage. "Lieutenant Richards! To what do I owe this pleasure?" She came toward him with hands outstretched, just as if she were in her drawing room and he a society caller.

He kept his hands on his notebook and pen, leaving her to drop her arms awkwardly. She covered her confusion by smoothing the folds of her gauzy multicolored skirt.

"I need the gloves Matthew Sweet was wearing the other night. For that matter, I could use all the gloves from all the cast members."

Cordelia swept her arm toward a box on a table piled with white. "All there, Lieutenant. But they're rented—I have to return them by tomorrow."

"Not gonna happen, I'm afraid. I'll give you a receipt for the rental company. Any record of who wore which pair?"

She gave a silvery laugh. "Hardly. I have a check-in sheet where I recorded who returned their things, but once the gloves came in, they went straight into that box."

Hell. He'd been afraid of that. "They haven't been washed, have they?"

"No. That was next on my list."

At least he could check visually for bloodstains. If he found any, the lab should be able to get DNA from the inside of the glove and determine who'd worn it.

He went to work on the pile. Lots of dirt, a few food stains, but nothing that looked like blood. Cordelia returned to her sorting. Halfway through his task, he said casually, "By the way, turns out you weren't quite straight with me last night. I have a witness says you left your table right after Jake went up."

He had her inconspicuously in his sights as he spoke. She froze and went as white as the fake ermine wrap she was folding. After a split second she let out that silvery laugh again. "Of course. I had to go up and make certain everything was in place. Didn't I say so?"

"No, ma'am. You said—or at least strongly implied—you stayed at the table till it was time to dismiss everybody upstairs."

She waved a beringed hand. "A simple oversight, Lieutenant. You must forgive me. I was distraught. We all were. Such a tragedy." For a second he thought she was going to bring her hand to her brow, but that would have been too stagy even for her. She smoothed her hair instead. "But after all, what difference does it make where I was? The poor boy simply fell down the stairs—didn't he?"

"I'm afraid there's a little more to it than that. We're assuming homicide."

Cordelia's eyes went wide. She clutched the wrap to her chest. "Homicide! You mean murder? Oh, that poor, poor boy! Oh, Lieutenant, whatever I can do to help—his murderer must be brought to justice." She gazed at him with soulful eyes.

He gritted his teeth to keep from biting her head off and took up his notebook and pen. "Just tell me anything you might have left out last night. What exactly did you do when you went upstairs the first time? Who did you see and where?"

She darted her tongue out over her lips. "Let me think. Oh, yes, I went up the back stairs—just to be inconspicuous to the guests, you know. I didn't see anyone on the stairs or in the hall. I went into the master bedroom and then into the stairwell to make sure Jake was in position." A pink flush came and went on her heavily made-up cheeks. "He was, all prepared, so I came back down—the back stairs again—and looked into the library to be sure all my cast members had left their table. Then I went to the different rooms and made my announcement."

"You didn't see anyone else? Besides Jake?"

"I heard some of the cast coming up as I left the bedroom, but I didn't turn to see who. And some of the waiters were busy in the kitchen, of course. But I saw no one else."

Luke flipped his notebook shut and slipped it into his back pocket. Her story was plausible on the face of it, but she wasn't a good enough actor to convince him she wasn't still hiding something. Not necessarily murder, but something. Maybe Emily could worm it out of her.

Jeremiah didn't show up Monday morning; nor did he call to explain. Roman appeared, along with another guy, so Emily sent them up to repair the roof, which Roman assured her he could handle without Jeremiah's supervision. A possible murderer on her roof made her less nervous than one inside her house.

Emily settled down to read *Jane Eyre* for a while. But as she read of Jane's restlessness toward the end of her time at Lowood, her own restlessness grew too strong to bear. If only she could help with the investigation. But she had no clue where to begin, and she didn't feel like asking Luke at this point.

She had to do something active or go mad. Maybe she could begin the redecorating process. She'd need Katie's help with that. Not finding her in the house, she slogged her way across the still-muddy lawn to Katie's apartment.

As she raised her hand to knock, she heard voices from inside. Katie's and another girl's—faint and weepy. One of her sisters? She paused with her fist poised, but couldn't make out any words.

Chiding herself for even attempting to eavesdrop, she knocked. Instead of calling her usual cheerful "Come in," Katie came to the door, opening it only the width of her own body. "What's up, Mrs. C?"

"I thought we might get started on the redecorating. If you're not too busy." Emily tried to be inconspicuous about peering over Katie's shoulder. Was that a blond head on the couch?

"Oh—oh, sure. Abby and I were just talking. Give me a minute and I'll be over?"

"Abby could come, too. I'd be happy to pay her for the day—there's plenty to do." Luke had mentioned Abby had been less than forthcoming when he questioned her. In the course of a day working together, perhaps Emily could get her to be more frank.

"Um—I don't—"

Abby's voice cut her off. "It's okay, Katie. I'd like to help."

"Well—all right. Lizzie's napping, so I'll have to take the baby monitor."

Back at the house, the three of them wiped their feet on the kitchen mat. "Where do you want to start?" Katie asked.

"Let's start with the Dickens room. No furniture to move

out." That room's serviceable but rather generic bedroom suite had already been moved into Katie's apartment.

"What do we need to do in here?" Abby's mouselike voice piped up.

"We'll start by taking down the drapes and stripping the wallpaper. That'll probably be enough for today. Then we'll need to hang new paper and wax the floor. The furniture will come down from the Montgomery room when it's all ready."

Katie brought in a stepladder and began taking the heavy brown canvas drapes off their hooks. Emily and Abby set to work on the wallpaper, a prim brown-and-beige stripe, undoubtedly chosen by no-nonsense Agnes Beech. Emily, who did not do ladders, peeled back a lower corner, expecting to see bare wall underneath. Instead, she found another layer of paper—this one a faded daisy pattern that had once, no doubt, been bright and gay.

Her heart misgiving her, she peeled the corner of the daisy paper as well. Under that was a tone-on-tone blue, and under that again, a subdued floral stripe. Under the stripe, she at last found bare plaster.

"Oh, dear. I wasn't expecting this," Emily said as the reality hit her. "I thought it would just be the one layer." She turned to Katie. "I suppose we could just paper over it again."

Katie picked at the strip next to the window. The top layer came away easily, crumbling in her hand. "It's too fragile. This top layer must have been here for years. If we paper over it, it won't stick worth beans."

Emily sighed, feeling her earlier restless energy drain out of her fingertips into the layers of wallpaper. "All right. Here we go."

They pulled and scraped for an hour without finishing the first wall. Emily forced herself to make small talk, trying to draw Abby out, but received mostly monosyllabic replies. Then a cry sounded from the baby monitor. "There's Lizzie," Katie said, putting down her putty knife and dusting off her hands. "I'll get her, and then I think it's about time for lunch, don't you?"

Emily gratefully agreed. She and Abby bent close over one particularly stubborn section of wall where the layers of paper had glued themselves together into a pulpy mass.

"I'm a little worried about Katie," Emily said as soon as she heard the back door close. "Don't you think she seems, well, tense?"

Abby glanced up at her, then down again. "Wouldn't you be if you were suspected of murder?" She added almost inaudibly, "And couldn't even remember whether you'd done it?"

"Surely you don't think Katie could be guilty? I can't imagine her killing anyone, can you?"

Abby's knuckles whitened on her putty knife. "Not normally. Of course not. But—" She bit her lip and tears came to her eyes.

"But what?"

"She's—always protected—" Abby clamped her mouth shut and shook her head so violently, her whole body followed suit. "No. I can't talk about it."

Emily put a motherly arm around the girl's thin shoulders. "Abby, you know I love Katie, don't you? Like my own daughter. I won't let anything bad happen to her, no matter what. But hiding the truth won't help her. Or you. If you know something about the murder, please, I beg you, tell me what it is."

Abby dropped her knife, covered her eyes, and leaned into Emily's embrace. Her frail body heaved in Emily's arms. Emily eased them both down to sit on the floor and held Abby until she calmed. She dug a clean tissue from her pocket and gave it to the girl. "What happened that night, Abby? What did you see?"

Abby blew her nose and took a deep breath. "Jake had been—after me. Just trying to get me to go out with him, you know? And I liked him. I didn't know about—Katie never told anybody about that till after. I never knew who Lizzie's father was."

She shuddered. "To think I might have—well, anyway. He asked me to meet him in the stairwell that night. I watched until he went up and then I slipped out, up the back stairs. I went into the bedroom and the stairwell door was open. I went up to the door and I saw—" She took a gasping breath and her tears began again.

Emily made her voice as gentle as if she were talking to baby Lizzie. "What did you see?"

"I saw—*her*. That drama woman. That old, fat, ugly—" Abby darted a sidelong glance at Emily, who was quite aware of having at least a decade and more than a few pounds on Cordelia Fitzgerald. "Sorry, it's just—she was way too old for Jake. And she had her arms around him."

Emily absorbed this information. It didn't greatly surprise her, but it certainly threw a new light on the situation. "Did you hear them say anything?"

"I didn't stick around to hear. I felt sick. I ran out of there and down the stairs as fast as I could go. Katie was in the kitchen. I ran straight into her arms and blabbed out the whole story."

What would Katie have felt at that moment, learning for the first time that her rapist had been pursuing her own beloved sister—a sister even more fragile and innocent than she herself had been?

Emily knew how she would have felt in Katie's place. Murderous.

· eighteen ·

"I wrote to him; I said I was sorry for his disappointment, but Jane Eyre was dead: she had died of typhus fever at Lowood. Now act as you please: write and contradict my assertion—expose my falsehood as soon as you like."

—Mrs. Reed to Jane, *Jane Eyre*

Luke took the box of gloves and drove to Tillamook. After a stop at Gifts from the Sea to collect the caterers' gloves—only to learn they'd already been sent to the laundry—he went by headquarters to drop off the ones he had for analysis. No results on any of the other clothes yet—analysts didn't have to work weekends like investigators did.

He was on his way out when Sheriff Tucker called him into his office. "Have a seat, Luke." Tucker eased his bulk into his leather desk chair and linked his hands over his ample stomach.

"What's up, boss?" Tucker could take his time coming to the point, and Luke wanted to get moving.

"Carter Newhouse came around to my house last night. Wanted to know what progress we're making on his boy's murder."

"Good grief, it's only thirty-six hours since it happened. I won't have labs back for days yet."

"I know it. But he's a grieving father and he's used to getting results. He asked—no, demanded—I put more men on it. My best men, he said. Or he was going to call in the state police."

"He doesn't have the authority to do that, does he? He's just a lawyer in private practice."

"That he is, but he has friends in high places. The commissioner's his cousin or some such."

Luke groaned. "Look, sir, I can handle this, I know I can. I just need a little time."

Sheriff Tucker leaned forward and put his elbows on the desk. "I have every confidence in you, Luke. In fact, I told Newhouse I already had my best man on the case—you." Luke breathed again, but the sheriff continued, "But I had to promise him, if we haven't made an arrest by Friday, we'll call in the state police."

Friday. He'd be lucky to get anything back from the lab by then. He'd have to rely on his wits—and Emily's intuition. Nothing like a nice little ticking clock to make life exciting.

He drove back to his office, where he went through the pile of statements again and plotted out the exact times and positions of everyone involved, hoping to find someone else with means and opportunity. If he found those, he could pretty much take motive for granted with this victim. He was left back where he started: The only people who could have been in the stairwell during the crucial few minutes were Matthew, Roman, Cordelia, Abby, Devon, and Katie. Everybody else was vouched for as being elsewhere—unless somebody else was lying.

He would've so loved to eliminate Matthew, Abby, Devon, and of course Katie on character alone. But if he was going to do that, he might as well pick up the phone right now and call in the state police himself. And turn in his badge to boot. He'd just have to pray the lab came through with negatives on all of them before Friday.

At the bottom of the statement file he found the photos of fingerprints taken from the walls and rail of the stairwell, the bedroom, and the upstairs bathroom. How had he missed these yesterday? Distracted by the gloves issue and then Jamie's fake confession, he guessed. He went through them now, painstakingly matching them all up to the prints taken from the people present Saturday night. That fingerprint training course he'd taken last year was sure paying off—if he couldn't do this himself, he'd have had to wait days or weeks for a forensics report.

The bathroom yielded prints from Devon, backing up his story, but none from Abby. No surprise there—they couldn't have both been using it at the same time, and he'd known Abby was lying, anyway. The bedroom was a mass of smudged and overlaid prints from all the guests who had crowded in there after Katie screamed and before he himself could secure the scene.

The stairwell was a little cleaner. His own prints came up at the bottom of the stairs, some from his investigation—he hadn't had any gloves on him at the time—and some probably dating back to when Emily had first shown him the secret passage. He smiled at that memory, but it had a kick to it—Emily hadn't kissed him that way in a while.

On the paneling at the top of the stairs was a good clean set of Matthew's prints, where he'd huddled against the wall while Luke was examining the body. More Matthew on the top railing; not much in that. Jake's on the railing, too, overlaid by Matthew's. Luke stopped and thought that out. Suppose they'd struggled and Jake leaned on the banister for support. Matthew stabbed him and pushed him down the stairs, then leaned on the banister to watch him fall. But if it'd played out that way, Jake would have had his hands behind him. Luke stood up and experimented on the edge of his desk. The way the prints were arranged meant Matthew and Jake both must have been leaning forward. That didn't fit with any scenario he could think of for Jake being stabbed in the chest. So he had nothing more on Matthew than he'd had before. Which was actually a relief.

He turned back to the pile. Cordelia Fitzgerald's prints here and there, but she would've been in there legitimately, planning out the play. Devon Penhallow's on the library entrance. Luke perked up at that until he saw Veronica Lacey's right next to them. Devon had told him Emily showed the two of them over the whole house—apparently that included the secret passage. The library entrance made no sense for Devon as the murderer, anyway; if he'd gone in, it would've been from above.

Then he found it: a clear set of Roman on the wall of the upstairs landing. Left hand only. Say he steadied himself on the wall with his left hand before stabbing Jake with his right. Luke checked the photographs for blood on the floor near that spot. No, the bloodstains began right at the top of the stairs, a couple feet away. So the prints were only suggestive, not conclusive. Dang. Could Roman have been there at some other time, for some other reason? Or did he go in and see Jake, either alive or dead, but not kill him? Or did he lean on the wall while talking to Jake, then stab him at the top of the stairs? Absolutely no way to know, short of Roman suddenly getting talky.

Another set of prints mingled with Roman's. Both hands this time, in several different spots on that section of wall. They didn't match any in Luke's pile. He stared at them, went back through the stack and compared them again. No joy. Agnes or

Beatrice? But Katie had cleaned the place pretty thoroughly since their time. He'd have to ask Emily if any of the workers had been there on some lawful errand. Or if she'd had some visitor in there other than the people at the party. The prints were big, spread like a big hand, now that he thought about it—almost certainly male. He gritted his teeth at the thought of Emily being in the secret passage with some other man. But he shook off that thought. No matter how mad at him she was, she wouldn't go behind his back with somebody else. And anyhow, she hadn't been mad at him before Saturday night.

He was still puzzling over the prints when the phone rang. "Luke? It's me. You'd better come over here. I persuaded Abby to talk."

Abby had left for her shift at Gifts from the Sea by the time Luke arrived, and Katie was busy about her regular duties. Emily'd had quite enough wallpaper stripping for one day; she'd changed into decent clothes and was relaxing in the library with *Jane Eyre*. Levin snoozed on her lap while Kitty and Bustopher curled on the hearth.

She nodded Luke to the opposite chair. "Abby had to go to work. She asked me to tell you what she told me." That wasn't strictly true. In fact, Abby had agreed under pressure to allow Emily to pass on a carefully edited version that would implicate neither Abby nor Katie.

Luke took out his notebook. "Won't be admissible evidence, y'know. Gotta hear it straight from the witness's mouth to use it in court."

"If it turns out to be important, you can always talk to her directly." She crossed her fingers under her skirt, praying it wouldn't be important—at least not for the Parker sisters. If it implicated Cordelia Fitzgerald, Emily's compunction would fit easily within the tightly laced bodice Cordelia had worn for the party.

"So. Why'd she really go upstairs?"

Emily had worked this all out as she waited for Luke. "Oh, she did go up to use the restroom. But then she heard a noise from the bedroom and went to investigate." Levin lifted his head and blinked at her. She hadn't thought cats could frown, but he seemed to be frowning.

"Why'd she do that? Didn't she know there were supposed to be people up there at that point?"

"She said it sounded suspicious for some reason."

Luke cocked one skeptical eyebrow. Levin's expression echoed his uncannily. "Then what?"

"She saw the door to the stairwell was open, so she peeked inside. And she saw Cordelia Fitzgerald with Jake."

"Cordelia told me this morning she'd been in to check Jake was in position."

"Well, according to Abby, it was a bit more than that. Apparently they were embracing."

He whistled. "No wonder she didn't want to admit where she'd been at first. Doesn't sound like a motive for murder, though. Doggone it."

"But we don't know the whole story. Abby said Cordelia had her arms around Jake, not the other way 'round, and she only saw them for an instant. Maybe he rejected her advances and then she stabbed him."

"Could be. That all Abby had to say?"

"That's the gist of it. She saw them and ran downstairs."

"What was she crying about in the kitchen, then?"

Emily had hoped Luke wouldn't ask that. "The episode just shocked her. Their age difference and all." That didn't sound very convincing even to Emily. She improvised. "Abby had admired Cordelia, and it was devastating to see her with one of her former students."

At this Levin jumped off her lap and marched to the hearth to join the other two. All three cats now glared at her as if she were no longer worthy to be called their mistress. Great. Her own conscience was sore enough without this feline Greek chorus to chastise her for covering up the truth. She ignored them and turned to Luke. "Abby's a very sensitive girl."

"I'll say." He flipped his notebook shut, put it in his pocket, and stood. "Guess I better go talk to Cordelia. Again. That woman gives me a pain in the you-know-where."

Flush with her success in getting the truth from Abby, Emily said, "Would you like me to talk to her? She might be more open woman-to-woman."

"Would you?" Relief flooded Luke's face. "That'd be fantastic. I'll have to talk to her myself eventually, but if you could soften her up, that'd help a lot."

He shot her a glance as if sizing up her attitude, and she realized her offer might have sounded as if she were relenting toward him. She steeled her expression against any such presumption and watched his face fall. Her rebel heart threatened to melt at that, but she willed it frozen again. Not until Katie was well and truly crossed off his suspect list would she let Luke back into her good graces.

He headed toward the door, then turned back. "Say, I almost forgot. I found some prints of Roman in the stairwell. On the wall of the top landing."

Emily leapt to her feet. "Do they prove he did it?"

"No such luck. Don't prove a dang thing except he was there at some point. He ever go in there before Saturday that you know of?"

She frowned, remembering. "I did take him and Jeremiah in there a while back. I had some idea of maybe replacing the stairs with an elevator all the way to the third floor."

"That could solve another mystery—bunch of prints I couldn't identify. Could be Jeremiah's. One set was pretty high up, like a tall man made it."

"Yeah, he's too tall for his own good. Come to think of it, he banged his head on a doorframe on Saturday and refused to let me call a doctor—maybe that's why he didn't come in today."

"Could be why he disappeared Saturday night, too. I better go check on him, get his prints while I'm at it so we can rule that set out."

She followed him to the door but kept her distance as he put on his coat. "Call me after you talk to Cordelia?" he said.

"Of course." She almost invited him to come to tea and re-connoiter in person but stopped herself just in time. She couldn't allow him to enjoy Katie's cooking until her name was cleared.

After closing the door behind Luke, Emily went in search of Katie and found her cleaning the upstairs bathroom. "Katie, I need an excuse to talk to Cordelia Fitzgerald. Did she leave anything behind that I could return to her? Or mess up anything I could complain about?"

"Actually, yeah. I found one of the feathers from her head-dress in the hall. I left it on the hall table."

"Perfect." Emily phoned Cordelia at the high school and asked her to come by after work. Emily would need the slight advantage she might get from being on her own turf—and the site of the murder.

As she waited, Emily attempted to conjure an appropriately disarming sleuthlike façade. Kindly, gossipy old lady like Miss Marple or Miss Silver? Dithering upper-class twit like Lord Peter Wimsey or Albert Campion? Absentminded, clueless detective like Columbo? Unfortunately, Cordelia had already met her being simply herself, and Emily knew from long experience that people rarely mistook her for being less intelligent than she actually was. Must be something about the eyes, or perhaps her habitual reticence was presumed to conceal wisdom. She'd have to try for sympathetic fellow middle-aged woman and see how far that took her.

Cordelia arrived at four o'clock. Perfect. Emily handed her the feather and said, "Won't you stay for tea? Katie's teas are to die for, and you look like you could use a break." Cordelia did look rather haggard—dark shadows showed through the careful makeup under her eyes, and her whole face sagged as if it had just taken off its corset.

She hesitated, then said, "That sounds heavenly, thank you. I've been on my feet all day, getting all those costumes sorted and cleaned and ready to return. And all the while, knowing poor Jake is lying cold on a slab in the county morgue, his murder unavenged. It wrings my heart." She clasped her hands over her bosom, but the black ostrich plume waving over her shoulder rather spoiled the effect.

Emily led the way into the library, where the tea was already laid out. She'd asked Katie to keep a low profile this afternoon. "I imagine you must get quite attached to some of your students. I know I did when I was teaching."

"Oh, indeed I do. They're all wonderful young people, of course, but once in a while one comes along who has that extra special something, you know? Good looks, charm, talent—real star potential."

Emily tried to look worldly wise as she poured the tea and handed her guest a cup. "I had a student like that a couple of years ago." True—she'd had one young man who reminded her of Luke, except that he was headed for a brilliant career as a writer. She'd had a bit of a struggle to keep her feelings strictly professional in his case. "They can make you feel like a teenager yourself again, can't they?"

Cordelia drew herself up. "My art keeps me ever young. To act, one must always keep one's passion near the surface and draw on it freely."

"And sometimes, no doubt, life imitates art? Passion over-flows into real relationships. Even if the man is younger in actual years."

Cordelia flushed but kept her eyes full on Emily's. "When hearts are aflame, age is irrelevant. Soul calls to soul across any merely conventional gap."

What a nice fantasy. Emily wondered if Cordelia could ac-tually believe it. "That's true of us *femmes d'un certain age,* as the French say. But young men don't always hear that call of the soul so clearly. The call of a firm young body can sometimes shout it down."

Suddenly, shockingly, Cordelia's carefully constructed face seemed to crack apart, and a raucous sob burst from the ruins. Her cup rattled in its saucer so violently that Emily took it from her hand before it could break. She handed Cordelia a handker-chief and patted her back, waiting as she cried herself out.

"He said he loved me," Cordelia managed between sobs. "He said he adored older women, we were so experienced and mysterious, so much more interesting than young girls. He asked for that role, you know—I was going to use only my current students, but he wheedled and cajoled until I gave it to him. And then Saturday night—" She stopped to blow her nose and seemed unable to go on.

"You went to meet him in the secret stairwell, didn't you?"

"We hadn't had a minute alone all evening. It seemed like the perfect opportunity. I'm ashamed to say I practically threw myself into his arms. But he—oh, I can't talk about it, I can't!" She wrung the handkerchief in her hands, her head tossing against the high back of the wing chair. Even in the midst of her obviously genuine distress, Emily wondered if she was capable of any gesture that wasn't pulled from melodrama.

"He rejected you?" she said as gently as she could.

Cordelia sat forward, eyes suddenly flaming. "He *spurned* me! He called me—" Her voice lowered to a whisper as her eyes dropped. "An old hag. He admitted flat out he'd only been using me to get the part."

Why would Jake have wanted that role so badly? Certainly not in service of any inflated dreams of a theatrical career. More likely as an excuse to get back into Windy Corner—and back to Katie. A confrontation—a live one—between those two during the party was looking more and more likely.

"You must have been terribly angry."

"Not then. Anger came later. At that moment I was simply devastated. I had to summon every ounce of my training to appear normal so I could go back downstairs and dismiss the guests."

Emily chose her words carefully. "You didn't—hurt him? You must have wanted to."

Cordelia blew her nose again. "Oh, I was tempted. He had

a knife, you know—he was playing with it when I went in. At first I thought it was the stage knife, but Matthew had that. Jake's knife was real." She sat back in the chair and closed her eyes. "For one moment I considered trying to get the knife away from him, but I knew I'd never have the strength. I'd been humiliated enough already, I didn't need more. He was quite well when I left him, I assure you. Well—and *whistling*."

With a sinking heart Emily accepted her story. Drama queen though she was, Cordelia had dropped her guard to reveal what was possibly the most painful humiliation of her life. Emily didn't think at this moment she was capable of a lie.

Which meant Katie was deeper in the soup than ever. If Emily didn't find a lifeline soon, Katie would be sunk.

nineteen

"I am glad you are no relation of mine . . . if any one asks me how I liked you, and how you treated me, I will say the very thought of you makes me sick, and that you treated me with miserable cruelty."

—Jane to Mrs. Reed, *Jane Eyre*

From Windy Corner Luke drove to the south side of town to check on Jeremiah Edwards. His small one-story house stood out from its neighbors with its immaculate paint, tidy lawn, and porch bare of all clutter. When Edwards answered the door after Luke's third knock—looking like the villain of a zombie movie with his pasty skin, deeply shadowed eyes, and crumpled overalls—the contrast between the house and its owner set Luke back a pace.

Edwards stooped in the doorway, open only far enough to admit his skinny frame. "Sheriff. Is there a problem?"

"Emily was worried when you didn't show up for work today. 'Fraid that knock on the head you got Saturday night might've laid you up. I knew you didn't have anybody here to take care of you, so I thought I better come by and make sure you're okay."

"Fine. I'm fine. Worked Saturday, took today off. Thought

she knew." He spoke as if each word had to be pushed out of him with all the force his lungs could muster.

"You don't look fine. You look like hell. I'd go see a doctor if I were you."

"No doctor. I look to the Lord for healing."

"Better pray harder, then. And get some sleep." Edwards started to close the door, but Luke put his palm against it. "While I'm here, I would like to ask you a couple questions about Saturday night."

Edwards didn't budge, only stared at him as if he didn't comprehend the words. "Saturday night . . ."

"Maybe you didn't hear what happened. What time did you leave?"

"Nine thirty, ten. Don't remember."

"Did you realize Jake Newhouse had been killed?"

Edwards passed a hand over his face. "Mrs. Cavanaugh told me."

"Did you go downstairs at all during the evening?"

He shook his head slowly, as if it cost him all his strength.

That squared, as no one had reported seeing him anywhere other than the third floor. Luke took out his notebook to check the details of Roman's story. "Did you see Roman when he came back up, somewhere around eight thirty?"

"No. Front room whole time. May have dozed off. Not working at that point, just there to keep an eye."

Luke tapped his pencil on the cover of the notebook. "Sounds like you weren't actually keeping an eye. Not an open one, at any rate."

Edwards raised a hand as far as his waist and let it drop. "Long day. Tired. Good worker, Roman. Trust him."

"Even though Emily doesn't?"

"Trust him for work. Not women."

"I see. So there's nothing you can tell me that might help this investigation?"

Again the labored head movement, a few degrees to the left and back to center.

"All right. You get some sleep now, and be sure to call me if you need help, hear?"

"The Lord helps those that help themselves."

Luke headed back to his office. As he rounded the corner onto Third, he saw a black BMW parked square in his own spot in the office driveway. What the heck?

He parked the SUV on the street and strode into the outer office. Heather, sitting at the front desk, mouthed at him, "Trouble," with a tilt of her head toward his office door. "Mr. Newhouse."

Oh, hell. Just what he needed to round off a frustrating day.

He squared his shoulders and strode into his office. Carter Newhouse stood by the window in a tailored gray suit and camel's-hair overcoat, drumming his manicured fingers on the sill.

He faced Luke square on with fists at his side. "What are you doing to find my son's killer?"

"Good afternoon, Mr. Newhouse. Won't you have a seat?" Luke swung an arm toward the guest chair as he rounded the desk to sit in his own. He wasn't about to be intimidated by a bully like Carter Newhouse, no matter how much money and influence he flashed around.

Newhouse strode to the chair but stood behind it, gripping

the back. "Don't toy with me, Richards. I want to know what's going on."

"If you'll sit down, I'll be happy to fill you in. I've had a long day and I don't like craning my neck to talk to people." He kept his voice calm, friendly. Newhouse hesitated, then yanked the chair out and perched on the edge of it, palms flat on the desk.

"We have about half-a-dozen possibles—people who were seen at or near the scene of the crime during the time window for the murder. I'm working at eliminating them. When I've finished eliminating all those who are innocent, we'll be left with the guilty party. Simple as that. I've spent the last two days going over evidence and interviewing suspects. I have an idea of who's likely and who's not."

Newhouse slapped a palm on the desk. "I don't want your harebrained ideas. I want an arrest!"

Luke swallowed his anger and pride. "I understand your frustration, Mr. Newhouse. But there's no point in arresting anybody if we can't prove him guilty. Since we don't have any eyewitnesses, the final elimination—the actual proof of guilt or innocence—can only come from the lab's analysis of bloodstains and DNA."

Newhouse opened his mouth, but Luke held up a silencing palm. "Sheriff Tucker has already asked the lab to make this case their top priority. That's all anybody can do to make them work faster. So I suggest you go home and let us do our jobs. I give you my word we will catch whoever killed your son, and he will pay for his crime." He added reluctantly, "Or she."

Newhouse might be caught up in the angry stage of grief, but he was also a lawyer. He must know firsthand how a case could fall apart in court if the evidence wasn't strong enough.

Luke watched his need to blame someone, to force action, wrestle against his common sense.

Newhouse buried his head in his hands, clutching his fingers in his perfectly groomed hair. Then he let go, smoothed his hair back, and stood. "You have until Friday." He strode out of the office without a backward glance.

Infected with Newhouse's impatience, Luke reached for the phone to call the ME about autopsy results. But it rang before he picked it up.

"Luke? I've had an interesting conversation with Cordelia." Emily told him what the drama teacher had said.

"Think she's telling the truth?"

"On the whole, yes. She dropped her guard completely. I don't think she's a good enough actress to pull that off unless it was genuine."

Luke rubbed his neck. He'd told Newhouse he just needed to eliminate people. So why did he get this sinking feeling in his gut as suspects dropped away? Of course, none of those who looked innocent could be completely cleared until the lab results came in. He cheered up a tiny bit at that thought.

"Listen, Em, I really appreciate all you've done. Could you do one more thing for me?"

"What is it?"

He didn't like the cautious note in her voice. "Could you go see Jake's mom? She's a mouse of a thing and I'm afraid I'd intimidate her. She might speak more freely to you."

"What do you want me to ask her?"

"Just try to find out anything you can about Jake that might shed some light. We've got half-a-dozen people with some kind of motive, but there might be something else we don't know about."

"Should I go see her tonight?"

"Nah, better wait till tomorrow when Newhouse isn't home. She'll never peep when he's around."

"All right, tomorrow morning it is." He gave her the address, and she said a curt good-bye.

At least she was still willing to help him. She couldn't be too mad at him.

Or could she? She wasn't helping him solve the case regardless of outcome; she was only trying to clear Katie. If she ran across anything that threatened to implicate Katie, would she pass it on?

Luke couldn't answer that question to his own satisfaction. And it raised another one: Could he continue to love a woman who would not only lie to him personally, but deliberately pervert the course of justice?

Tuesday morning Jeremiah showed up as usual, looking far worse than he had on Saturday, but apparently ready to work. He mumbled some excuse about the day before, which Emily decided not to question. She wasn't his mother, after all.

After breakfast she drove to the Newhouse home. The building was clearly intended to have the status of a mansion, but she couldn't accord that title to such a modern monstrosity. It was a successful man's monument to his own success—certainly not a home.

The impression was only strengthened when the maid ushered her into the reception room, in which the unfriendly black leather club chairs were the warmest element. All else was metal and glass, creating an effect so coldly masculine it froze Emily's blood in spite of the quite adequate radiant heating. She couldn't believe a woman had been permitted to have any influence on the design or decoration of this place.

When Mrs. Newhouse entered, her shuffling steps noiseless on the white carpet, Emily's impression was confirmed. Beneath the immaculately groomed façade, her shrinking form and ruined face told a story not only of fresh grief but of a lifetime of being beaten—perhaps literally—into submission. She doubted Mrs. Newhouse had any say even in her choice of clothing.

Emily had planned her strategy, but now she said her opening speech with more sincerity than she'd intended. "Mrs. Newhouse? I'm Emily Cavanaugh. It was my house where—the party took place. I just wanted to tell you how terribly sorry I am and ask if there's anything I can do to help."

Mrs. Newhouse touched Emily's fingers in greeting, then subsided into a chair. She clutched a lace-trimmed handkerchief, but her reddened eyes were dry. Emily suspected she'd cried herself out over the last two days. She waved Emily to the opposite chair.

"Thank you, you're very kind." She spoke barely above a whisper, putting one word after another as a weary wanderer still miles from shelter drags his unwilling feet. "But I really don't see what anyone can do. Jake is gone. Nothing can bring him back."

"Is he—was he your only child?"

"I have an older son, Robert. He lives in Portland. A lawyer, like his father." She stared out the massive window. "So much like his father."

A volume of history seeped through the cracks of those few words. "You were closer to Jake, then?"

Mrs. Newhouse heaved a sigh that seemed to come from her toes. "For a while. When he was little. But then I lost him, too."

She turned to face Emily. "Truthfully, Jake has been gone from me for a very long time. All that's changed now is I've lost any hope of ever winning him back."

Emily felt some guilt at exploiting the woman's unearned confidence. She must never have the opportunity to speak to a sympathetic human being, or she wouldn't open up like this with a stranger. But Emily reminded herself she meant to use any revelations to help catch Jake's killer, not to exploit them to his mother's harm. She forged ahead.

"What drew him away from you?"

"What draws any boy away from his mother? He was desperate to please his father. And being close to me would never accomplish that."

Emily's shock must have showed on her face. She'd known going in this wasn't a happy marriage, but she was nevertheless appalled by the depth of dysfunction that statement implied.

Her hostess shot her a sidelong glance. "My husband despises me, Mrs. Cavanaugh. There's no secret about that. And because I've never been able to stand up to his bullying, Jake grew to despise me as well."

Without thinking, Emily said, "I got the impression he despised women in general. Except as sex objects, of course."

Mrs. Newhouse winced, and Emily immediately regretted her lapse into bald honesty. "I'm so sorry—I didn't mean—"

She waved a hand weighted with a diamond bracelet that might as well have been a handcuff. "Don't apologize. What you say is no news to me. I know Jake—behaved badly with girls. I've heard the gossip, and I always dreaded the day would come—" She sat straight and peered into Emily's eyes. "Tell me truly—may I call you Emily?"

"Of course."

"And I'm Mildred. Tell me—was Jake killed by a girl he'd wronged? Or a jealous husband or boyfriend?"

Emily hated to answer that, but Mildred had asked her for the truth. "We—Lieutenant Richards isn't sure yet who killed him, and until we know who, we can't know exactly why. But it does seem fairly likely to have been one or the other of those."

Mildred collapsed back into her chair. "I knew it. I knew he would bring down judgment upon his head. My poor, poor, foolish boy."

She lay there for a minute, then with an energy Emily would not have thought she possessed, she sprang from her chair and faced her guest with blazing eyes. "It's all his father's fault. Jake wanted to make him proud, wanted to be the golden boy like his brother. He didn't have the brains for law school or even college, but he had the looks." She shuddered as if remembering how his father's version of those looks had ensnared her in her youth. "He had the looks, and he knew how to use them. Just like his father did."

She seemed to re-collect herself and walked to the window, where she pounded her fists against the glass of her prison. "And it worked. His father was proud of him for being such a 'ladies' man.'" She turned back to Emily. "What an ironic phrase that is. A man who cares nothing for women except to use them for his own pleasure and ego is called a ladies' man. Ladies' bane would be more like it."

Emily stood to face her. Clearly this woman had some backbone if she could make a speech like that. Hesitantly she asked, "Why have you put up with it all these years?"

Mildred's eyes were as bleak as the gray, tempestuous sea that made her backdrop. "I kept hoping Jake would come back to me. I knew if I left his father, I'd never see him again." Then realization visibly dawned. "But there's no point in staying now."

She looked around as if seeing the room in its true character for the first time. "I could leave. I could leave all of it. I have my own money, you know. Not a lot, but enough to live on. I could walk out of here right now and never look back."

She lifted her hand and stared at the diamond cuff. Then with a savage movement she tore it off her wrist and dashed it against the window. The diamonds screeched their way down, marring the smooth surface of the glass. "You thought you could tie me with trinkets and threats, Carter Newhouse? You never tied me at all. Only my own doting foolishness did that. Well, now the worm has turned." She strode to the door, then turned back as if remembering Emily's existence. "If you'll excuse me, Emily, I have some packing to do. The clothes on my back and a few things I brought with me into this travesty of a marriage. I won't take anything that came from *him*."

Emily was flabbergasted. While she applauded Mildred's decision, she felt it would be irresponsible to leave her in this fevered state. "Do you have anywhere to go? You'd be welcome at Windy Corner until you decide exactly what you want to do." Then she mentally kicked herself. Of course the woman wouldn't want to stay in the house where her son was killed.

"Thank you, but no. I'm going as far away as I can get, and the sooner the better. He won't let me go easily, you know. So it's better if no one knows where I am."

"Won't you even stay for the funeral?"

A spasm of pain crossed the pale face, where two bright spots of color now burned. "No. If I stay even an hour, I might lose my nerve. But if I might—call you and find out where and when it will be held—?"

"Of course." Emily scribbled her number on a sheet of the small notebook she carried in her purse and handed it to Mildred. She'd even be willing to force herself to attend as Mildred's proxy. What a terrible life this woman must have led, to be willing to sacrifice her own son's funeral in order to escape it.

Mildred took Emily's hands. "Thank you. You'll never know how much you've done for me." She leaned forward and kissed Emily's cheek, then turned and hurried from the room. As Emily left the house, she heard Mildred telling the maid to take the rest of the day off.

Stunned, Emily drove down the hill into town to report to Luke. She'd learned nothing that would help the case. But about the dark side of marriage and parenthood she'd learned a great deal. Perhaps being childless had not been an unmixed curse after all.

twenty

I was going back to Thornfield: but how long was I to stay
there? Not long; of that I was sure.

—*Jane Eyre*

S oon after he arrived at the office, groggy from a near-
sleepless night, Luke got a call from headquarters. The autopsy report was ready. Quick work. But of course a county like
Tillamook didn't have a lineup of bodies like they would in
Portland, for instance. Medical examiner was a part-time job
around here and a murder victim a welcome diversion. The labs
would take longer—Tillamook County didn't have a forensic lab
of its own; they had to outsource and wait their turn.

Luke drove to the morgue so he could go over the results
with the ME in person. George Tomlinson moved in the same
social circles as the Newhouses and made sure everyone knew
it. Luke always had to fight a sense of inferiority in his presence—
and beat down the defensiveness that went with it. They were
two competent professionals doing their jobs. If Tomlinson
chose to talk down to Luke like he was a raw recruit straight
out of a cattle barn, that was his problem, not Luke's.

Luke strode into the morgue and put out his hand to shake Tomlinson's, then pulled it back as he realized the doctor's gloved hands weren't fit for shaking. Great, he'd put his very first foot wrong. Tomlinson bit back a smile, but not before Luke saw it.

"Here he is, Lieutenant." The doctor lifted a sheet off a body on a table, already barely recognizable as Jake Newhouse. Once the life had gone out of a face—no color in the cheeks, no twinkle in the eye, no smirk in the mouth—it was tough, especially with a young kid, to tell one lump of flesh from another. Hotshot doctor and humble lawman, Casanova and lonely nerd, all came down to lumps of flesh in the end. And if they ended up in this morgue, those lumps all had angry red Y-shaped scars roughly stitched together across their unmoving chests.

Luke shook off his morbid thoughts. "What'd you find?"

"As you can see, there were two potentially fatal wounds: the deeper puncture wound to the thorax, and the blunt trauma to the back of the skull. My primary job was to determine which of those wounds actually killed him."

Luke nodded. "We figured the puncture wound was made by that knife—" He nodded toward the evidence bag on the counter. "And the head trauma resulted from falling down a spiral staircase. That consistent with what you found?"

Tomlinson continued as if he hadn't spoken. "The puncture wound severed the coronary artery, causing severe bleeding. The victim would have died of blood loss within a few minutes. The bruising all over the body occurred while the victim was still alive. The amount of blood in the hair also suggests the head wound was sustained before death. But that wound would likely not have killed him instantly. It's most probable he died of blood loss from the wound."

"Any sign of the victim being pushed down the stairs?"

"Look at this." Tomlinson pointed to the stab wound, which lay horizontally between two ribs. The skin had closed around it, but the gash was surrounded by a purple bruise that extended about a half inch from all its borders.

"So the killer pushed the knife all the way into him," Luke said. "That bruise is from the handguard."

Tomlinson assessed Luke as if he were a pupil who turned out to be brighter than he'd expected. "Exactly. If the victim happened to be standing at the top of the stairs when he was struck, the impact could have toppled him."

"We're looking at a pretty strong killer, then?"

"Not necessarily. A woman could have done it in the heat of passion."

Heat of passion likely applied in this instance, woman or man. "Can you tell me anything about the attacker? Height, left- or right-handed?"

"Probably right-handed, but I can't be certain. The weapon entered the body square on. Remarkable, really. Almost mathematical precision."

"So would you say the killer knew what he was doing, anatomically speaking?"

"There I'd say no. His—or her—first blow was quite ineffective. And the second—"

"Wait a minute. *First* blow?"

"Well, yes. I assumed you'd seen it." He pointed to a smaller gash that ran vertically a few inches above the left nipple. "This one hit a rib. It would have bled, but not copiously. It didn't do much damage."

Luke mentally kicked himself. How had he missed that? And Sam? Maybe she'd seen it but assumed he had, too, and didn't think to mention it. He could see in Tomlinson's eyes he'd lost that tiny bit of respect he'd gained by guessing what caused the bruise. "And the second blow?"

"As I said, that blow severed an artery but did not come especially close to the heart. So I would say the killer was not trained in either medicine or killing."

All of that got Luke exactly nowhere. None of the suspects was a physician or an ex-soldier or a secret agent—at least, not that he knew of—so the amateur placement of the wound didn't rule any of them out. Left-handed Cordelia Fitzgerald was unlikely, but not impossible. And the precision of the angle—either Roman or Devon would have a carpenter's or cabinetmaker's eye and might line up the blade without thinking. But there was no reason any of the others might not have done the same by pure accident.

"What about blood spatter? Would the attacker necessarily have gotten blood on his hands or gloves? On his clothing?"

"As I said, the first wound would have bled but not spurted. It's likely the killer would have blood on his hands or gloves, but not certain. There's no reason to think he'd have blood elsewhere on his clothing unless he was standing quite close, almost embracing."

"But the second wound would have bled?"

"Not hugely unless the knife was removed before death. Since it did strike an artery, there would likely have been some seepage around the knife. Once it was pulled out, blood would have spurted with decreasing force until death occurred, and then the bleeding would have stopped." Tomlinson stripped off his gloves and moved to the sink. "You'd know better than I how much blood was at the scene. The amount I saw on his clothing suggests the knife was removed before death, but probably not long before."

But the amount of blood on Katie's clothing told another story. She could well have pulled the knife out of him while he was still alive. Jake probably hadn't had more than one good spurt left in him by that time. But most of it hit Katie's apron. No wonder the girl had blocked the scene from her memory.

Emily would never forgive him if he arrested Katie. And he'd lose his almost-adopted daughter as well.

Luke stared at Jake Newhouse's savaged body and almost wished he could trade places with him. His own future was looking bleaker by the hour.

Emily returned exhausted from her interview with Mildred Newhouse. Witnessing all that emotion had drained her, and besides, her whole body ached from her exertions the day before. She gave herself the day off from redecorating and retired to the library with *Jane Eyre*. By early afternoon she'd read up to the terrible revelation of the existence of Rochester's crazed but living wife. She wasn't sorry to be interrupted when the phone rang.

Her tenant in Portland was on the line. "Emily? Lillian. Listen, we have a problem here. The pipes in the bathroom sprang a leak and soaked through the living room ceiling. We were out and didn't catch it till all the plaster had come down."

Emily groaned. "I'll call the insurance rep. He'll have to look at it first before any repairs can be done."

"We had to shut off the water completely. How long will all that take?"

"Heavens, I don't know, but it probably won't be quick. The insurance should cover it if you need to go to a hotel for the duration."

Lillian grumbled a bit, but finally accepted there was nothing more Emily could do. Emily called her home insurance agent and explained the situation.

"I can get an adjuster over there first thing tomorrow morning to assess the damage. But I'll need you to meet him if the tenants are clearing out."

Emily would have to drive to Portland tonight and stay over with Marguerite if she didn't want to be up and out at some ungodly hour tomorrow. Well, there was nothing for it. "I'll be there."

She made arrangements with Marguerite, who said cryptically, "I told you to come to Portland, and *voilà*! You are coming."

"So what did you do, sneak into my house and loosen a join on my pipes just to get me up there?"

"*Moi? Certainement pas.* It is destiny, *mon amie.* You are meant to be here now."

Emily hated to leave with everything still so uncertain. Even though she'd extracted what she believed to be the truth from Abby and Cordelia, and Luke himself seemed to have eliminated Matthew and Devon, they still had no real proof against Roman. He had motive, means, and opportunity, but so did Katie. Only Emily's instinct—or, it could be argued, her blind affection—told her Roman was guilty and Katie innocent. And Luke didn't seem to share that instinct. What if he arrested Katie in her absence?

And then there was Roman himself. In the house with Katie. A man whose unhealthy passion for the girl had already possibly—probably—almost certainly driven him to murder. And herself not there to protect her girl.

Inconceivable.

She sent Katie upstairs to ask Jeremiah to come down to the

library. "I have to go to Portland for a few days, and I'm nervous about having Roman in the house with Katie while I'm not here. I'd like you to let him go."

Jeremiah's bushy brows drew together. "Roman? He's the best worker I have."

"I'm sorry, but he has feelings toward Katie that make me very uncomfortable. He'll have to go, at least for the time I'm away. After that, we'll see."

Jeremiah's already grim face went gray as death. "Can't put the girl in danger. I'll get rid of him right away."

Emily imparted her plans to Katie. "Oh, Mrs. C, do you really have to go? I don't like being alone in the house with—them." She cut her eyes upward toward the third floor.

"It's all right, I've told Jeremiah to let Roman go. At least until I get back."

Katie twisted a lock of hair. "Well—all right. I guess. Although Mr. Edwards is kind of creepy himself."

"Agreed, but he'd never do anything to hurt you. He seems almost as anxious to protect you as I am."

She gave Katie a reassuring hug, then as an afterthought, called Luke.

"I have to go to Portland for a couple days. There's an issue with my house I have to take care of in person. You'll—keep an eye on Katie while I'm gone, won't you?" The irony of asking for protection for Katie from the man who stood in the position of greatest threat to her just now did not escape Emily. She hoped Luke could hear between the words of her request her real message: *And don't arrest her while I'm gone.*

"So it isn't going to Portland you object to—just going there with me." He spoke teasingly, but she could hear an undercurrent of actual hurt. Too bad.

"This isn't a pleasure trip. I *have* to go. Oh, and I've told Jeremiah to lay Roman off for the duration."

"Wise move. Don't worry, I'll look in on Katie and make sure she's okay." Between the words of his assurance she heard, *And make sure she doesn't skip town while you're not looking.* Why, Lord, why did that pipe have to burst right now? It wasn't even winter yet.

She packed quickly. Dark came early at this time of year, and she wanted to make Portland in daylight in case the weather was as bad there as it was here. She said her good-byes to Katie, Lizzie, and the cats, and drove off into the storm.

Emily reached Marguerite's apartment in time for dinner. Marguerite was waiting with flowers on the table, a quiche in the oven, and a glass of wine in each hand. "I am sure you need this, *chérie,*" she said, handing Emily a glass.

Emily kicked off her shoes, flopped on the couch, and drank gratefully. "Do I ever." She looked around the bright, spacious, white-walled room with its clean-lined furniture and subdued color scheme. An abstract painting hung on one wall, while clusters of black-and-white photographs in ebony frames were dotted about the rest of the room. "You know, Margot, I always used to think your style was a bit—well, sterile, no offense—but right now it seems really restful. Windy Corner is so—*full.* Not just of stuff, but of people and events and disturbances. I still love the place, but it's good to have a break."

Marguerite gave her a wise, slightly smug smile. "What did I tell you? You should listen to Marguerite. Marguerite knows what you need."

"I guess she does." She closed her eyes, sipped her wine, and thought of absolutely nothing while Marguerite put dinner on the table.

They talked of college politics, gossiped about mutual friends, touched on recent films Marguerite had seen and concerts she'd heard—Emily had hardly been inside a theater since moving to Stony Beach. Nostalgia for the life she'd left behind washed over her. She should have come up with Luke a couple of weeks ago. If she couldn't find some way to integrate her two worlds, she'd always feel like half a person, whichever one she happened to be in. She went to bed resolving to find a way to spend a weekend with Luke in Portland as soon as this case was solved and life returned to normal. That is, assuming the case was solved to her satisfaction.

At eight o'clock the next morning she unlocked the door of her little Tudor cottage on Woodstock Boulevard. This act brought its own nostalgia, but before that feeling could take hold, she entered the living room—and saw utter chaos. A mound of disintegrated plaster covered the sopping rug. Somewhere under that mound, she suspected, lay the ruined remains of the antique coffee table she'd inherited from her maternal grandmother. Looking up, she could see the bare joists of the ceiling. Good thing she didn't actually live here anymore.

The insurance adjuster came in right behind her, only pausing in the entryway to knock on the open door. He was already disheveled—comb-over flapping, shirttails dangling, tie askew—although this must have been his first appointment of the day. He shook her hand without introducing himself or even looking her in the eye, then proceeded immediately to the war zone. His head bobbed mournfully as he walked around the pile of plaster.

"Bad, oh, very bad," he intoned. "This is going to cost a

bundle. Yes, indeed. Quite a bundle." His voice reminded Emily of Puddleglum from the Narnia stories. Any minute she expected him to start discoursing on fricasseed frogs and eel pie.

She followed him upstairs, where she glanced into the bedrooms and office while the adjuster addressed the ruined bathroom. Her tenants were no messier than she'd expected— average for two college instructors—but it gave her gut a peculiar wrench to see someone else's belongings strewn about her own dear rooms. Maybe next year she'd keep the house empty so she could use it herself whenever she took the notion to come to town.

In an hour he was finished and on his cell phone, making arrangements for the repairs. "How long will it take?" Emily asked.

He shook his long-jawed head. "We're looking at two weeks, maybe three," he droned. "Lot of work to be done. Real plaster's not a quick process. Or a cheap one." He glared at her over his glasses. "You sure you won't go for drywall?"

"No. I want the ceiling to look just as it did before. The whole house is plaster—one drywall ceiling would stand out as badly as a plate-glass window in this cottage." All the windows still held their original diamond panes.

"I guess that's your prerogative. The policy does say 'restore to original condition.'" He spoke as if he prognosticated untold troubles arising from her decision.

"Will the policy cover my tenants staying in a hotel that long?"

"Beats me. Have to ask your agent about that. I only handle the damages."

Emily steeled herself for a possible steep bill landing on her desk. On top of her own remodeling and redecorating, plus the catering and whatnot for the fundraiser, this was going to sting. At least no guests had asked for their money back after the genuine murder disrupted the party. Maybe they felt they'd gotten more than they paid for instead of less.

When the adjuster had left with a final mournful shake of his head, his comb-over waving like seaweed behind him, Emily checked her watch. This would be a good time to catch some of her colleagues between classes. She walked the block down the hill to campus and headed for the faculty common room.

"Well, well, well, if it isn't our prodigal sister come back to the fold at last." Her department head, Richard McClintock, greeted her without moving from the coffee machine. At least he stood aside to let her pour herself a cup. "What's the matter, did the millions run out? Or have the innumerable charms of small-town living paled for you already?"

With an effort Emily ignored his sarcasm. She couldn't be certain she herself would have reacted with perfect grace and generous well-wishing if one of her colleagues had come into the fortune that fate had chosen to drop into her lap. Though she certainly would have made more of an effort to act the part. "I had an issue with my house here. Poor Lillian and Henry came home to a living room full of fallen plaster last night. I'm afraid they'll be camping at a hotel for a couple of weeks while it all gets put back together."

McClintock's lip curled. "So even the mighty have their little troubles, eh?"

"And big ones." She didn't feel like telling him about recent events at Windy Corner, though. He'd probably find a way to make even the murder of a rapist on her property sound like some privilege of the wealthy.

She turned from him to examine the college magazines

strewn about the table until a couple of other professors came in. These slighter acquaintances from other divisions made polite small talk, but clearly were no happier to see her there than McClintock was. Emily finished her coffee and took her leave. She might regret leaving Portland, but at least at this minute, she didn't in the least regret leaving Reed.

A visit to Powell's would wash the bad taste from her mouth. The "City of Books" that filled an entire block downtown would likely have a good selection of volumes on period decor, and maybe something on running a bed-and-breakfast—not exactly what she and Katie would be doing, but close enough that they could profit from others' experience in that field.

Emily spent several happy hours browsing the shelves and perusing her selections in the small café, where patrons were allowed to bring in books, purchased or unpurchased, and to sit at the long communal tables as long as they pleased. She left with as many books as she could carry, well equipped to complete the transformation of Windy Corner into a writers' retreat. Ah, she had missed Powell's.

But she certainly had not missed downtown rush-hour traffic. Nor, really, downtown itself, which had become almost unbearably hip in recent years. Merely walking down the sidewalk past trendy boutiques and organic eateries, surrounded by skinny young people in tight black clothes with devices attached to their ears, made her feel old and hopelessly out-of-date. She had a sudden sharp pang of longing for Luke, who adored her exactly as she was—long swishy skirts, upswept hair, Luddite tendencies and all. And for the beach, where she could walk for miles in the early morning without encountering another human soul.

She'd promised Marguerite to stay another night; otherwise

she would have headed back to Stony Beach there and then. Instead she turned her PT Cruiser back toward the southeast side of town. She just had time to catch Wednesday night vespers at St. Sergius. Her church was the most fundamental thing about Portland she still missed.

• twenty-one •

Laws and principles are not for the times when there is no temptation: they are for such moments as this, when body and soul rise in mutiny against their rigour; stringent are they; inviolate they shall be. If at my individual convenience I might break them, what would be their worth?

—*Jane Eyre*

Luke stopped by Windy Corner on his way into the office Wednesday morning to check on Katie. Normally they had an easygoing, teasing relationship, such as he'd always imagined having with the daughter he never had. But now she seemed skittish around him, as if she expected him to whip out the handcuffs if she turned her back. He asked as gently as he could if she'd remembered any more about the night of the murder. She shook her head, not meeting his eyes.

Maybe if he arrested Abby, that would get Katie to talk. She'd do anything to exonerate her sister, even if it meant implicating herself. But that would be a mean trick to play on both sisters. Only as a last resort would he even consider it. And things weren't quite that bad yet. It was only Wednesday morning. He had till Friday to solve the case.

Lab results came in during the day. Newhouse must have a

cousin in the lab as well—or some old client he could put pressure on—otherwise they'd never have been so fast.

The reports were exhaustive and tedious to read through, but they boiled down to this: None of the gloves or clothing he'd sent in showed any traces of human blood. Except, of course, for Katie's outfit, which was drenched in it.

He told himself that wasn't conclusive. Tomlinson had said it was only highly probable—not certain—the killer would have gotten blood on his hands or gloves. Not very likely he'd have blood on the rest of his clothing. And even if Katie had pulled the knife out of Jake while he was still alive, that didn't mean she knew what she was doing. Nor did it mean she was the one who put the knife in. And none of this went any way to clear Roman, whose prints were on the knife and who'd had a nice little rain shower to wash any blood off him before Luke saw him. Katie wasn't any closer to the top of the suspect list than she'd been before.

So why was his gut still tied in knots?

I love my job, and I love Mrs. C, but I thought it might be fun to have her gone for a couple of days—just me and Lizzie on our own, pretending we're queens of the castle. We could sleep in, eat pizza for breakfast, trek into town to the Friendly Fluke and catch up with our friends. Maybe invite Abby and Erin to tea in the library. Have ourselves a fun little break.

I was wrong.

This morning actually was fun. We took our time getting up, then puttered around our own little apartment, doing some finishing touches I never had time for when we first moved in, what with the fundraiser to plan and all. The weather was too nasty to walk anywhere, but still, it was a nice, relaxing morning.

But this afternoon—!

I'd thought it was a good idea of Mrs. C's to lay Roman off, if only temporarily. He's really been freaking me out lately, the way he stares at me and follows me around when Mr. Edwards isn't looking. But he did not take kindly to being laid off. Not one little bit.

I don't think it's the work he cares about. He didn't lay into Mr. Edwards or anything when he told him. But when Roman left here last night, he looked at me like his life was over. And sort of like it was somehow my fault.

And then this afternoon, when the weather had cleared and I was strapping Lizzie into her stroller to walk to the Friendly Fluke, here comes Roman down the drive. He marches right up to me and says, "Katie, I can't live without you. I can't stay away. Don't make me. I'm not asking anything from you, but I have to be able to see you or I'll die."

What on Earth do you do with a statement like that? Especially if you can't return the feeling?

I tried to be kind. "Roman, I don't know what to say," I said. "You're a nice guy and all" (that was a bit of a stretch) "but I just don't feel that way about you. I'm sorry, but I think you need to honor Mrs. Cavanaugh's wishes and not come here anymore."

His face—oh my God, his face! I've never seen anyone look like that. First he went white, then he went purple. His eyebrows seemed to grow to twice their size and his mouth shrank to this hard white line. He sort of convulsed, and then he said through clenched teeth, "I thought with Newhouse out of the way you would love me."

I was blown away. Surely he didn't think I actually cared for Jake? And then I thought about what he'd just said. Did that imply he'd gotten Jake out of the way—on purpose?

I just stared at him. His hands started to come up, sort of like he couldn't control them, and for a second I thought he was going to strangle me. But he just put his hands on my shoulders and squeezed. I can still feel the bruises. "What can I do to make you see?" he hissed.

I was really creeped out at that point, and not at all sure he was going to let me get away unharmed. I didn't think he would—do what Jake did—but I was kind of afraid he might kill me with the sheer force of his passion. But thank God, just at that moment Mr. Edwards came up behind him and yanked Roman away from me. Mr. Edwards is so skinny, he doesn't look that strong, but Roman was like a straw in his hands.

He put his face down in Roman's face and said in this voice that was so quiet it rang in my ears, "You will not touch Miss Parker ever again. You will not bother her in any way. You will leave this property and my employment this minute, and you will never come back."

Roman didn't flinch. He didn't talk back. He just turned on his heel and left. But he looked back at me for a second with a look that meant no way was he leaving me alone.

Mr. Edwards isn't here 24/7. Roman will be back.

Mrs. C, where are you when I need you?

Emily got caught on the Burnside Bridge as it was being raised, so she was a few minutes late for vespers. She crept in and stood at the back, underneath the icon of St. Emmelia—the mother of the great saints Macrina, Basil, and Gregory, as well as the lesser-known Peter and Naucratius. Emily could have taken a different saint as her patron when she was baptized into the Orthodox Church, but she liked the idea of being associated with a famous mother—though she could never be a mother herself.

And if Katie was arrested for murder, she'd no longer be able even to pretend.

Emily willed herself to breathe deeply and let the familiar chanting of the psalms and hymns wash over her. Her parish was blessed with a few good singers who could do justice to this music that had lifted the hearts and calmed the spirits of generations of worshippers. It calmed her now, washing away the superficial cares of the last few weeks and replacing them with the bedrock assurance that "all shall be well, and all manner of thing shall be well." Her favorite lines of T. S. Eliot quoting Julian of Norwich.

But at the very core of her being, the music met its match: the black involuted mass that was her guilty conscience. She had falsified some details in relating Abby's confession to Luke in order to avoid implicating Katie. Not only her own faith, with its commandment *Do not bear false witness,* but every murder mystery she'd ever read—in which information withheld inevitably led to the wrong person being blamed—chastised her and held her up to judgment.

If Katie was arrested, it would be Emily's own fault. Whether she spoke or kept silent, it could still be her fault.

The service ended, and the few worshippers stopped to chat with Emily in the narthex on their way out, reminding her by their gladness at seeing her how long she'd been away. She was turning to leave when Father Paul came up to her and enveloped her in a hug. She'd missed those bear hugs of his, the way his long beard tickled her face as he kissed her on both cheeks in the Russian manner. Even more so since she'd deprived herself of Luke's embraces.

"Emily! How good to see you! What brings you to Portland? I assume you didn't come all this way just to attend Wednesday night vespers?"

"No. My tenants were flooded out. I had to meet with the insurance adjuster. But I couldn't leave town without coming to church—lucky for me it was Wednesday."

He wagged a finger at her. "You know how I feel about the word *luck*. God brought you here." He paused and scrutinized her face. "Is anything troubling you, Emily? Would you like to talk for a bit?"

She hesitated, knowing the black knot of her guilty resolve could not long hold out against Father Paul's gentle compassion. But she couldn't make her mouth shape the word "no," nor her feet move toward the exit. She nodded and followed him back into the nave. He put his stole around his neck—which meant he was prepared to give her absolution if this turned into a formal confession—and sat with her on a side bench near the front icon screen.

With only the slightest prodding, she poured out the entire story of the murder, pausing for breath only when she came to her own dereliction in reporting Abby's confession to Luke. But that had to come out, too.

"If I tell him, he'll know Katie had an even more powerful motive for killing Jake than avenging her own rape—she'd just found out he'd been after her sister. I can't give Luke that kind of ammunition."

"But if you don't tell him, he'll be acting on false information. He could end up arresting the wrong person."

"I don't care, as long as it isn't Katie." Emily gasped, unable to believe she'd just said that. But it was true.

"It could be Katie. He could arrest her by mistake, although she's innocent. You can never tell where a lie will lead. Once you've loosed it into the world, it can turn on you to your own destruction."

Emily's eyes and nose burned with unshed tears. She opened her purse to get a tissue, exposing the copy of *Jane Eyre* she'd brought with her to read in odd moments. Father Paul reached for it.

"Ah, *Jane Eyre*. One of my favorites. Where are you?" He opened the book to her marked page and skimmed a few lines. "I see you've left Jane just before her great moment. When she's about to sacrifice her love, everything in the world she holds dear, for the sake of her conscience. Now that is a true heroine." He closed the book and slid it back into her bag.

That was a low blow. Using her own beloved literature against her.

"It comes down to this, Emily: Do you truly believe in Katie's innocence? If you do, you must know the truth can only serve to clear her in the end."

Emily drew in a breath so deep the lingering incense in the air burned her lungs. Could she, in truth, imagine Katie stabbing Jake—not just to wound, to disable, but deliberately to kill—under any circumstances whatsoever?

No. She could not.

What Jane Eyre sacrificed came back to her in the end, though wounded, humbled. She was able to enjoy her love with a clear conscience, even with a greater sense of equality than would have been possible before.

Could Emily trust that Katie would be restored to her as well?

She must. Or her love for Katie would be poisoned forever, as would her love for Luke. For she did still love him, in spite of everything. He was only doing his job. And he couldn't do it properly unless she told him the truth.

Luke ran by Windy Corner again on his way home that evening to make sure Katie was okay. He knocked but got no answer, so he walked in and found her sitting in front of the library fire, drinking sherry, playing Celtic folk music loud on the stereo, and watching Lizzie try to crawl on the hearthrug. *While the cat's away,* he thought, but when he took a look at Katie's face, he thought different. Something had happened. She needed that sherry.

"What's up, Katie?" he asked, keeping it light just in case he was mistaken.

She jumped two feet. "Oh, Lieutenant Richards! You startled me. But I'm so glad you're here." She seemed to remember her manners and turned off the stereo. "Can I get you something? Tea? Sherry?"

"No, thanks, I'm good. Sit down and tell me what's going on."

She sat, and she told him a tale that made his hair stand on end. Thank God Edwards had been there to save the situation. It sounded like Luke and Emily had come within a hair's breadth of leaving Katie alone with a murderer.

"Tell me again what he said about Jake? His exact words, if you can remember."

"He said, 'I thought with Newhouse out of the way you would love me.' Just like that."

"Holy crap. We may have found our murderer."

"That's what I thought. If you could have seen his face! He looked capable of *anything*."

"I just hope the judge'll see that as probable cause to swear out a warrant on him. I've got indications, but it's all circumstantial—nothing solid enough to pin the murder on him. But I'll go see the judge first thing tomorrow morning." He shot a concerned look at Katie. "Meanwhile, though, I'm not leaving you and Lizzie alone. I think you should sleep over here in the main house tonight and let me stay with you." He realized how that sounded, blushed, and quickly added, "In another room, of course."

Katie bit her lip. "Fine by me, but don't you think we ought to ask Mrs. C? It is her house, after all. And I'd feel a lot better if she were home."

"Absolutely. I'll call her right now." Luke had insisted Emily charge her cell phone and take it with her. He just prayed she'd remembered to turn it on.

Emily had remembered. Her cell rang just as she was getting in her car. "Luke! Is everything okay?"

"Not entirely." She listened in horror as he told her about Katie's encounter with Roman. "I think it'd be best if you came on home."

"I think you're right. I'll have to go back by Marguerite's—I'm at church right now—and then I'll head out. Can you stay with Katie till I get there?"

"I think I better stay the night, if that's all right with you. No offense, but I have a feeling Roman may not consider himself subject to your authority anymore. You ladies need some beef in the house."

Emily smiled to herself in spite of the seriousness of the situation. "All right, Mr. Porterhouse. Pick a room, and I'll be there in a couple of hours."

She drove as fast as she dared and arrived around nine thirty. She walked into the library and found Luke and Katie playing Scrabble, with the cats asleep on the hearthrug and Lizzie nowhere to be seen.

"Well, isn't this domestic! And here I thought I was coming home to a war zone."

Luke gave her a sheepish grin. "All quiet on the western front tonight, ma'am." He stood awkwardly, as if wanting to hug her but unsure whether she'd consent to be hugged. Fortunately for her, Katie rushed into the breach and squeezed her hard.

"I'm so glad you're home. Windy Corner just isn't itself when you're not around."

Emily's heart glowed at those words. "Any chance of a cup of tea?"

"Right away."

She hurried to the kitchen, and Emily turned to Luke. "Is there anything you didn't tell me on the phone?"

"Just that I'm pretty sure now Roman's our murderer. First thing in the morning I'm going to swear out a warrant for his arrest."

So her great confession and revelation scene might not be necessary after all. Emily felt oddly let down, although on a conscious level, at least, she'd been dreading that conversation. But now it seemed all question of Katie's possible involvement had been set aside. Emily had been right all along—it was Roman. Heathcliff would get his comeuppance at last.

twenty-two

Jane Eyre, who had been an ardent, expectant woman—
almost a bride—was a cold, solitary girl again: her life was
pale; her prospects were desolate.

—*Jane Eyre*

Luke left right after breakfast the next morning to get his
warrant. Jeremiah and his crew arrived as usual, sans
Roman, of course. Emily was still debating how to spend her day
when the doorbell rang. Katie was busy washing up, so Emily
went to the door herself.

Roman stood on the doorstep.

Emily summoned Beatrice's shade to augment her own
rather shaky authority. "Roman, you are not welcome in this
house. Katie does not want to see you, and neither do I."

He scowled somewhat sheepishly. "Left my hammer on the
roof. Came to get it back."

Emily waffled for a moment. Allow Roman in her house, or
send someone else to get the hammer? A gust of wind blew up,
driving the rain almost horizontally before it. No, she couldn't
risk another person's life on that roof for the sake of Roman's

hammer. If he cared about it enough to go after it in this weather, let him.

She watched him up the main stairs, then went to the kitchen to warn Katie to stay put so she wouldn't be in Roman's path. That is, unless he came down by the back stairs. Emily mounted the back stairs herself to make sure that didn't happen.

She hung around in the deserted hallway for several minutes, half her mind on Roman and the other half on the slightly faded wallpaper of the hall: Should she replace it? And if so, with what? It wouldn't do to favor one end of the nineteenth century over the other when she had author rooms covering the whole span.

Her attention was arrested by a sliding sound from above, followed a second later by a loud thud, a second sliding sound, and a crunching thud from the front of the house. She raced through the Brontë room and onto the balcony where, by leaning out, she could get a view of the drive just in front of the house.

On the drive to the right of the porch steps lay a crumpled form with a pool of blood oozing around its head.

Luke had stopped by his office and was only a couple of miles down the road when his cell rang. "Call an ambulance and come back right now!" Emily commanded him, offering no explanation. He used the radio to make the call as he turned on his siren, flipped a U on the highway, and headed back. It couldn't be Emily herself who needed the ambulance, since she was able to call him. He prayed it wasn't Katie or Lizzie. If he was too late with that warrant, he'd never forgive himself.

He crunched to a halt on the wet gravel of the drive and ran to where Emily stood with her arms around Katie, huddled against the rain. Next to them a dark shape lay on the ground. "What happened?"

"It's Roman. He fell off the roof."

Luke bent over the body, checked the pulse and respiration, even though Roman was obviously dead. His eyes were glazed, his head bashed in. Near his right hand lay a hammer.

He straightened. "What the hell was he doing on your roof?"

"He left his hammer up there the other day. Came back to get it."

Luke looked up, pulling his cap brim forward to keep the rain out of his eyes. "Up there by the tower?"

"Yes."

"Three stories. That could kill a man, all right."

"I think he hit the porch roof on the way down."

"Yup. That makes sense. It'd break his fall a little, but it's still far enough to be lethal." He looked down at the crumpled remains. "Even if he was a murderer, that's a hell of a way to go."

He went up on the sheltered porch and pulled out his cell phone to call his deputies and tell the ambulance not to hurry. What he needed here was an ME, not a paramedic.

He waved Emily and Katie up onto the porch. "Now tell me exactly what happened."

Emily related what she'd heard and seen.

"Anybody else go up on the roof with him? Or see him go up?"

"I don't know. I didn't go past the second-floor hall. You'd have to ask Jeremiah." He turned toward the door, but Emily stopped him with a hand on his sleeve. The jolt that went through him spoke of how long it had been since she'd touched him.

"Luke—there's something else you need to know." She lifted Katie's face from where it was buried against her coat. "Katie? Do you feel up to talking about it?"

She nodded.

"Talking about what? You see something, Katie?"

"Not today. I was in the kitchen. But when I saw him lying there—and all the blood—" She shivered, and Emily held her tighter. "I remembered. What happened before."

Luke sized up Katie's condition and said, "Let's get you inside and get something hot into you." He led the two women into the library and seated them in front of the fire, then poured them each a brandy—faster than making coffee or tea.

"Now take your time and tell me what you remember."

Katie groped for Emily's hand and squeezed it hard. Emily said, "It's okay, sweetie. You can do this."

Katie nodded, closed her eyes for a second, then spoke. "I needed to go upstairs, like I told you before. I opened the door to the secret stairwell and I saw something lying on the floor. It was dark in there with only the candlelight from the library coming in. I couldn't tell what it was, so I went closer." She shivered. "I knelt down beside the thing and then I saw it was a person. A man. I saw the knife sticking out of his chest and I reached for it. I don't know why. It just looked so—*wrong*—sticking out of him like that. I didn't really think, I just grabbed the knife and pulled it out. And then the blood—"

She went pale, and for a second Luke thought she was going to be sick. But she took another sip of brandy and went on. "It spurted out of him. All over me. And that's when I screamed."

That all fit in with the evidence he had. Except one thing still didn't make sense. "Katie—what were you going upstairs for?"

She glanced at him, wide-eyed, then looked down again. "I—well, I guess I can tell you now. If you're sure it was Roman who killed him."

What the hell—?

"I was going up to confront Jake. He'd messed with Abby, and I was so mad I couldn't see straight. I was going to go all she-wolf and make sure he never bothered any woman in my family ever again." Then she seemed to realize what she was saying. "I mean—I wasn't going to hurt him. Just give him a really big piece of my mind. But then—I guess Roman saved me the trouble."

Luke's head was swimming. "Let me get this straight. Abby had some kind of run-in with Jake?" He glanced at Emily. If Abby had told her that, why hadn't she passed it on? Emily's face was as red as her hair. She must have known. And deliberately concealed it from him.

Katie nodded. "He'd been flirting with her. I'd never told her about him being Lizzie's father. She didn't know what a dick he was. She went up the back stairs to meet him in the secret stairwell, but then she saw him there with Ms. Fitzgerald. She thought they were—you know—and she was devastated. She came running down and I caught her in the kitchen and made her tell me everything."

"And you didn't tell me this—why?"

Katie squeezed her eyes shut. "I was afraid Abby might have gone back up and confronted him. I knew she wouldn't kill anybody on purpose, but—well, I didn't know what to think. I didn't want to get her in trouble."

Luke caught Emily's gaze and held it. He could see in her face she'd known all of this. She'd seen how it gave Katie an even stronger motive for killing Jake, and she'd chosen to keep it to herself.

He could understand Katie keeping quiet to protect her sister. But he'd foolishly believed Emily's first loyalty would be to him—and to the truth. Obviously he'd been mistaken.

How could he ever trust her again?

Katie was still shivering under Emily's arm, although her brandy glass was dry. "Can Katie go now, Luke? She needs to get into some dry clothes."

"Yeah, all right."

He stood and turned his back on them as Katie left the room. Emily felt cold to her core, and not just from standing in the rain over Roman's body. She'd left her confession too late. Would Luke ever believe she'd intended to make it at all?

"Luke—I was going to tell you."

He spun to face her. She'd never seen him look like that— not only hurt and angry, but stone-faced, all the love-light gone out of his eyes.

"When? When were you going to tell me? When we're old and gray, sitting around swapping stories about the good old days?"

Every word of his was a dagger, but she knew she deserved each one. "Today. I was going to tell you today. I decided in Portland I'd have to come clean. I would've told you last night, only when you said you were going to arrest Roman—well, it didn't seem that urgent anymore."

"It didn't occur to you it might make a difference?"

"Well—no. I mean, the fact that Katie had a stronger motive didn't make her guilty."

He passed a hand over his eyes. "It isn't so much that you didn't tell me last night. It's that you didn't tell me in the first place. You heard the whole story from Abby, didn't you? Three days ago?"

She nodded dumbly.

"And you just glossed over all that—made it sound like Abby seeing Jake with Cordelia was a pure accident, of no significance to her at all."

"I thought—the fact that she'd seen them together was the important thing. Not why she was there to see it."

"No, you didn't. You thought if you told me the truth, you'd be handing me ammunition, which I would then turn around and use on Katie."

Why didn't he just cut her heart out and get it over with? She'd admitted just that to Father Paul last night, but to hear it now from Luke was like surgery with no anesthetic.

"I'm sorry, Luke. I was distraught. I had to protect Katie."

"Against the truth?" His voice dropped from the high pitch of anger to a nearly inaudible whisper of pain. "Against me?"

She couldn't answer.

"Couldn't you trust me to have her best interest at heart? Don't you know I love her almost as much as you do?"

Emily noticed he didn't say *almost as much as I love you.* Oh God, what had she done?

"I—I wasn't thinking clearly, I guess. I was desperate." Justification was pointless now. "I was wrong, Luke. I know I was wrong. I acted against everything I believe in. But I never thought—"

"What? Never thought I'd find out? So you think I'm stupid into the bargain?"

Her chest was so tight she could hardly speak. She shook her head. "Never thought I might be doing something that could cost me your love."

"And I never would have thought that could happen." His expression offered her no hope.

This conversation had reached a low from which Luke could see no recovery. Meanwhile he had a second death to investigate.

"You better go get dry. I need to talk to Edwards."

He followed her into the front hall. Dumbly, with an air of beaten-down hopelessness, Emily started up the stairs. Luke followed her at a distance, wondering if he'd ever be able to look at her the same way again.

She turned off into her bedroom, and he went on up to the third floor, where Jeremiah and his two workers stood clustered around the window of the front room. They turned to greet him with shocked faces. "Any of you see Roman on his way up?"

"We all did." Edwards spoke for the three of them. "He came up, and I asked him what he was doing here, since I'd dismissed him yesterday in no uncertain terms. Said he'd left his hammer on the roof. I let him go up and followed him to be sure he didn't cause any trouble."

"How'd he get to the roof?"

"Window of the tower bedroom."

"You follow him all the way onto the roof?"

"No, I stayed inside. By the window."

"Could you see him from there?"

"Not the whole time. He disappeared around the corner. Few seconds later I saw him fall. Roof's slick as greased lightning in this rain."

Luke nodded. "All right. You can get back to work." Jeremiah headed into the soon-to-be bathroom, and the two young men turned to follow him. "Just a minute, you two."

Luke knew them—Bobby and Bertie Fillmore, two brothers who looked alike enough to be twins, though they were actually a year apart. Good kids. Luke waited till Jeremiah started hammering, then asked them, "You confirm what he said?"

Bobby, the older one, spoke up. "We saw him go into the tower room after Roman. Then a while later we heard Roman fall. That's all we know." Bertie nodded his confirmation.

"All right. Off you go."

Wheels crunched on gravel, and Luke went back outside. The ambulance was pulling up to the door with Pete and Heather in the department SUV, plus Sam Griffiths in her Subaru, not far behind. Luke stood by while Heather photographed the body and Sam examined it.

"Story is he fell off the roof. That what you're seeing?" he asked Sam.

"Injuries consistent, I'd say. Nothing to suggest otherwise. Have to get him on the slab to be sure." She scratched her head. "One thing's funny, though. Way his head's bashed in, looks like he fell headfirst. If he slid off a slick roof, wouldn't you think feet first?"

Luke studied the body's presumed trajectory. "Yeah. I would. But maybe he didn't slip—just lost his balance and fell backward."

He turned to Pete and Heather. "We'll assume accidental death for now. But you two be thorough just in case."

Luke went back inside and up to the third floor. In the tower bedroom, he examined the window closest to the adjoining roof. The sill was wet, as he'd expected, with one pair of muddy bootprints in the water. The casement was damp, too, but he did his best to dust it for fingerprints. Not that he really expected to find any evidence of foul play. Roman may have been a nuisance, even a murderer, but as far as he could see, nobody in this house had reason to want him dead.

He opened the window and leaned out. He wasn't about to risk his own neck on those shingles in this weather, but from what he could see the roof looked undisturbed. He pulled his head in and shut the window.

He found Emily, changed into dry clothes, huddled with a blanket in front of the library fire, a coffee tray on the table next to her. She looked so small and defeated sitting there, he was tempted to forget everything that had just passed between them and take her in his arms.

But that would be to build their relationship on a lie.

She looked up as he came in, and gestured toward the coffeepot to ask if he wanted a cup. They'd been so close, they didn't need words to communicate. And yet she hadn't been able to trust him to make proper use of the truth.

"No, thanks. I'm going into town to close the case."

"So you're sure Roman really was the murderer?"

"Why wouldn't I be? I was about to arrest him. And you've been saying Roman was the culprit all along."

"I know." Emily picked cat hair off the hearthrug—pointless, since the three cats were still sitting there, lined up facing her like the no-evil monkeys. "I just have a funny feeling about it. It doesn't feel as if everything is over."

"Your feelings just haven't had a chance to catch up to reality yet, that's all. You've had trouble in this house for what, almost a month now? Since Jake first came? You've gotten used to trouble. It'll take a while to get used to it being gone."

"I guess you're right." But she didn't sound convinced.

And even if the murder trouble was over, the trouble between the two of them was far from done.

Jake, and now Roman. And my memory came back. I should be relieved. And I am, kind of. But also freaked.

Two guys were after me, one way or another. And both of them are dead.

Am I some kind of jinx? Did some old hag put a curse on me—"Love her and die"?

Not that anyone would call what Jake had for me "love." Roman used the word, but his didn't feel like love on my end, either. "Lust after her and die," maybe.

I can't help but wonder if Jamie is safe. He actually loves me, I'm pretty sure of that, though of course he hasn't said so yet. So if the curse says "lust," he's probably okay.

But I'd better stay away from him just in case. At least for now. That hurts, because I was really starting to care for him. But I can take it. I'm used to being on my own.

It's just you and me now, Lizzie-lou. Now and maybe forever.

· twenty-three ·

Zealous in his ministerial labours, blameless in his life and
habits, he yet did not appear to enjoy that mental serenity,
that inward content, which should be the reward of every
sincere Christian and practical philanthropist.

—*Jane Eyre*

The body had been taken away; Sam and the deputies had
left, and Luke along with them. The incident of Roman's
death was closed as far as Emily was concerned. She'd have to
testify at the inquest, but Luke assured her that was a mere for-
mality. Life could go on.

Theoretically. But Luke had not forgiven her, nor did he
seem likely to anytime soon. What kind of life was that to go on
with?

And even apart from that, it didn't seem right to plunge into
her everyday activities when a man had just died in her driveway, even if he was a man she was grateful to have out of Katie's
way. But what else could she do?

She could pray for his soul. She did that, and felt a little better. But she would need something more than reading in front
of the fire to keep her from brooding over the situation with

Luke—a situation it seemed at this point only time might be able to heal. If it could be healed at all.

She still had plenty of redecorating work to do. She recruited Katie to work with her, guessing the girl needed the occupation as much as she did. Together they tore through the Montgomery and Austen rooms, taking down drapes, stripping wallpaper— only a single layer in each of these rooms, thank God—and moving some smaller items to different rooms. The heavy furniture and rugs could wait until they could enlist some masculine help. That would give Billy Beech something to do—the weather had precluded any gardening lately, and the remodeling made his handyman efforts pretty much superfluous.

"We're making pretty good progress, aren't we, Mrs. C?" Katie said when they broke for tea.

"We certainly are. At this rate we should easily be done by Christmas."

"Do you want to open for Christmas? I thought you were thinking the first of the year."

"I was, but it occurred to me a lot of working people have time off around Christmas. That might be a good time for them to take a writing break. And I kind of like the idea of having a full house for the holiday. The guests will probably be people I know to begin with—Reed friends, or friends of friends."

"Well, that's fine with me. The more the merrier."

Emily sensed a sadness under Katie's bright tone and thought perhaps she was looking forward to a bustling Christmas to help her forget the events of the last few weeks.

The doorbell rang. Katie sprang up—to the amazement of Emily, who was sure she herself would need a crane to lift her out of her chair—and went to answer it.

Emily heard subdued voices from the hall, but couldn't make

out what they were saying. After a couple of minutes Katie returned, looking downcast. Emily heard Jeremiah and his workers clomping down the stairs and out the door. They must be finished for the day.

"Who was that?"

"Jamie."

"Why didn't you ask him in?"

"He just came to check on me. He heard about Roman."

"Is that any reason to send him away?"

Katie dropped into her chair without looking at Emily. "I don't want him to get hurt."

"I thought you liked him."

"I do. I like him a lot."

"Then why would he be hurt? That's what he's hoping for." This conversation was hard work. It wasn't like Katie to be so uncommunicative.

"I don't mean that kind of hurt. I mean physically hurt. Or—worse."

"Katie, what on Earth are you talking about?"

Katie looked into her eyes at last. "I think I'm cursed, Mrs. C. Jake went after me, and he died. Roman had some weird thing for me, and he died. Jamie—well, I think he might be in love with me, and I don't want him to die, too."

Emily was stunned. She went over to Katie's chair and put her arm over the girl's shoulders. "You're right about one thing—Jamie is in love with you. But the rest of it—it's pure fantasy, sweetie. It has to be. Curses like that aren't real. And anyway, who would curse you? Think about it. We don't have any witches in Stony Beach. It just doesn't make sense."

Katie sighed. "I know it doesn't make sense. But how do you explain those two deaths?"

"Roman killed Jake out of jealousy. Then he lost his footing on a slippery wet roof and fell. That's all there is to it. Roman's death is pure coincidence."

"I don't know, Mrs. C. It doesn't feel that way to me."

And despite her assurances to Katie, Emily had to admit that deep down, it didn't feel that way to her, either.

Once again Luke stood outside the towering wall of glass that reflected the perfect outward image of the Newhouse family. Again the double doors opened and he greeted the cute young maid. Only now she had a few hairs out of place, and her white apron was wrinkled and stained. She looked bewildered.

She showed him into the reception room without a word, and soon Newhouse came in, his walk closer now to a shuffle than the strut of a few days before. "Have a seat, Lieutenant," he said in a weary voice. He waved Luke to one of the black leather club chairs and sank into another, shifting his weight as if hoping to find a softer spot. But no softness was to be found in this house.

Luke had seen this kind of reaction to a loved one's murder before—initial anger and disbelief, but then when the truth finally sank in, depression followed. But the stages didn't usually move this fast, and especially not before the bereaved had found closure through the arrest of the murderer and the burial of the victim. Anger generally held out until then.

He spoke more gently than he would have a few days before. "Mr. Newhouse, I've come to tell you I believe we've found your son's killer."

Newhouse perked up a bit at that. "Have you arrested him?"

"As a matter of fact, that won't be necessary. He's already dead."

"What? How?" The anger was back, and Luke understood why—the killer's death deprived Newhouse of his revenge.

"He fell off a roof. Seems to've been accidental. I guess you could say God passed judgment on him—which is a good thing, 'cause our evidence was kind of slim."

Newhouse rose and walked to the window. "Who was it? And why?"

"Roman Martinez. Young fellow Jake had been working with on Edwards's crew. They were both after the same girl." That was the kind way of putting it.

Newhouse turned back to him with amazement written on his face. "A girl? Jake was killed over a *girl*?" As if he couldn't conceive of any female being worth killing over.

"That's what it looks like." Luke weighed his words, then decided not to mince them. "Not exactly jealousy in the usual way. This was a girl Jake had raped over a year ago and was harassing again. Roman was obsessed with her—he probably killed Jake to protect her. Or avenge her, or something."

Newhouse's mouth settled into a sneer. "Raped? Come now, Lieutenant. We're men of the world. We know what girls will say. A handsome, charming guy like Jake comes along, they can't resist him, then he moves on and out of spite they accuse him of rape. Happens all the time."

Luke stood and faced Newhouse square on. "This happens to be a girl I know pretty well, and I know she doesn't lie. She didn't even like Jake. He drugged her at a party and raped her." He was about to add, "and got her pregnant," but just in time it occurred to him it might not be a great thing for Newhouse to know he had a granddaughter. Instead he added, "And I'm pretty damn sure she wasn't the first. Or the last."

Newhouse's sneer wavered and died. "All right, so maybe my

boy wasn't perfect. But whatever he may have done, he won't be doing it anymore." He turned back to the window, and Luke was astonished to see a tear snake down the side of his cheek.

"You may as well know my wife has left me, too." His voice had a dead finality to it. "I'm alone now. Except for Robert, of course. But he has his own life in Portland."

In the window's reflection his eyes locked onto Luke's, and he blinked as if coming to himself. He turned and shook Luke's hand. "Thank you for telling me, Lieutenant. Thank you for solving the case."

Luke showed himself out. This was the least satisfying closure of a case he'd ever experienced. He just couldn't quite put his finger on why.

Emily and Katie kept working at a fevered pace all through Friday, trying to keep at bay the unsettled feeling that the business of Jake's and Roman's deaths was not in fact over. By the end of the day, the Austen room was newly papered and ready for its transformation. So on Saturday, when Devon called and said Hilary had returned during the week and his load of furniture had arrived from England, Emily felt it was perfect timing. She drove to Remembrance of Things Past to look over the loot.

Devon greeted her at the street door with a white face and shaking hands. "I'm sorry, Emily, I'm not at my best just now. We've had an—incident." He gestured toward the shop window.

Hilary, whom Emily had met only briefly last summer, stood in front of the window. He stood a head taller than Devon and was fair where his partner was dark, but he was just as immaculately dressed—except that at the moment his shirtsleeves were rolled up and he held a bucket of soapy water and a sponge. For the first time Emily looked at the window.

Scrawled across it in bright lavender paint, each letter a foot high, were the words, SODOMITES GO HOME—OR ELSE.

Emily felt ill. She herself was not a hundred percent comfortable with having a gay couple as tenants, but whatever her private feelings about their lifestyle might be, they had a right to live unmolested like anyone else. But where her own faith taught love for all sinners—including herself—she knew there were others who twisted the same scriptures to teach only judgment.

"I have a feeling I might know who's responsible for this." It had Jeremiah Edwards—or at least his church—written all over it. "Don't wash it off just yet. You need to show it to Lieutenant Richards."

Devon and Hilary exchanged a look. "We don't want to make a fuss. We're the newcomers, after all. It's not unusual for people to react this way in the beginning. After a while they get used to us and we get along fine."

Emily looked from one to the other. "You've been through this before? How many different places have you lived?"

"A few." Devon shifted his weight uncomfortably. "Please, Emily. No real damage was done. Just forget it. Let us show you the furniture."

She hesitated, then nodded. Devon and Hilary went inside. Internally, Emily resolved to investigate and give whoever was responsible for the painted message a piece of her mind. She told herself that as the landlord she had a responsibility to prevent vandalism. A painted window was relatively mild as vandalism went, but who knew what would be next? A brick through the window? A personal attack?

She took out her cell phone. With difficulty she remembered how Luke had shown her to take a picture and snapped a quick shot of the window before following the two men to the back of the shop. They might not want to report the incident, but she'd find some unofficial way to make sure Luke knew about it.

Hilary's finds proved to include the ideal furnishings for the Austen room—a delicate Sheraton bedroom suite of satinwood inlaid with rosewood and birch, and a lovely Aubusson rug that coordinated with the new wallpaper. They haggled a bit, weighing the value of the pieces she wanted against that of those she was selling to them, which Devon had already valued. She paid the balance and asked that the pieces be delivered the following Monday.

Now to corral some vandals.

Jeremiah wasn't working today, so she would have to track him down at home. She consulted the local phone book and found an Edwards on the south end of town, below the beach rentals, where the fishermen and most of the other year-round residents lived.

Jeremiah's black Ford pickup stood in the driveway at the listed address. But when she parked her PT Cruiser and knocked on the door, she received no answer. A quavery voice reached her from the neighboring porch. "Preacher ain't here. Gone to bury his daughter down Tillamook way."

Emily couldn't believe she'd heard properly. She peered into the dimness of the porch and saw an ancient woman, bent almost double, with a few strands of white hair raked across her pink skull into a tiny bun atop her head.

"Hello. I don't believe we've met. I'm Emily Cavanaugh. Mr. Edwards is working on my house right now."

"Gladys Elliott. Pleased to meetcha. Come on over and set a spell."

The house with its leaning steps and peeling paint did not look inviting, but Emily felt she was on the scent of something and was not about to let it slip away. She climbed Mrs. Elliott's steps—avoiding their sagging centers—and sat in the rocking chair the old woman indicated to her, across from where she sat on the porch swing.

"Preacher's daughter died at college back East last week. Last Saturday it was he got the word. Took 'em a while to ship her body back."

"How terrible," Emily said sincerely. Jeremiah's appearance and behavior over the last week suddenly made sense. But why hadn't he told her? She would have gladly given him the week off. "What happened? Was it a car accident?"

Mrs. Elliott shook her head knowingly. "That's what's being put out, but I don't believe it for a minute. I reckon she took her own life."

"Committed suicide? Why would she do that? A young girl with everything to live for?"

The old woman leaned forward on the swing to whisper confidentially in Emily's ear. "She was in the family way."

"Oh, dear." Unwed pregnancy happened all the time these days, and in many families it would be no big deal—but not for the daughter of a man like Jeremiah Edwards. "Did Jeremiah know?"

The ancient head wagged from side to side. "Not a bit of it. Well, they probably told him after she died. Nobody here knew but me, and she never *told* me." She nodded wisely. "I just knew."

"But surely—these days—"

"Even in these wicked days, Preacher'd never've stood for such a thing. He'd've disowned her if he ever so much as suspicioned."

Emily could well believe that. "Didn't she have anyone else she could turn to?"

"Not a soul. Her mother died last winter. Preacher got even stricter after that. No other family I ever heard of. Only way she could get away was to go to college. And she had the devil's own time getting him to go for that."

Given what Emily knew of campus life, she was not surprised. "What convinced him?"

"Rachel went to a Bible college. Said she wanted to become a missionary. He couldn't argue with that."

"Then she got away—so why would she kill herself?"

The old woman snorted. "Gettin' away to Bible college ain't exactly gettin' away. Soon's she started to show, she'd've had a handful o' trouble. They'd be writing to her daddy, telling him to come and take her away from there before she spread moral pollution amongst their student body."

"So what was the point of going then?"

Mrs. Elliott shrugged. "Buying time, maybe. Hoping she'd lose the baby natural. Wouldn't dare get rid of it on purpose. That'd be a mortal sin."

But suicide was also a mortal sin. And for a pregnant girl, it involved murder as well.

How terribly tragic. And for Jeremiah, how horrible to learn that he himself had driven his daughter to her destruction.

"Do you have any idea who the father was?"

"That I never could figure. Rachel never had a boyfriend that I ever saw. Her daddy wouldn't let her date outside his congregation, and there wasn't but one young man in it—and he was sweet on another girl. But Rachel was a real pretty girl, I will say that."

She fumbled in an old handbag that lay on the table and brought out a wallet, which she flipped open to show a typical school picture of an attractive brunette. Emily took the picture and looked closer. The girl could have been Katie's cousin—the features were different, but she had the same clear complexion, sweet smile, and girl-next-door wholesomeness.

Mrs. Elliott took the wallet back. "She coulda had any boy she wanted if her daddy'd let her date."

Emily was so absorbed in this narrative that she completely forgot to ask about who might have painted the nasty message on Devon and Hilary's shop window. It seemed unlikely Jeremiah himself would have spite to spare for a gay couple when he was facing such tragedy in his own home.

After a hard afternoon of painting and papering with Katie and Veronica, Emily flopped in the library with *Jane Eyre*. Jane had found refuge after her headlong flight with her as-yet-unknown cousins, the Rivers siblings. St. John Rivers made Emily almost as impatient as did Heathcliff, though for completely different reasons. Every time she read the book, some part of her irrationally feared Jane would fall under St. John's self-righteous spell, accept his proposal, and never see Rochester again.

As she read about St. John—his rigid self-control; his passion for Rosamond Oliver, which he would not allow himself to indulge; his determination on a missionary life, his insistence that Jane was called to share it with him, and his condemnation of her when she refused—she was inevitably reminded of Jeremiah Edwards. He had dedicated his daughter to a missionary life. Had he indeed been informed about her pregnancy when she died? Did he know, or suspect, who was responsible?

Emily thought back to the previous Saturday night—the night of Jake's murder. She hadn't understood the reason for it at the time, but Jeremiah had looked then like a man who had just lost his whole world. What would happen to his rigid self-control if he felt he had someone other than himself to blame for his daughter's ruin and death?

Those who are supple can bend in the wind of life's misfortunes and survive. But the brittle who insist on remaining upright will ultimately break.

twenty-four

"He is a good and great man; but he forgets, pitilessly, the feelings and claims of little people, in pursuing his own large views. It is better, therefore, for the insignificant to keep out of his way, lest in his progress, he should trample them down."

—Jane to Diana Rivers, *Jane Eyre*

Emily invited Jamie for dinner Sunday night, partly so they could finish up the paperwork on the Reed trust but also to try to force Katie to abandon her superstitious belief that Jamie's love for her was putting him in danger. She'd told Katie only to plan for an extra person, not mentioning Jamie's name so Katie wouldn't have an opportunity to protest.

Jamie arrived fifteen minutes late, which was quite unlike him. Emily opened the door to see Luke standing behind him and the sheriff's department SUV on the drive. Jamie's ancient Honda was nowhere in sight.

The young redhead's freckles stood out against his white skin. As she took his coat she saw his hands were shaking.

"What's going on? Did you have an accident?"

"He near as all get-out got himself run off the road." Emily chose to attribute the steel in Luke's eyes to that incident alone. "Damn lucky to be alive."

Emily was stunned. Could Katie's superstitious fear have grounds in reality after all? Had she herself endangered Jamie's life by inviting him here?

"Come into the library. You need some sherry."

She settled Jamie in her own chair in front of the fire with a generous glass of Harveys Bristol Cream. "Now tell me what happened."

Jamie gathered breath with difficulty. "I was on the highway north of Tillamook. You know that bit where it runs right up close to the bay on the west side and the marsh on the east?"

Emily nodded. That section of road always made her uncomfortable, although it was safe enough under ordinary conditions.

"This car came up behind me. Big old thing, one of the old gas-guzzlers. Pontiac, maybe, I don't know. First thing I knew, he was right on my bumper. I would've pulled over and let him by, but there's no shoulder to speak of along there." Jamie shuddered and took another drink of sherry. "So I sped up instead. But he sped up right along with me till it wasn't safe to go any faster. Not on that winding wet road."

Luke took up the tale. "Thank God I was right behind the bugger. Saw him nuzzle up to Jamie's bumper—didn't know it was Jamie at the time—and put on my siren. Guess he hadn't seen me before that. He swerved left, sideswiped the Honda and pushed it onto the shoulder, and roared off down the road. Jamie was past the marsh by that time so he ended up on firm ground."

Emily's heart was racing as fast as the unknown car. "Did you go after him?"

Luke shook his head. "Stopped to make sure Jamie was okay—recognized his car at that point. But I called in the other guy's license number, so he should've been picked up by now.

Distinctive car—light blue Pontiac, 'bout a '78, I'd say. Hard to hide in that."

She turned to Jamie. "You weren't hurt?"

"Just shaken up. I may have to break down and get a new car, though." He gave a pale smile. "I hate to think what would've happened if Lieutenant Richards hadn't been there."

"Did you recognize the driver?"

"No. I was too busy trying to stay on the road to get a good look at him."

"Who'd want to hurt Jamie?" she asked Luke. "It's not like he's a criminal lawyer who's put some killer away for life. He handles property transactions, for pity's sake."

Katie spoke from the doorway. How long had she been standing there? "I know who'd want to hurt him. Or rather what. I told you, but you wouldn't listen. It's the curse."

It's true. I am cursed. And now the curse has fallen on Jamie.

None of them will believe me—though Jamie, sweetly, looked as if he wanted to—but I know it. The curse is real.

I will never be able to allow a man to love me, lest he die.

And somehow I know it just has to be all Jake's fault. If he weren't already dead, I'd kill him. He may as well have killed me.

Luke stayed for dinner at Emily's, then took Jamie back to his own place for the night. Dinner with Emily was excruciating given the way he felt about her right now, but he wanted to keep an eye on the boy until he had a better idea of what was behind the incident on the road.

Monday morning he drove Jamie back to his car to wait for

the tow truck, then at Jamie's insistence took him to his office. "I won't be driving anywhere for a while," Jamie said, and Luke couldn't argue with that.

He went on into the office. The guilty driver had not been caught the night before, but Heather had left Luke the name and address of the owner of the vehicle—a name he didn't recognize, and a house on the south side of town, near Jeremiah Edwards's place. Luke drove down there. No one was home, and the car was nowhere to be seen. The mailbox bulged as if the owners had been gone for several days.

Strange. Luke checked the DMV report—the only phone number listed was a local one, no cell. Not much point in calling then.

He was turning to go when a quavery voice called to him from across the street. "Jenkinses are out of town."

Luke squinted toward the voice and saw an old woman leaning on her porch rail. He started toward her. "How long they been gone?"

"'Bout a week. Flew to California to see their kids."

"Flew? Where's their car?"

The old woman shrugged. "Preacher drove them to Portland to the airport. Maybe he's using it."

"Preacher?"

"Preacher Edwards. He lives right there." She gestured toward the house to her left, which Luke remembered from his previous visit. "Not home now, though."

No, he wouldn't be. He'd be at Emily's, working. Luke tried to picture Edwards behind the wheel of the old blue Pontiac, zooming up on Jamie's bumper with apparent intent to kill. He couldn't put it together. What on Earth could Edwards have against Jamie?

Maybe the Pontiac had been stolen, or lent to someone else. He needed to find that car.

He called Heather and asked her to relay an APB to points north of Stony Beach all along the coast. But he didn't expect results from that. If the driver had kept going, he either would've been picked up or he'd be in Canada by now. More likely he'd ditched the car, especially if it wasn't his own.

Luke drove slowly back toward the spot where Jamie's Honda had left the road, scanning both sides of the highway. About a mile south of Stony Beach he spotted a flash of sky blue amid the green of the forest and undergrowth along the right side of the road. He pulled over and walked back, his coat sleeves and trouser legs snagging on blackberry brambles as he pushed through the brush.

Yep, there it was, an old blue Pontiac. He checked his notes—the license number matched.

The car was locked and showed no signs of forced entry. The paint along the right side was badly scratched, consistent with its having scraped the driver's side of Jamie's car. Luke shined his flashlight inside but couldn't see anything of significance. The interior was neat and mostly clean, with only a bit of dried mud on the driver's side floor mat off somebody's boots.

If he could get at the mud, he might be able to match it to the perp's boot treads. Long shot, but it was all he had. He jimmied the window down, unlocked the door, leaned in, and took flash photos with his pocket camera. Photos of the position of the mud clots would be a lot more useful than the clots themselves, which would no doubt crumble as soon as they were touched.

While he was there, he checked the glove compartment. Car

manual, registration in the name of Howard Jenkins, a flashlight, and a first aid kit. Nothing personal, nothing whatsoever to show who'd been driving the car. He trained his own flashlight along the back of the driver's seat, hoping for a hair or two. No joy, but he ran a tissue along the smooth vinyl. It came away greasy, and he dropped it into an evidence bag to be tested for DNA. He also dusted the door handles, steering wheel, and dashboard for fingerprints but found nothing usable, only smudges. Apparently yesterday's driver had been wearing gloves.

He called for a tow, thankful he'd found the car on his own turf. The incident itself had happened outside his bailiwick, but finding the car here would give him reason enough to claim the case. And he had a gut feeling the car was going to lead him a lot farther than to this lonely spot in the woods.

When Luke got back to the office, the autopsy report on Roman was waiting for him. It showed a number of injuries consistent with his three-story fall, but one finding had the ME puzzled: a wide bruise that wrapped most of the way around the left ankle, made shortly before death.

Luke studied the photo of the bruise and thought about the trajectory of Roman's fall. Several things he might have run into on the way down—drainpipe, porch roof, even creepers on the porch columns—but nothing that would wrap around his ankle like that. Nor could he see how the final impact with the driveway could cause such a mark.

That bruise looked like it was made by a hand. He grabbed his hat and headed out to Windy Corner.

The work on Emily's private sitting room was drawing to a close, and she went up Monday morning to inspect it. She stood in her new sitting room and pivoted slowly, imagining how her chosen furniture—assembled from the Windy Corner attic, Lacey Luxuries, and Remembrance of Things Past—would fit into the space. The love seat would go nicely under the window, chairs and end tables to the sides. But once she put the long bookcase along the inside wall, the extra two feet occupied by that inexplicable paneled wall Jeremiah had uncovered were going to seriously cut into the space she had to move around in. Of all things, she hated a crowded room.

She pulled out a tape measure to be sure her instinct was correct. Yes, once the furniture was in place, she'd have only about a two-foot-wide passage between the chairs and the bookcase. Definitely not enough.

Emily hadn't forgotten the peculiar feeling that came over her when she touched that wall nor the reason for her decision to retain it. But she couldn't live in a cramped space. Funny feeling or no funny feeling, that inexplicable wall would have to go.

"Jeremiah!" she called.

"Yes, ma'am?" he answered from the small storage room that was being transformed into a bathroom.

"We're going to have to get rid of this wall."

Jeremiah ducked his head under the lintel. He was looking even more haggard since his daughter's burial. Emily hadn't dared let him know she knew about that; he was such a private person, and lately a bit frightening. The dark shadows under his eyes, combined with his drawn cheeks and lantern jaw, made him look like crazy Jonathan from *Arsenic and Old Lace*.

Now he frowned deeply, accentuating the resemblance further. "Don't think that's a good idea, ma'am. That wall has some good reason to be there. Could be structural."

"How could it be when it isn't even in the plans?"

"Maybe the plans were bad. Builder realized that as he worked and put this wall in to fix it. Better leave it alone."

Emily looked askance at him. When they'd discussed the wall before, he'd been ready to do whatever she decided. Why change his mind now? If he'd discovered any legitimate reason to leave the wall alone, he would tell her, but instead he was making up silly excuses. His daughter's death must be affecting him even more deeply than she'd guessed.

Under the circumstances, she decided not to press the issue. She'd get Charlie Cartwright to come over when Jeremiah wasn't around and give her a second opinion.

Luke banged on the front door of Windy Corner with more urgency than usual. Within seconds Emily opened it. "Luke! What brings you here?"

He winced at the appropriateness of that question, which only a week ago would have been no question at all. Emily would have brought him there—no excuse required.

"Developments. Is Edwards here?"

"Upstairs. They're working on my bathroom. Why?"

"I've got several little matters I want to go over with him." An understatement, but he didn't want to worry her.

She frowned. "As a matter of fact, I'd like to talk to you about Jeremiah myself. Come into the library."

Luke listened in growing concern as Emily told him about her conversation with Mrs. Elliott a couple of days before. So Edwards's daughter was dead—pregnant and dead. He narrowed his eyes, remembering his talk with Charlie Cartwright weeks ago. "I wonder . . . Charlie told me Edwards had accused his boy Eli of making improper advances toward Rachel at a party.

Maybe he suspected Rachel'd been raped. Must've known it wasn't really Eli. Knowing Jake's reputation, wouldn't be that much of a stretch to pin the rape on him."

"You think Jeremiah's capable of *murder*?" Emily's voice became a shocked whisper.

"To avenge his daughter's death? I wouldn't put it past him. And I haven't told you what I found out this morning. It could've been Edwards who was driving the car that tried to run Jamie down." He related the trail that had led him to the Pontiac. "On top of that, there's some reason to believe Roman might have had a little help falling off your roof. He has a bruise on his ankle I can't see any other way to account for."

"And Jeremiah was the only one near him when he fell."

Luke nodded. "Nothing conclusive, but facts seem to be piling up against the good preacher."

Emily's brow furrowed. He'd always liked that look on her, loved her braininess and the way she always tried to see all sides of a question. If only she hadn't put blinders on where Katie was concerned. "I can see why he might kill Jake. But what about Roman? He couldn't have thought them both responsible for Rachel's pregnancy."

"Maybe Roman knew something. Saw him near the stairwell when Jake was killed."

"Why wouldn't Roman have spoken up right away? I don't see him having the kind of loyalty to Jeremiah that would make him lie for him."

Luke shrugged. "Maybe he was blackmailing him. Edwards went along for a bit, then decided to put an end to it."

"Hmm. Maybe." Emily didn't look convinced. "But why in the world would he go after Jamie? That makes no sense at all."

"Yeah, you got me there." Katie's idea of a curse wasn't even worth considering.

"And besides—if Jeremiah killed Jake, he would have had to come out of the stairwell through the bedroom. Even if he came out of that room before Roman, it couldn't have been more than a couple of seconds before. Wouldn't Matthew have seen him, too?"

That point had been bothering Luke as well. The time was so tight, no way the murderer could've escaped unseen. "That's one hell of a wrinkle, all right. But like Sherlock Holmes says—"

"'When you've eliminated the impossible, whatever remains, however improbable, must be the truth.'"

"That's right." Here she was finishing his sentences again. The two of them made such a good team, professionally as well as personally. Why couldn't she have trusted him?

He stood. "I'm going up to talk to Edwards. You better stay here—just in case he gets nasty."

• twenty-five •

"It is not violence that best overcomes hate—nor vengeance that most certainly heals injury."

—Helen Burns to Jane, *Jane Eyre*

Emily stayed in the library, chewing over everything she and Luke had just discussed. What would make Jeremiah want to kill all three of the men who'd been interested in Katie? Katie's curse theory looked more likely by the minute.

No. It wasn't a curse that linked Jake's murder, Roman's fatal accident, and Jamie's frightening near miss. It was one man's intention.

Little facts and incidents to which she'd attached no importance at the time suddenly sprang vividly to her mind. Rachel Edwards's resemblance to Katie in the photograph Mrs. Elliot showed her. The fact that Jeremiah had very likely overheard Katie talking to Emily about Jake's rape of her. His ferocity, as reported by Katie, in dismissing Roman after he accosted her. Jeremiah could also have overheard, and misinterpreted, the conversation in which Katie asked Jamie to stay away for his own good.

What if Jeremiah had somehow transmogrified his rage and grief over the death of his own daughter into an obsessive desire to protect Katie from sexual harm? What if he'd taken his extreme judgmental attitude toward lustful indulgence a step further and appointed himself a vigilante to make sure all such offenders were punished?

The contraction in her gut told Emily she'd hit on something very near the truth. But that still left the practical problem: How could Jeremiah have escaped the stairway after Jake's murder without being seen?

More jagged shards of memory clicked together like the tumblers of a lock. Jeremiah's unreasonable reluctance to take down that paneled wall. The odd feeling it gave her. And the Clean Scene man, Fred Senior, had said something about Windy Corner being full of secret passages. She'd only shown him the one. Had he found another?

As if drawn by a magnet, she rose and approached the curved shelf that led to the stairway. She hadn't opened it since the day after the murder, hadn't planned to open it ever again; in fact, she'd nearly decided on putting in that elevator, as the stairs were forever poisoned for her by Jake's death. But now she reached for the fake volume of *Arabian Nights* and gave it a pull.

The curved wall creaked open. Emily took the flashlight that nestled in a little hollow in the side of the shelf and lit her way up the stairs. Clean Scene had done their job well; she couldn't see the bloodstains left by Jake's falling body. But she could still feel them.

At the top she paused and shined the flashlight in a circle. She saw no crack in the paneling, no possible place for a release lever to be concealed. If there was a passage here, it had been constructed very cleverly. Emily wondered whether Beatrice had even known of it.

Logically, if the passage came out in the third-floor sitting room, the opening should be on the wall nearest the hall. Probably right there, on the curve that fronted the corner where the side wall of Beatrice's bedroom met the wall of the hall. Emily held the flashlight under her left arm so she could feel around the wall with both hands, applying gentle pressure in various spots.

At last she heard a soft click, and the panel swung outward under her hand. She set the opening wide and trained her flashlight into the tiny space—no more than a corner with one concave side. A rude ladder consisting of blocks nailed to the wall ascended to her right. Several spiders skittered away from the light.

Emily did not do ladders. Not even clean ones in well-lit, spider-free rooms. And she certainly didn't do spiders. She could just leave this for Luke to investigate later.

But some instinct told her later would be too late. And perhaps if she could provide Luke with the last piece of the puzzle about Jeremiah's opportunity for killing Jake, he would forgive her for lying to him.

She stretched up and laid the flashlight on the highest rung she could reach. Taking her courage in both hands, and heartily wishing those hands were at least gloved, she began her ascent.

The first rung wasn't so bad. The floor was still comfortingly close below her. The second rung required her to make a withdrawal from her courage account. At the third rung, she felt something brush across her fingers. Instinctively she snatched her hand away and shook it, shifting her balance so that for a moment she hung precariously in space. A chasm yawned below her, and her stomach rose into her throat. Her heart beating like a tom-tom at a primitive dance, she swung her body back toward the wall and clung tight with both hands, breathing hard and uttering a frantic "Lord have mercy" on every breath.

When her heart had calmed to a mere polka, she screwed her last remaining bit of courage to the sticking point. *You can do this,* she told herself. *Make Luke proud.* She wiped one sweaty palm on her skirt, then the other, took a deep breath, and climbed another rung. Now her hands met the flashlight. One more rung. She picked up the flashlight and trained it above her head. The ladder ended two rungs beyond her eye level, and a dim opening stretched out above.

She used the flashlight to scan the remaining rungs for spiders and squash the one she found, then laid the light at the top of the stairs. In one deep breath she raced up the few remaining rungs, gained the upper floor, and stepped onto it with the gratefulness of a mountain climber reaching a towering peak. Voices reached her from the other side of the wall—Luke's raised in accusation, Jeremiah's muttering in self-justification.

Now to find the way out.

Luke found Edwards working in the soon-to-be bathroom. "Need to talk to you a minute, Edwards. Come in here." He led him into the sitting room, where as yet there was no place to sit.

"I understand you've been using Howard Jenkins's car while he's out of town."

Edwards's eyes immediately went wary, so Luke knew he was on the right track. Violent he might recently have become, but the man was not an accomplished liar. This might not be too hard.

"Who told you that?"

"Your neighbor. Mrs. Elliott. Seems like not much gets by her, sitting on her porch all day."

Edwards cleared his throat, probably weighing how much he'd have to admit to be plausible. "Drove Jenkins and his wife to the airport week ago Sunday in their car. Took it out for a spin yesterday to keep the battery going."

"Go to Tillamook, did you?"

"No, just around town." His eyes were all around the room as he said that. That much was a lie.

Luke would leave that for the time being. "I also have reason to believe you helped Roman Martinez off of this roof."

Edwards froze, his eyes narrowed on Luke's face. "What reason?"

"There's a nasty bruise on his ankle. And according to what you yourself told me, you're the only one who could've put it there."

"I—I reached out to him when I saw him fall. Trying to save him. May have caught at his ankle, don't remember. Anyway, he was too heavy. Slid out of my grasp."

"Now I wonder why you didn't tell me that in the first place?"

"It—simply slipped my mind."

"Slipped your mind. Just like his ankle slipped out of your grasp. Your very firm grasp, judging from the severity of that bruise."

"Go ahead, twist my words. You can't prove it didn't happen like I said. Besides, why would I want to hurt Martinez? Already fired him. That was enough."

"I'm still working on the why, to tell you the absolute truth.

I only have the how. But I think I know what reason you had to kill Jake Newhouse."

"Newhouse! What makes you think I had anything to do with that?"

"He's the fellow that raped and impregnated your daughter. Or at least you believed him to be."

Edwards's face went an ugly red. "I never went into that bedroom. If anyone says he saw me there, he's a liar. The Lord hates a liar."

Out of nowhere Luke heard a familiar, if muffled, voice, pitched an octave lower than usual: "But He also hates hands that shed innocent blood. Don't forget that, Jeremiah."

Edwards's eyes looked as if they would fly out of his head as he whipped around, searching floor, ceiling, everywhere for that disembodied voice. "Innocent! How can you call him innocent? He was a viper, a snake in the grass, the lowest vermin that ever disturbed the peace of Eden. He seduced my girl, I tell you! He stole the most precious treasure she had. And then he stole her from me. She killed herself to destroy the evil seed that was in her. And he had the gall to come back here and stand in that stairwell—*whistling*!"

"What about Roman?" came the spectral voice. "And Jamie, for pity's sake? Jamie is innocent if any man is."

"They were bothering Miss Parker. I had to defend her. She's so much like my Rachel. . . ."

At this inopportune moment, Katie's head appeared around the corner from the hall. "Lieutenant, have you seen Mrs. C?"

Luke waved her back out of the room, but it was too late. Edwards had seen her, and he was closer. In two strides he'd reached Katie and caught her in his arms. "Rachel!" he cried.

"You've come back to me! The Lord has rewarded His faithful servant."

His sunken eyes lit with a triumphant, maniacal fire. "I had to rid the world of all that evil. It was my Christian duty. The scripture says the penalty for rape is death." He held Katie's arm in a viselike grip as he stared around the room, his voice rising. "God appointed me as His minister to purge the Earth of bloodthirsty and deceitful men who would prey upon a young girl. I am not to blame." He raised his free hand to heaven and cried out, "I am not to blame!"

Katie hung limp in Edwards's arms. Her terrified eyes fastened on Luke's, mutely begging him to deliver her—which he must do, at any cost. He fought down panic as his mind filled with calculations—his own weight versus Edwards's greater height; the time it would take him to cross the room and tackle Edwards versus the time it would take Edwards to lock Katie's throat in a stranglehold. Luke had brought his pistol from the car, anticipating trouble; but he couldn't use it without endangering Katie. He didn't delude himself the girl was safe because Edwards had mistaken her for his daughter. The man had flipped, gone clean over the edge. No one within his reach was safe.

But Edwards still answered to one authority—the voice of God. And it came in right on cue. "If you do not forgive others, you will not be forgiven. You may have memorized the whole Old Testament, Jeremiah Edwards, but you've ignored the words of the Lord Jesus Christ. Your actions are not pleasing in His sight." The unseen voice escalated in volume and authority as it lowered in pitch. "The bloodthirsty and deceitful man is *you!*"

A look of horror crossed Edwards's wasted features. He pulled

Katie in front of him, one wiry arm across her throat while the other hand still gripped her arm, and edged toward the window. "This world is not our home, Rachel. We must go to our Maker. He will receive us into His everlasting mansions!"

It was now or never. Luke shot a look at Bobby and Bertie Fillmore, who'd been watching in fascinated horror from the bathroom. They were big, muscled young guys; he prayed they'd have the wits to cooperate. He launched himself toward Edwards, aiming to land between the maniac and the window. Bobby and Bertie rushed Edwards from the other side, one wrenching his arm away from Katie's neck while the other slammed his wrist to loosen his grip on her arm.

Seeing himself overpowered, Edwards suddenly wilted. His arms fell limp at his sides and he hung his head, his breath coming in giant gasps. Bertie pulled Katie out of reach as Bobby yanked both of Edwards's hands behind his back.

Luke pulled out his handcuffs and began: "Jeremiah Edwards, I'm arresting you for the murders of Jake Newhouse and Roman Martinez, and the attempted murder of Jamie MacDougal. You have the right to remain silent . . ."

The back wall opened and Emily stepped out into the room. "I think it's a little late for that."

· twenty-six ·

Reader!—I forgave him at the moment, and on the spot.
There was such deep remorse in his eye, such true pity in
his tone, such manly energy in his manner; and, besides,
there was such unchanged love in his whole look and
mien—I forgave him all.

—Jane Eyre

Luke took Jeremiah away, not pausing for conversation; but
the look he gave Emily as he left filled her with hope. She
gave the Fillmore boys the rest of the day off with bonus pay
and called Jamie to come and comfort Katie. Meanwhile Emily
cradled her on the library love seat, stroking her hair. The poor
girl had been through hell.

"You see, sweetheart, there was no curse after all. Only a
crazy man who thought he needed to protect you."

"I guess you're right. I think I was a little crazy myself to
believe that."

"It's been a crazy time. But you're safe now."

"I don't know, Mrs. C. I don't know if I'll ever feel safe again."

Jamie arrived, and Emily told him what had happened. He
folded Katie in his arms, and she clung to him as to a lifeline as
he murmured endearments into her hair. Gently he led her

across the lawn to her own apartment, where little Lizzie had slept through the whole crisis. Thank God for that.

Emily watched the new couple from the porch with a divided heart. Katie was safe: that was the important thing. She had to focus on that. And not think about the fact that she might be about to lose her in a different way—to Jamie. After all she'd gone through, all she'd done to protect Katie and Lizzie— including possibly destroying Luke's trust in herself forever— she was still going to lose the girls she loved.

But that was what mothers did. They protected their daughters all through childhood, only to send them away in the end to be protected by a husband. Or to face the world on their own.

Emily hadn't had all the years of Katie's childhood, or Lizzie's, either. She'd only had a few months, into which she'd poured a lifetime of frustrated mother love. And now she would have to let go. Move straight into empty-nest and grandma mode without the usual transition time.

And without a husband to support her through it all.

Once Jeremiah was safely in jail, Luke searched his house for evidence to corroborate his confession. The man was clearly insane, and without hard evidence a good defense lawyer might be able to persuade a jury to discount his admission of guilt.

In the backyard incinerator Luke found the remains of a pair of stained work gloves. With any luck they'd yield traces of Jake's blood. Inside the house, in a drawer of Edwards's painfully neat desk, was a letter from Rachel's college along with an autopsy report confirming suicide and stating that she was pregnant when she died. Motive and means—he had Cordelia's testimony that Jake himself had the knife, which Edwards must have wrestled away from him. And Luke could supply evidence of opportunity from his own investigation—thanks to Emily. No doubt Edwards would be committed to a psychiatric facility instead of a regular prison, but one way or another he'd be put away for life; Luke was confident of that.

And as a bonus, in the same desk he also discovered a box of toddler-size crayons and a can of lavender spray paint. Emily had shown him her picture of Devon and Hilary's window smeared with this same paint. Finding the can wasn't proof positive Edwards had been responsible for those threats, but it was pretty damn suggestive. Apparently the man saw his mandate from God as extending to the harassment of homosexuals. If he hadn't been stopped in time, who knew how that might have escalated? He might've seen the gay couple as worthy of being purged from the Earth along with Jake and Roman.

Thank God Luke and Emily had managed to stop that maniac before he killed again.

With the case now well and truly closed, Jake's and Roman's bodies were released for burial. Roman had no family to escort him out of this world; if his body were left to the state's tender care, it would be cremated, and Emily's Orthodox faith forbade cremation. Even for a man she'd disliked and feared, she couldn't let that happen simply by default, so she took it upon herself to arrange and pay for his funeral. He would be buried at St. Bede's.

It was Father Stephen's idea to give Jake and Roman a joint funeral. Emily had no objection, but she was sure Carter Newhouse would never stand for it. To her amazement, however, Father Stephen approached him and he agreed. Emily checked to be sure the funeral was announced in the *Wave* so Mildred Newhouse would be able to see it and attend if she changed her mind.

A few dozen mourners—mostly, Emily guessed, business associates and social acquaintances of the Newhouses—dotted the pews behind the two coffins. Emily had made sure Roman's casket gleamed as brightly and held as many flowers as Jake's. Heathcliff or no, she had more sympathy for Roman; at least he had been driven by a specific passion for Katie, rather than a generalized lust mixed with contempt toward women in general.

Father Stephen neatly avoided eulogizing the two young men. Instead he spoke of mercy and forgiveness, the qualities that had been so notably lacking in the theology of their murderer. And he spoke of community, of its power to heal and become stronger through suffering. By the end of his homily, Emily had found a tiny corner of pity in her heart even for Jake. And for his father, whose ruined countenance met her gaze across the aisle in the first pew. She stole a glance toward the back of the church and caught sight of a figure in a veiled black hat in the darkest corner. So Mildred had made it after all. For Mildred she felt the most compassion of all.

Mildred kept herself inconspicuous at the graveside as well. Emily watched her assess her husband in wonder at how humble and passive he had become. She need hardly fear him now. Nevertheless, Emily was sure Mildred would not attend the reception Newhouse had organized in Jake's honor.

When the cavalcade of mourners had departed, Mildred lingered by the grave, dropping wildflowers one by one from the posy she held. Emily approached her quietly.

"Mildred?"

Mildred started and looked up, wide-eyed, but relaxed when she recognized Emily. "Emily. Thank you for coming."

"It was the least I could do." The grieving mother dropped the last of her flowers into the grave, then looked around her as if she'd never seen the place before. Emily felt she ought not to be left alone. "Would you like to come to Windy Corner for tea?"

Mildred nodded absently. "Thank you, you're very kind."

Emily drove her down the hill, as she didn't seem in a fit state to drive; she'd bring her back to her car later. Katie had stayed home from the funeral, not wishing to be an object of curiosity to anyone who might know or have guessed the motive for the murders, and she had tea all ready. Emily introduced Mildred to Katie—without, of course, mentioning anything about Katie's connection with Jake.

Katie took one look at Mildred, whose pale drooping face above her stiff black suit seemed to forbid joy from ever visiting there again. Then she whispered something to Emily, left the room, and came back with Lizzie in her arms.

"Mrs. Newhouse? I'd like you to meet your granddaughter."

The transfiguration of Mildred Newhouse's face rivaled anything Minerva McGonagall could accomplish. She held out her arms to Lizzie, who gurgled and went to her gladly. The baby played with Mildred's black beads while the newly elevated grandmother examined every inch of her as if she were a miracle dropped straight from heaven. Which, of course, she was.

When she had a moment of attention to spare from Lizzie, Mildred said to Katie, "I won't ask how this child came to be. I have a feeling it would be better for me not to know. But I can't begin to tell you what this means to me. Thank you so very, very much for allowing me to meet her just this once."

"It doesn't have to be just this once. You're welcome to see Lizzie as often as you like."

Mildred gave a sad smile. "I'm moving away from here. I'd thought of going to Portland, or farther, but—Emily, you saw Carter today. Do you think I'd be safe going only as far as Seaside?"

"I'd hate to pronounce on that, but he certainly seems like a changed man to me. I think he's accepted that what happened to Jake was partly his own fault—and that includes his abuse of you."

Mildred planted a kiss amid Lizzie's red curls. "Maybe I will be seeing more of you after all, little Lizzie. I always wished I could have a daughter. Though I wouldn't have wanted to raise one in *that* house." She shuddered. "Having a granddaughter will be even better."

So even Emily's remaining role as adoptive grandmother would have to be shared. But that, too, was in the nature of things, and she could hardly begrudge Mildred this comfort after the miserable life she'd led. Emily would just have to learn to live with a reduced role in Lizzie's and Katie's lives.

One last entry here, just because I've written so much angst in this journal and now I want to write some joy to counteract it. After tonight, I'm going to be so busy and so happy I'll never want to write in here again.

Jamie asked me to marry him. With all the trappings. He took me to dinner at Gifts from the Sea, with champagne in an ice bucket and everything. When I finished my champagne, there at the bottom of the glass was the most gorgeous ring I'd ever seen. He went down on one knee, right there in the restau-

rant, and said, "Katie Parker, queen of my heart, will you do me the immeasurable honor of becoming my wife?"

I was kind of startled, naturally, and he explained that he knew it was "precipitous" (he actually uses words like that, just as if we were in a Jane Austen novel), but he wanted to be sure I knew that I was safe and loved after all I'd been through. And I didn't have to answer him right away if I didn't want to, but his feelings would never change.

Well, of course I said yes. And not just because of the ring and all. (I mean, imagine—me, Katie Parker, from the wrong side of the tracks, engaged to a lawyer, with a diamond the size of the Twin Rocks on my hand? No way.) But I really do love him. I don't even know him all that well yet, but I feel safe with him, like I thought I would never feel again. Safe and whole.

But then when he brought me home, I looked around at my sweet little apartment that I've only just gotten fixed up exactly the way I wanted it. And I thought about Mrs. C and all our plans for Windy Corner, and I thought, no way can I leave here now.

I didn't say it, but Jamie saw something was wrong. He's really intuitive like that, which I've never seen in a guy before. It's pretty nice. He asked me if I was having second thoughts, so I told him.

And he said, "No problem. I can move in here." Just like that. I handed him a problem, and he handed me a solution. Just like Mr. Knightley offering to move in with Emma and her dad. I asked wouldn't he mind commuting to Tillamook, and he said no, he liked the drive. And his own place was just a bland apartment with hardly any furniture and no personality at all; he'd be happy to leave it.

Well, of course I kissed him then. I'd been a little nervous *about that side of things because of—well, history. But honestly? I don't think it's going to be a problem. He's happy to take it slow, and so am I. We agreed on a longish engagement because we need some time to get to know each other.*

Lizzie woke up while we were talking—Mrs. C had been keeping an ear on the monitor for me—and Jamie went in and picked her up. I looked at their two red heads side by side. He might as well be her biological father. After a year or two, people will forget he isn't. We'll just be a family like any other.

Only happier.

I can't wait to tell Mrs. C.

Katie's news made Emily feel as if she'd been given the most gorgeous, decadent chocolate cake ever baked and told she could keep it and eat it, too. Katie happily married but still on the property—what more could she possibly ask?

She could ask for Luke. In the days since the arrest, the ache his absence left inside her had grown to a gnawing emptiness that wouldn't let her sleep or settle to either work or play. All she'd been able to do was walk on the beach, and that brought back so many memories of their early times together, she only did it once. He hadn't called or come by. She'd only glimpsed him at the funeral, on his way out while she was talking to Mildred.

Now she stood on the front porch of Windy Corner, debating whether the drizzle was light enough that she might venture into town on the Vespa. It was close to lunchtime; she could just casually stop by the Crab Pot and have a ninety-percent chance of finding Luke there. If he asked her to join him, all would be well. If not—then she might have to reevaluate her plans for the future. Living in Stony Beach while being permanently estranged from Luke was unthinkable.

The drizzle was thickening into real rain. She turned back to the door to get her umbrella and car keys and caught sight of the three cats, arrayed in the parlor bay window, watching her with unblinking eyes. "What? What have I done now?" she asked them. Was the innocent ploy of pretending to run into Luke by accident too deceptive for their sensitive collective conscience?

Then she heard the crunch of wheels on gravel. She turned and watched, her heart fluttering like a teenager's, as Luke's SUV rounded the bend of the drive and pulled up to the house.

She told herself he must have come on some official business, though she had no idea what that might be. It was a bit late to gather evidence, and anyway he had Jeremiah's confession; he shouldn't need more than that.

But Luke mounted the porch steps slowly, his cap in his hands despite the rain, and stood before her like a suppliant. "Hey, beautiful," he said in a husky parody of his old teasing tone.

"Hey." She scanned his gray eyes but found no steel there— only the infinite sadness of the stormy sea. "Does this mean you forgive me?"

He took her left hand and caressed her fingers with his roughened thumb. "I've been doing a lot of thinking the last few days." He cut his eyes up toward the attic. "Up there when Edwards grabbed Katie—I would've done anything to keep her safe. *Anything.* Even killed him, if I could've done it without hurting her. So I guess what I'm saying is—" He cleared his throat and squeezed her hand hard. "I guess I can understand you withholding a bit of evidence. Even if it was from me."

She covered his hand with her right. Their hands, at least,

were back where they belonged. "And I can understand you were only doing your job. Even if it did mean suspecting Katie."

His brow was still troubled. "But listen, Em—I've got to know you trust me from now on. And I've got to know I can trust you."

She brought their joined hands to her heart. "I think I went a little crazy for a while—chalk it up to change of life, maybe. But it was miserable being on the outs with you. I give you my word, I will never doubt you or betray your trust again."

Dawn broke over the stormy sea of his eyes. "So we're good now?"

She smiled, her heart expanding till the empty ache melted away. "We're good."

He took her in his arms and kissed her for the first time in weeks. The chorus of cats, still arrayed in the parlor window, looked on and blinked their benediction.